Among the Stars

Denise Clanin

Morgan Pierce Media & Publishing

Cover Illustration & Design: Laurie L. Mach

Published in the United States by Morgan Pierce Media & Publishing
www.MorganPierceMediaPublishing.com

Paperback ISBN 979-8-9919514-2-5

Ebook ISBN 79-8-9919514-3-2

Library of Congress Control Number: 2025932366

Contents

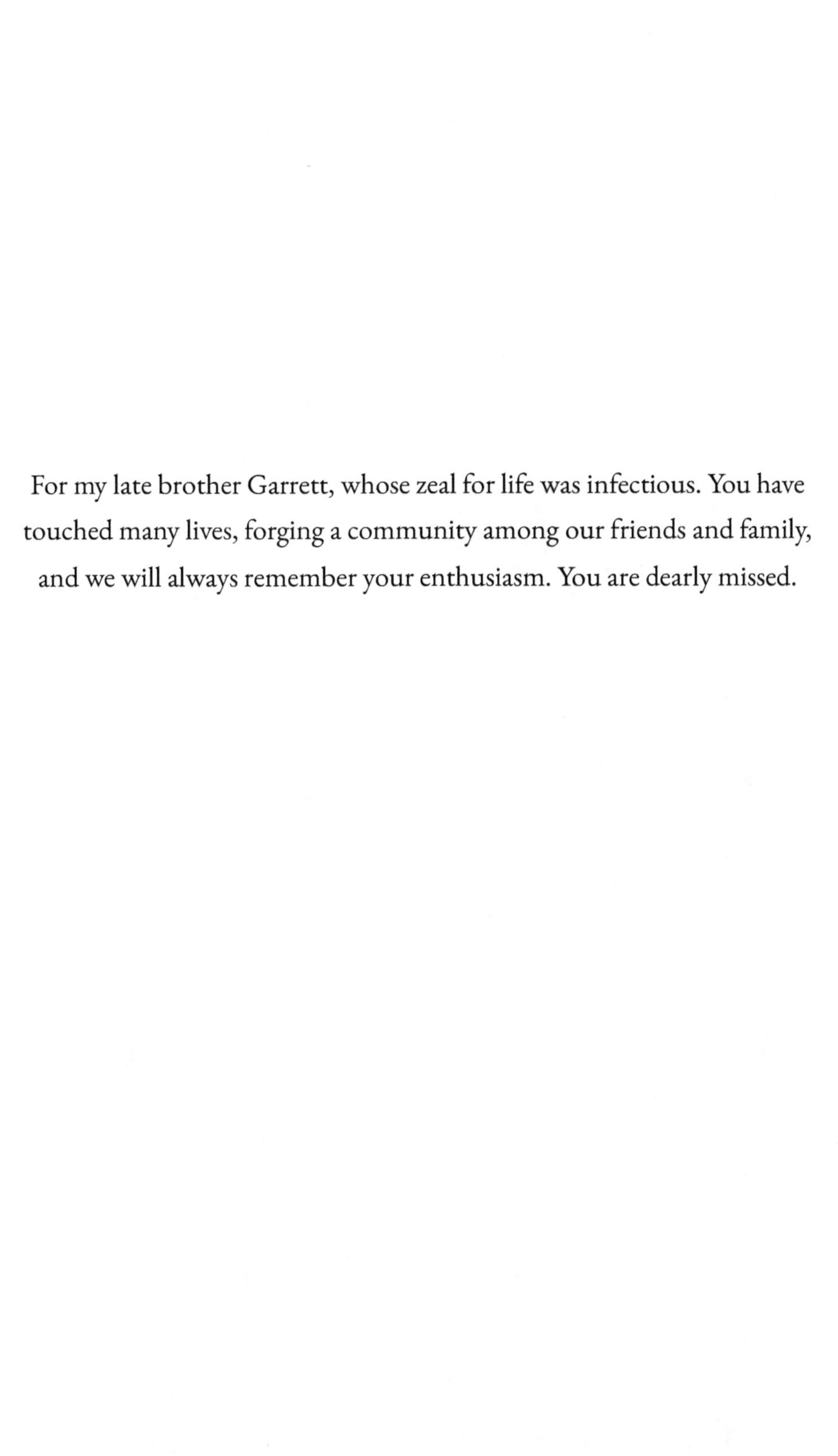

For my late brother Garrett, whose zeal for life was infectious. You have touched many lives, forging a community among our friends and family, and we will always remember your enthusiasm. You are dearly missed.

Chapter One

- -

I find myself dreaming of Ville du Lac—almost as much as I find myself dreaming in color. A little slice of heaven. My hometown. The land of vast lakes and winding rivers. Lush forests and sloping mountaintops. The one place that holds the titles to my most cherished and tragic memories—both spanning within the same 24-hour period...

"Starlight. The end of an era. I miss it already!" My aunt Liz stated, bringing a glass of Chardonnay to her rosy-red lips.

I was suddenly snapped back into reality: my relatives and I were seated along the ocean-front window of an upscale restaurant as a celebration of my recent graduation from medical school.

"Well, the theater should've managed their debt more wisely," my uncle Chris said. "You don't file for bankruptcy due to a simple drop in attendance. Doesn't work that way. Poor financial decisions would turn off their lights faster, especially when employees are missing their pension payments."

"Still, it's sad. The newer generation will never enjoy a musical theater performance underneath the stars."

"And underneath the landing path for the San Diego Airport."

Aunt Liz laughed at her husband's statement. "But that's part of the experience—the actors freezing every few minutes as the airplanes fly overhead. There was nothing like it!"

My mom nodded in agreement. "In the meantime, Natalie here will be starting her residency next month. Can you believe it?"

I stared down at the stiff, white tablecloth, trying to avoid eye contact—instead focusing on cutting my filet mignon and green beans in a precise manner. *I'd rather be eating some street tacos right now.*

"I can! You were the valedictorian of your high school, after all," Uncle Chris pointed out.

"Where did you end up getting matched for your residency again?" my grandmother asked. "Is it also at UCSD?"

"Yes. I'm keeping the family tradition alive," I explained to her.

Grandma gave me a puzzled look.

"John and Chris both went to UCSD for graduate school," Mom clarified.

"But unlike his brother, Chris only made it to dental school," Aunt Liz teased him, removing a lock of her short brown hair from underneath her black-framed glasses.

"Only dental school? Those four years weren't a cakewalk, let me tell you!" Uncle Chris pointed out.

It sometimes slipped my mind that my dad and uncle were twins—I recalled them looking almost nothing alike. My uncle was stockier and taller, with darker hair and a short beard, while my dad had a slimmer, fairer complexion. A complexion I remembered as if it were yesterday. I felt a twinge of sadness.

Aunt Liz rubbed his shoulder. "I'm only joking, dear. I know dentistry is tough. Not as tough as what Natalie's about to go through. That's why we're more than happy to open up our home to her again. It's the least we can do."

"Is your residency in the same place as the medical school?" Grandma asked.

"Not the classrooms themselves, but I'm quite familiar with the clinic and hospital from my rotations," I replied. "I've been told it'll be a very different experience, though."

"Different, that's for sure. You'll be saying goodbye to all your free time now," Aunt Liz joked, "but we'll finally have another doctor in the family!"

"Yes, that'll be wonderful!" Mom agreed.

Grandma shook her head disapprovingly. "No free time? How is that wonderful? How on earth will she ever find time to meet a man?"

"Really, Barbara? That's all you can think about right now?" Aunt Liz remarked. "My niece just graduated with one of the most prestigious degrees out there, and you just want her to get married?"

"No, no. It's up to her what she does with her time," Grandma said. "I'm concerned that as she gets busier with work, she won't have time to invest in a family. She'll be too busy delivering other women's babies. It'll be a shame if she doesn't have any of her own."

"I don't think that'll be a problem," Uncle Chris quipped. "It'll be hard for her to keep men away once they realize she has an MD to her name."

In frustration, I forcefully set my fork and knife onto my plate with a loud clang. The entire restaurant went quiet for a brief second. "You know, I'm right here—if anyone would like to ask me about my life rather than speaking for me."

"I'm sorry, Natalie," Aunt Liz apologized, "I was just trying to point out logic to your grandmother."

"It's alright," I said. "To be honest, I'm not really looking to date at this time. Olivia has set up enough awkward blind dates for me to last a lifetime. The right guy probably doesn't even exist in this neck of the woods."

Changing the subject, I added with a hopeful tone, "But I'm looking forward to having a month to myself before my residency begins."

"That's wonderful! You deserve a break," Grandma affirmed. "Are you planning on traveling during that time?"

I shook my head. "I wish! I'm pretty knee-deep in med-school debt. My part-time job at the Coffee Bean barely pays the bills. Maybe one day, once my debt is paid off. But I'm planning to see a movie with Olivia tomorrow evening. And yoga in the morning. I've got a busy day ahead of me."

Although I was looking forward to spending the day with my best friend, I still wished I had more of a breather. A chance to catch my breath—to figure out how I wanted to spend the next month of my life. My last real window of free time.

Chapter Two

That evening, up on tiptoe, I reached for the top level of my bookshelf. With my hand, I nudged my photo album forward—sitting between my Bible and one of my anatomy textbooks.

"Got it!" I said to myself, as I felt the large, bulky book slide into my grasp. I lowered my heels to my bedroom carpet—well, my uncle and aunt's guest room carpet, to be fair. I let out a satisfied sigh. At five-foot-three, I was no stranger to climbing counters.

I sat cross-legged on the carpet, the red leather album resting in my lap; as I flipped open the cover, my eyes skimmed through years of memories—beginning with high school. Photos of my classes and extracurriculars: Key Club, Academic League, Latin Club, Science Team, and their corresponding awards: all stepping stones toward my college journey. And my friends—whom I met from those aforementioned extracurriculars. I was then met with numerous straight-A report cards, SAT scores, college admittance letters, and graduation honor cords, all tucked neatly inside the album.

Upon flipping past a single blank page of a clear sleeve, I arrived at my college photos—or lack thereof. After freshman orientation, I only came across one or two standalone photos per year of undergrad. The rest of the pages were filled with certificates, transcripts, MCAT scores, additional admittance letters, and honor cords.

Eventually, I came to the end of the album, marked by the UCSD Undergrad Commencement program. I stood up, making my way over to my desk. Grabbing my Class of 2015 School of Medicine program, I returned to the floor, sliding it into the adjacent empty sleeve of the album. The two UCSD Commencement programs lay side-by-side on opposite pages. Perfect. A nice way to conclude my academic career.

As I pushed myself up, closing the cover, a loose photograph suddenly slipped out of the album's contents, falling to the carpet.

Bending down to retrieve it, I studied the lone 4x6 photo for a moment. To my surprise, it didn't belong with my high school or college photos. It was a photo of my childhood friend Justin Sanders and me when I lived in Ville du Lac.

It was a later photo of us taken during my last summer with him. We were standing side-by-side, Lake Awl to our backs, our arms shaded by the surrounding ponderosa pines. Justin was only standing an inch or two above me—he'd just begun his growth spurt. I wore a pink tee with green cargo shorts; hair pulled into a ponytail—my usual summer attire. My smile was casual, my eyelids relaxed, and my head slightly tilted in Justin's direction. He smiled widely with excitement as if he had a secret he couldn't contain. His brown hair was gently wind-swept, his sky-blue eyes expressive—engaging with the camera, complemented by his teal T-shirt. His hands were resting comfortably in the pockets of his beige shorts.

Funny, I should come across this photo. How did it end up here, in this album? I shook my head in puzzlement as I leaned the lakeside photo against the lit lamp on the dresser beside my bedside.

Catching a glimpse of myself in the dresser mirror, I took a moment to observe my appearance. As it was close to bedtime, I was wearing pajamas: a UCSD T-shirt and loose striped pants. My brown hair was flat against my head, with no bounce or movement whatsoever. My hazel eyes were soft, no longer hiding underneath the mascara and eyeliner from earlier. My freckles spread across my face in almost a perfect T-formation, from the bridge of my nose to my cheeks—also no longer concealed by makeup.

Yawning, I made my way over to my bed, tossing the numerous throw pillows onto the floor. As I pulled up the covers, I rolled over to face the dresser, glancing at the photo of Justin and me one more time—with our wide-eyed, baby-faced smiles and youthful demeanors. We were only kids at the time—kids who could only dream of the future—a future of endless possibilities.

I thought back to the last time I saw Justin. Almost thirteen years ago, walking home from the treehouse—where we'd shared our first kiss. It was the first time a boy had ever touched my lips. Or my heart...the memory came flooding back in a torrent of warm emotion.

***

"Can you believe freshman year is only a few days away?" I remarked, slipping my halfwet feet into my sandals.

Justin and I had just finished drying off from our swim at the lake. As he put on his blue Quicksilver T-shirt over his swim trunks, I noticed his shirt emphasized his eyes. I consequently turned away from him, trying not to blush. Adolescent hormones were no joke.

"Yep. It's hard to imagine," he said.

As we walked down one of the quaint tree-lined streets of our suburban neighborhood, I took a deep breath, inhaling the fragrant warmth of the last summer days. Autumn would be here before we knew it—a beautiful time of the year.

But it also meant school. High school.

"How come?" I wondered.

As we arrived at our favorite treehouse, I sat on the bottom step to unstrap my damp sandals.

"Well, Hillview High is such a huge school," Justin said, climbing up to the first level of the treehouse. "Like what, two thousand students total? I mean, coming from Riverstone Charter, any grade level with more than thirty students is a lot."

"Yeah. That makes me nervous, too, when you put it that way. At least there's a lot more activities to join."

"True."

I observed the community treehouse for a moment. It was nestled against a few pines in the corner at the end of the street. The wood was the shade of sable, with a narrow ladder leading to its first and second stories—the structure still seemingly in decent condition. Neither of us had any idea who had originally built it or whose property it was considered—it wasn't private property, and the iconic "City of Ville du Lac" sign was missing from its base. Thus, we adopted it as our own.

"Do you remember when I first brought you here? To the treehouse?" I asked Justin, joining him on the first level.

"Yep. Eight years ago, the morning after we moved to the block," he remembered, pushing a strand of his wavy hair out of his face. "You came over to our driveway and introduced yourself. My mom and dad were still unloading the moving truck while Kyle and I were trying not to get in their way."

I nodded in remembrance. "That's right. You were frustrated about a broken toy when I first saw you."

"It was not a toy. It was an RC Jeep Renegade," Justin corrected me with a smirk. "Kyle threw it into the mud."

"Well, he was two at the time. What'd you expect?"

"For him not to throw my jeep into the mud."

"Right. Well, it was good of your mom to let you explore the neighborhood with me."

Justin climbed to the top level of the treehouse, sitting on the ledge. I sat down next to him, my bare feet and his black-and-white Converse sneakers dangling over the side. As my leg lightly brushed up against his, I felt a rush of hot energy flow through my body.

He smiled at me. "Yup. I'll never forget the first time I saw this view."

I adjusted the tie on my ponytail. "Yeah. Lake Awl is certainly a sight to see, isn't it?"

"You got that right."

We took a moment to admire the expansive lake before us. The water was a calm dark blue—the last rays of sunlight resting peacefully on its surface. Beyond the lake, on the horizon, dense forests of green gradually formed into lofty mountain peaks.

"I was thinking," I began. "Would you be interested in joining the drama club with me?"

Justin laughed loudly. His signature laugh. "What?! The drama club?! I don't know how to act!"

"Neither do I."

"You sure there aren't any other clubs you'd like to join?"

"Maybe, but I thought we should at least try it out and see how it goes."

Well, my dad certainly thought so. I still had some reservations about his suggestion, but I trusted him.

Justin sighed. "As long as I'm not expected to act in any plays."

"And what's wrong with that? Just saying you've been in a few plays already. Like in the third grade, when–"

He closed his eyes, shuddering. "God, no. Please don't recount that memory!"

I smirked at him. "Oh, you mean the one Christmas play where the tree collapsed as you set the star on top?"

"Yes, that one. Let's never bring up that disaster of a play again, ok? Because of that, my ankle was sprained for the rest of winter break."

"Ok, ok. I get it!" I giggled. "But seriously. High school is a new experience with a clean slate. We should take advantage of that."

I took a deep breath. "Maybe I'll finally fit in with the other girls."

Justin drew his eyebrows together in confusion. "Aren't you still friends with Megan and Christina? I thought all that drama got resolved last fall."

"I am. I just feel so behind, you know—when I compare myself to the other girls."

"With what? You're like the smartest girl in our class!"

"Thanks. It's a bit complicated."

He shifted in his sitting position. "I'm listening."

"You see, there are milestones girls are expected to meet. Basically, if we wanna be taken seriously in high school, we're expected to meet them."

"Really? That's ridiculous. Sounds like those girls are just looking for reasons to put down other girls."

"Pretty much."

"So what exactly are these 'milestones?' Like wearing makeup and dating and stuff?"

"Kind of. For instance, one is having our first kiss by the time we're in high school."

Justin looked at me, half-amused. In response, I turned my gaze toward the ground—trying to mitigate the awkwardness. I couldn't believe I'd just said that.

"I know. Lame, right? That's just how girls are, I guess." I forced a laugh.

He nodded. "Yeah, that is lame."

After a moment of silence, Justin spoke again. "Have you had yours yet?"

"What?"

"Your first kiss."

I shook my head as I felt my cheeks run hot. "No."

"That's ok. There's nothing wrong with that. In fact, I–" He stopped in mid-sentence.

I was intrigued by what he was about to say. "What is it?"

"Well, I was gonna suggest," Justin began, stammering a bit, "that maybe I could kiss you. If you wanted me to—for your milestone."

Instantly, my heart began to pick up speed. "I appreciate the offer, Justin, but I'm not sure it would count. Wouldn't it just be a sympathy kiss, not a real one?"

"I believe it'd count. I mean, who makes up the rules for these milestones, anyway?"

I looked up at the sky, trying to calm the flutters in my stomach. I noticed the first stars were beginning to appear, shining brightly against the backdrop of the twilight sky.

"Yeah, I'd be ok with that. As long as you are..." I said, feeling the palpitations of my heart intensify.

"Yep."

"Ok. Let's not tell anyone about this unless they ask."

"Will do."

Justin and I leaned in toward each other, tilting our heads slightly. My nose lightly brushed against his, as I closed my eyes. I felt our lips meet. In that moment, I felt peace. Bliss. The only thing that mattered then was Justin and how his lips felt on mine—gentle, warm, soft. I exhaled deeply. There was no place I'd rather be. No place at all...

Though the moment was quicker than it felt—before I knew it, we found ourselves pulling apart. I opened my eyes as they met Justin's for a brief second before gravitating to the ground.

We didn't say anything for a while as we climbed down from the top of the treehouse. I fastened my sandals once again, glancing above the treeline toward the sky. A darker shade of clouds was beginning to roll in.

"We should probably get going if we wanna avoid the rain and all," I said.

"Oh yeah. Absolutely," Justin agreed.

The two of us walked back onto the main road for about a block until we reached our street. It was beginning to drizzle.

"I hope you have a good rest of your night, Natalie," he said, smiling widely.

"You too!" I waved to him as I walked up the steps to my house.

I leaned my back against the front door, pausing, overtaken by a rush of awe. I couldn't shake the feeling I'd developed during our kiss—the feeling of not wanting the moment to end. The way Justin looked at me was different than before, my body trembled with exhilaration and fear. Is our friendship worth risking—for the sake of something greater? Like love?

I dismissed the thought as I reached for the doorknob. It was locked. My dad must not be home yet from fly-fishing, I figured. My mom was always the more cautious one. I knocked on our door.

Almost immediately, the door swung wide open—my mom on the other end, sighing with relief. "Oh, good! I'm glad you've beaten the storm!"

I scurried inside—the rainfall, as if on cue, was beginning to pick up momentum. As I took off my sandals, I found that I was still smiling. A smile I'd wear for the rest of the evening—until the next morning. The morning when my life changed forever: when I'd learned my father had died—the police finding his body submerged within the rapids of the Atlas River, and my mom's subsequent decision to move us to Montana to live with my grandmother—a mere three days later.

***

Reaching over to turn off the lamp, I allowed my hand to rest on the photo of us as I wondered: Where was Justin now? Was he living the future he always wanted? Was he surrounded by his friends and family in Ville du Lac? Or was he living someplace else—another state or another country? Most importantly, was he truly satisfied at the end of the day?

I returned my hand from the photo, rolling onto my back. I never once blamed Justin for our lost connection—it was a hectic time for everyone. I adjusted the pillow underneath my head. As I closed my eyes, allowing my body and mind to rest, I was left with only one question: Did Justin ever think of me?

Chapter Three

- -

"Ah! That was glorious, wasn't it? Don't you feel so rejuvenated?" Olivia asked me with a relaxed sigh.

I glanced behind my shoulder at the small, heated yoga studio, light steam escaping from its premises. It might as well be considered a sauna.

"I wouldn't say rejuvenated as much as dehydrated!" I replied, bringing my Nalgene water bottle to my mouth, feeling the relief of its cool, refreshing contents.

"But that's the point—to detoxify. How else are you supposed to release all that pent-up negative energy?" Olivia untied her ponytail, releasing her honey-blond hair onto her shoulders.

"Uh, how about sleep? Isn't that the purpose of it? I doubt our ancestors practiced hot yoga in their spare time, and they turned out just fine."

"Yeah, but they could've been better."

She adjusted her yoga mat, rolled it up, and tucked it underneath her arm. "Come on, Nat. What do you say? One more try next week—same time, same place?"

I shook my head. "I don't know about that, Olivia. I do know I'm not a fan of nicknames..."

"Oh, right. Sorry," she apologized as we walked out of the building toward the parking lot. "What about regular yoga? No heated room this time—just you and your mat."

I shrugged. "Possibly."

"You know what they need?" Olivia brought her index finger up to her cheek pensively. "A little cafe right next to the studio. It could be called 'Namaste Cafe.' Pretty catchy, huh?"

I held a hand over my mouth, trying to hold in a giggle.

"Oh, you think you've got something better?!" She laughed. "You're the one with the dream of opening your own coffee shop, right?"

"Not like that," I said as we approached her Honda sedan. "A legitimate coffee shop and bakery—like the one I remember when I lived with my grandma. A place where all people can come together, not just downward-dog-enthusiasts."

Olivia shook her head in amusement. "Still think it'd work."

"Then that can be your project." I pointed my finger at her, as I made my way over to my car.

"Don't forget—movie tonight, at six!" she called out to me. "The AMC by my place!"

I waved a hand at her, still moving forward. "Yep. Haven't forgotten."

As I reached for my car key, I sighed to myself. It'd been a long time since I'd last stepped foot into a theater of any kind. Not since high school. It wasn't so much due to my scarcity of free time—more that I had very little interest in paying money to sit through fifteen minutes of previews beforehand. Time, like money, was a limited resource for me. Though I eventually caved into my best friend's pleading, I still held onto the notion that no movie was worth the inconvenience—no matter who was starring in it.

***

"It's about time you saw the world." Olivia panned her hand out in front of her. "We need to get you plugged in. How are you still avoiding social media, after all this time?"

Grabbing my bag of popcorn from the concession stand, I glanced over at the various posters of upcoming movies plastered on the wall. Since when did superheroes become so popular?

"It's worked out well for me this far," I said as we walked over to the ticket line, "and I doubt browsing through friends' Facebook posts and pointless YouTube videos qualifies as 'seeing the world.'"

"Hey! Not all YouTube videos are pointless! Remember when I couldn't figure out how to pop the hood of my Honda? That video was a lifesaver."

"You know, there's also this fairly useful book called the car manual," I informed her sarcastically. "All you have to do is open your glove compartment."

Olivia gave me a smirk, as we stopped in front of one of the movie posters. "Real funny. But don't you feel like you've missed out at all? I mean, look at all those missed relationship opportunities."

I dug through my backpack to find my ticket stub. "Real opportunities. I'd even consider retaking Step 2 of the licensing exam to avoid the awkward small-talk of those dates."

"But not all of them were duds! Some of those guys were decent. You wouldn't know because you didn't give any of them a chance!"

"Really? Like Trey Rosenberg?"

Olivia put her hand up to defend herself. "Ok. That pairing was not my greatest judgment call, I have to admit."

I shook my head, half-laughing. "You think? He thought he knew me—from an alternate universe!"

"What can I say? The dude must've been high."

"Or deranged." I popped a piece of popcorn into my mouth.

"But, c'mon! Not every guy was like that, but you act like they were."

"I do not. I just ... have high standards for men, that's all."

It wasn't that I was ruling out all potential dating opportunities. I was choosing to be pragmatic, not idealistic—the odds of finding someone with my preferred qualities was a tall order.

"Yeah, and how's that working for you?" Olivia quipped, tossing a piece of my popcorn into her mouth.

I shrugged. "I'm fine with it. Better than unnecessary heartbreak."

"Regardless, your antisocial nature is hard to work around."

I put a hand on my hip in a lighthearted manner. "I'm hard to work around? What about you? Your relationship status with Derek is impossible to keep up with. By the way, are you on or off now?"

"Off. That's why you're here tonight."

"Of course. I'm the rebound—and you also wanted to see a rom-com for a change!"

"Bingo." She pulled out her smartphone to check the time. "We should get our seats now before all the good ones are taken."

I sighed. "Even though it'll just be previews for a while."

"That's like the best part! Gets you all pumped for the new movies in store!"

"Or for the additional money to waste..."

As we waited in line for our tickets to be torn, I briefly looked over my shoulder, at the poster we'd passed.

" 'The Dalí Effect'? Huh. Never heard of it," I noted as we reached the front of the line.

I was only able to catch a glimpse of the title. I didn't care enough to turn my head again for the actors. Like it really mattered, anyway. I wasn't planning to return to the movies anytime soon.

***

"Ugh. Another one?" I groaned, checking the time on my smartphone.

Olivia and I were slightly reclined in our seats, legs crossed, as yet another green rating card flashed onto the theater screen. By that point, I calculated there'd already been about twenty-five minutes of previews. Twenty-five. That was a record for me.

I watched as the screen played a trailer for an action-based psychological thriller about the interconnection of dreams. If I have to watch one more of these previews, that's what I'll be doing!

"This one looks good!" Olivia said.

As the trailer progressed, I noticed one young man in particular who was present in most of the scenes. For some reason, he looked oddly familiar. As the trailer was fast-paced, I couldn't quite study him thoroughly, but it appeared he had brown hair and blue eyes. I was not able to identify him.

"He's looking good, too!" Olivia added.

Toward the end of the trailer, the movie title was displayed. 'The Dalí Effect'—the movie poster from earlier. So now, I could say I legitimately recognized one of the previews we were forced to sit through. Cool, I guess?

The trailer then proceeded to list the main actors' names. Immediately, it dawned on me why that one particular man looked so familiar.

The insides of my stomach lurched forward, as my bag of popcorn fell to the floor—my gaze still fixed on the screen, in shock. "Oh my God. I know him!"

"Don't we all…" Olivia said dreamily. "That's not a face you can forget."

"No, really! Justin—that's my childhood friend! He lived across the street from me when I was younger."

"Seriously?! For real?!" Olivia exclaimed, drawing the attention of the audience. "Sorry."

"I'll explain later," I whispered.

I returned my focus to the big screen—the opening credits of the feature film beginning to roll. My thoughts continued to stray from the movie as I found myself thinking back to the preview with Justin. It was hard to tell if he was the same guy as my friend. His last name was different—Anderson. That could be his screen name, or he could be a different guy altogether. However, he did seem to carry an air of familiarity about him.

If they were the same person, though … then wow. That'd be something!

***

"I believe this answers your question, Natalie," Olivia said.

As I joined her on her Ikea couch in the living room of her seaside apartment, she displayed the bright screen of her laptop to me—the full-fledged IMDb page of my childhood friend.

Wouldn't you know, Justin was indeed an actor. An A-list actor.

"'Justin Anderson was born Justin Daniel Sanders in Ville du Lac, Idaho, to Jennifer Sanders, a realtor, and Robert Sanders, a landscaper,'" Olivia read, scrolling down the page of her web browser. "Wow, I didn't know he began acting when he joined the drama club as a freshman! It looks like his family moved to LA when he was sixteen so he could pursue acting. And that was all right before he was selected to star in Midnight Club when he rose to fame. That is so crazy!"

I still couldn't believe what I was reading. Peering over her shoulder at the computer screen, I studied the current webpage listing all of Justin's filmography and credits. I was truly impressed by his repertoire—especially for someone with little to no acting experience before the age of fourteen.

"Wow, he's been busy," I noted.

"You've really never seen any of his movies before?" Olivia questioned.

I shook my head.

She laughed in disbelief. "Wow, where have you been?"

"Med school."

"Oh yeah. Right."

I continued to read the webpage over her shoulder. Toward the bottom, it displayed one of Justin's headshots. I recognized his brown hair and blue eyes from the preview earlier—not to mention from eight years of shared childhood memories. Those striking blue eyes were not easy to forget.

"This whole time, I never put two-and-two together: that your neighbor Justin—the same Justin who played with you as kids and made out with you in a treehouse—was none other than Justin Anderson," Olivia remarked. "My God! Is there anyone else on your block I should know about? Like maybe the other Justin—Justin Bieber? Oh wait, he's from Canada. Never mind."

I chuckled. "Ville du Lac's not that far north! It's not like we have moose crossing our streets … most of the time. But, hey! I did not 'make out' with him! It was just a quick peck on the lips to cross that milestone off my adolescent checklist."

"Sure, whatever you say!" Olivia teased. "But we've gotta meet him!"

I sighed. "I doubt it'll be that easy. One does not simply meet a celebrity on the street on any given day!"

"In LA, you might," she pointed out. "Maybe there's a movie premiere we can crash!"

I raised an eyebrow at her. "Crash? As in trespass? Isn't that illegal?"

"Not if it's like a public meet-and-greet. I recall some premieres allow fans on the sides as the celebrities walk down the red carpet."

"Really?! That cannot still be a thing. And even if it was, it's unlikely Justin will be attending a premiere in the next week or so."

Olivia turned her laptop away from me as she suddenly began to type vigorously. After a few minutes, she revealed her screen to me with a smug smile. "I believe you are mistaken. There's a premiere for 'The Dalí Effect' at the Chinese Theater in Hollywood on Wednesday. Since Justin is starring in that movie, he'll most definitely be at that premiere."

I shook my head. "What are you doing? We can't just show up at a movie premiere! Besides, I have a shift at the Coffee Bean that day, so it wouldn't work with my schedule, anyway."

"The Coffee Bean?! Do you hear yourself, Natalie?! This is the chance of a lifetime! Do you really wanna spend the rest of your life regretting not reuniting with your movie star friend—just to work a shift at a coffee shop? If I were you, I'd start looking for a shift replacement now."

"Fine, I guess," I agreed reluctantly. "But you know we probably won't be able to meet him, right? Most of this trip will probably be spent sitting in traffic."

"Don't be ridiculous! LA is only a few hours away! Traffic shouldn't be too bad if we drive before rush hour." Olivia closed her laptop. "For now, I'm assigning you some homework."

"Homework?"

"Yup, that's right. You're gonna watch all of Justin's movies, starting with 'Midnight Club'!"

I laughed to myself. "For real? What's he gonna do, start quizzing me at the premiere?"

"No, this is for your own good. So you can stay relevant."

"I am relevant!" I retorted.

"Oh, really? Ever heard of 'Gangnam Style'?"

I gave her a blank stare. "What?"

"My point exactly."

"I'm as relevant as I need to be," I muttered to myself, grabbing my backpack next to me.

Olivia could be a bit much, personality-wise. That evening, she was on a whole different scale. I was not holding my breath for meeting Justin Anderson at his movie premiere. That would be a movie plot of its own.

Chapter Four

- -

"Why is there traffic in the middle of the day? This doesn't make sense!" Olivia complained in mid-stride, trying not to trip over her black kitten heels.

We'd just parked my car almost a mile away from the Chinese Theater. Due to the typical state of the LA roads, we were running late for the premiere—literally.

"Because LA doesn't make sense," I huffed. "That's why we live in San Diego."

Olivia stopped to catch her breath. "I bet we can still make the premiere in time. Pretty sure the limos would get stuck in traffic, too; not every street can have an HOV lane."

I looked down at the sidewalk, raising a foot. "But they sure have a lot of these star plaques."

"Oh, the Hollywood Walk of Fame? I wonder if Justin has one!"

I laughed. "Let's not get ahead of ourselves."

Eventually, we arrived at the Chinese Theater. I observed hordes of people standing within eyeshot, roped off on the two sides of the iconic red carpet, which led to the grand theater entrance. The carpet itself was much skinnier in real life, I noted, almost resembling a sort of walking path—a pathway to the stars. Cameras, cell phones, and energetic fans were abundant. Out of my comfort zone would be an understatement.

I was glad I didn't follow Olivia's lead in the wardrobe department as she styled a halter dress and heels for the occasion. Instead, I opted for a simple olive-green peasant top, skinny jeans, and light-brown Teva sandals—like any other day.

"Olivia, this is not going to work," I said as we faced the backs of several dozen spectators. "There are a ton of people here. I can't see any conceivable way we can make it to the front. I bet they've been staking out their spots for hours."

"Don't worry, Natalie," Olivia reassured, putting a hand on my shoulder. "I have a plan. Do you have those photos I asked you to bring?"

I nodded, rolling my eyes.

Without hesitation, she pulled me by the arm toward a security guard off to the side, monitoring the rush of foot traffic. He was a larger man who had the intensity and concentration of a Secret Service agent. I did not want to see the outcome of this encounter.

"Excuse me, sir," Olivia began, catching his attention, "but is there a way we could possibly meet Justin Anderson? Natalie here was his best friend growing up, and would love to see him again, for old time's sake."

The security guard laughed, obviously not taking her request seriously. "Can't tell you how many times I've heard that one before. Nice try."

I sighed, unzipping my backpack. I couldn't believe I was about to do this. "No, it's true. We both grew up in Ville du Lac and went to Riverstone Charter together through the eighth grade. Here's some photos to prove it."

I grabbed two photos from my backpack—the one of Justin and me by Lake Awl and our eighth-grade class photo—and handed them to the security guard. He thoroughly inspected them, including the small list of students' names at the bottom of the class photo.

"You're both in here?" he questioned me, still reading the students' names.

"Yup. I'm in the front row, far-left corner. The name's Natalie Baker. And there's Justin, in the center—under his birth name, Sanders," I said, pointing to one of the boys in the middle row. "He wasn't tall enough to stand in the middle row until that year. In the seventh grade, with Mrs. Larsen, he was still in the front row with me. He was sort of a late bloomer."

I giggled to myself. "You can always check online—to confirm what I said is true."

The security guard shook his head. "Well, I don't believe you're lying. The roster speaks for itself."

He reviewed the class photo one more time and handed both photos back to me. "This is not something we normally do, so consider this your lucky day."

Olivia squealed with excitement as the security guard escorted us to the front of the crowd, mere inches away from the ever-enticing red carpet. Eyes of envious fans followed our every move as we passed by.

"Thank you so much!" Olivia enthused.

"We really appreciate it," I said.

He nodded as he promptly returned to his post in the back of the crowd.

"See, I told you I had a plan!" Olivia said. "Where'd you find that school photo, by the way?"

"In an album, on the top shelf of my aunt and uncle's closet," I answered.

I was surprised I even found that old family album of mine—a separate album from my high school and college photos. Judging by the accumulation of dust and clutter, no one had sorted through the top shelf in years.

"Did you know that Justin practices Jiu-Jitsu with Shia LaBeouf?" Olivia said, scrolling on her phone.

"What?! Where'd you hear that?" I laughed.

"Online."

"Yeah, that's almost certainly false!"

Within a few minutes, a shiny black limo drove up to the theater entrance. I studied the handful of people who made their way to the red carpet, all decked out in formal attire and surrounded by massive flashes of light. Celebrities.

"Has Justin arrived yet?!" Olivia asked eagerly, trying to catch a better glimpse of the star-studded individuals.

"I don't think so," I replied.

Suddenly, out of the corner of my eye, I spotted another jet-black limo at the head of the red carpet. Loud, high-pitched shrieks of exhilaration rang through the crowd as I watched the various finely dressed individuals climb out of the limo—including a young man who appeared to match the online headshot from the other day.

My stomach did a backflip. It was Justin.

Physically, Justin had changed considerably since the last time I'd seen him in person. But he still had that familiarity about him—nostalgia, if you will. Basically, like a grown-up version of the boy I remembered from across the street: the boy who'd knock on my door whenever he wanted to embark on a scavenger hunt through the woods or trek up the hill for a spectacular view of the Northwest wilderness. The boy who'd bike into town with me whenever we were craving some huckleberry ice cream. The boy who'd take a dive with me into the crystal-clear lake—only to discover he'd forgotten to bring a towel to dry off afterward. That boy.

Justin had certainly grown since then, but he was not overly tall or big—still on the slender side. He had wavy, brown hair that was a bit long but not unkempt, complementing his light skin. His smooth, chiseled jawline had matured, while his cheeks still held onto some of that baby fat from his youth. I recognized his wide smile and prominent blue eyes. He was styling a sleek, dark-blue Armani suit as he greeted some of his fans on the sidelines.

Needless to say, he was bona fide heartthrob material.

I couldn't pinpoint how I was feeling at that moment. Curious? Scared? Excited? Something more?

It had been years since the last time I'd seen Justin. It hadn't even crossed my mind that I'd ever bump into him again. Now, he was apparently a world-famous actor with an enormous fanbase. Within this context, it would seem even less likely now that we'd ever cross paths again.

But here I was—chilling on the sidelines at his film premiere.

Suddenly, Justin proceeded to walk down the red carpet.

Closer to us.

An intense wave of shyness hit me, my heart beating overtime. Instinctively, I turned my face to one side, away from the roped-off carpet.

"Natalie, what's wrong?" Olivia wondered.

"I can't do this!" I admitted.

Olivia whistled loudly, using both of her fingers. "Yo, Justin! Your friend Natalie from Ville du Lac is here to see you!"

That grabbed Justin's attention. He looked over at us, seemingly confused. After a moment, his eyes softened as his lips crept into a smile—a smile of recognition. He headed over to us.

My shyness was at its max. I desperately wanted to hide right then and there.

"Natalie?! Is that really you?!" Justin exclaimed.

He seemed surprised yet glad to see me.

"Yep, it's me," I replied, meekly.

"Wow, long time! How are you?"

"I'm doing alright. You're doing quite well for yourself, I see!"

Justin laughed loudly. *I remember that laugh.*

Olivia nudged me.

"Oh, yes. This is my best friend, Olivia," I introduced her.

He shook her hand. "Pleasure to meet you."

Olivia's eyes widened, starstruck. "The pleasure is mine! Your movies are awesome, by the way! I still can't believe you and Natalie were neighbors growing up! That's amazing! She's told me so many good things about her childhood friend, and I never realized she was talking about you the whole time!"

I glanced down at my sandals, trying not to blush.

"Thank you," Justin replied. "We have a lot to catch up on. Like twelve, thirteen years' worth of stuff? Will you both be in town tomorrow?"

Before I had an opportunity to answer, Olivia blurted, "Of course we will!"

"Cool! Do you have a pen and paper?" he asked us.

I nodded as I pulled out my pad of paper and pen from my backpack, handing them to Justin.

He flipped open the pad to its first empty page and quickly wrote something that was out of my line of sight. Closing the pad, he handed them back to me.

Promptly, I returned the pen and paper to my backpack.

"If you wouldn't mind keeping this to yourselves, that'd be much appreciated," Justin added.

"No problem!" I agreed.

He stepped away from the rope dividing us. "Thanks! We'll catch up tomorrow, then. Awesome seeing you both!"

"You too!"

Justin waved to us with a smile as he continued to walk down the red carpet, periodically stopping along the way to meet other fans.

Olivia and I broke away from the crowd, moving to a secluded corner about a block away. I then unzipped my backpack and pulled out the pad of paper.

"What does it say?!" Olivia anxiously tugged on my sleeve.

I flipped open the pad to the page with Justin's slightly messy handwriting—Olivia actively staring over my shoulder. I noticed an address was written down, followed by the time of 10 am. Now I realized why Justin had asked me for a pen and paper—the surrounding fans and press probably thought he was signing his autograph. Smart.

"Maybe it's his house?" Olivia guessed.

I closed the pad of paper. "Yeah, right. That's pretty private information for a celebrity to share."

"But you're his friend!" Olivia pointed out.

"Regardless, we have nowhere to stay tonight. I'd rather not drive back and forth to LA."

"No worries, I booked us a hotel."

I chuckled. "Of course you did."

"We packed our suitcases, didn't we?!"

"Yes, we did."

"So we're all set! Now, we can do some shopping!"

"What for? We're only here for one additional day."

She pointed her finger at me. "Exactly! We'll need to find the perfect outfit for you tomorrow. Something that says 'childhood-friend-looking-to-be-friendlier.'"

I shoved Olivia playfully.

As we began the long walk back to our car, I couldn't help but wonder. What would be in store for us tomorrow? A meetup with a celebrity was uncharted territory for me—especially a celebrity whom I kissed on a previous occasion.

That most certainly makes things weird.

Chapter Five

Awestruck, I watched as we drove by the countless large estates nestled within the hills of Malibu. I sighed—just a typical neighborhood for the rich and famous.

"That's it!" Olivia exclaimed.

I steered my car over to the chrome-gated entrance. Along with the car, I felt my heart lunge forward as I abruptly shifted into park. I took a quick glance beyond the lofty gates—noticing a private road leading to a large, beige house, mostly hidden away by tall hedges. I also noticed an intercom by the front of the gate.

"Called it! This is totally Justin's house," Olivia stated, beaming like the sunlight shining through my windshield.

Still in the driver's seat, I reached through the open car window, pressing the big, round button on the intercom next to the speaker. The intercom beeped, and a male voice that was not Justin's answered bluntly, "What is your business here?"

For a moment, I thought we may have stopped at the wrong house—before I realized that celebrities probably required additional security at their residences.

"Uh, yes. I'm Justin's friend, Natalie Baker," I began, trying not to stammer. "My friend Olivia is here with me, as well. Justin asked us to meet him here at ten."

"Yes. After the gates open, please follow the paved road to the main courtyard. You can park your car on the right side with the other vehicles."

"Ok. Will do!"

The front gate automatically opened, and we drove through it, heading down the private road as instructed. I parked my car in the driveway, sandwiched between two sports cars—a slick silver Audi and a dark-blue, high-end vehicle whose hood ornament I didn't recognize. Ferrari? Porsche? Nevertheless, my red, economy-size Volvo stuck out like a sore thumb.

As I gingerly opened my door, side-stepping around the sports cars, I observed my surroundings. The house and courtyard were Mediterranean style, with shrub pots hanging in every corner and tiles of various shades of brown encompassing the large driveway. The right side of the courtyard included a four-car garage with a similar tile design, just behind where we parked our car. The left side included the wide, burgundy front door to the house and an adjacent dome archway that looked like it led to the backyard. The house itself was a beige-cream color two stories high. It included a burgundy Spanish-style roof and long, arched windows with matching burgundy trim. This home seemed like a resort to me.

Suddenly, the front door opened, and Justin stepped through the high-vaulted entrance. He smiled and waved to us as he casually walked over. He was wearing a light-blue cotton polo shirt and dark wash jeans, his hands resting in his pockets. His smile was relaxed as he brushed a few strands of his hair out of his Paul Newman blue eyes.

I felt myself jolt slightly.

"Hey! Great to see you again!" Justin greeted us. "Were you able to find the place, alright?"

"Yeah, no problem at all," Olivia replied confidently.

"Well, we took a slight detour by Pepperdine, but we found our way back onto the main road after that," I added.

"Glad to hear. Would you like to catch up on the back patio?" Justin asked, gesturing toward the other side of the house.

"Sure, sounds great!" I answered.

"Yeah, I'm open to anything!" Olivia said.

"Cool," he said. "Follow me, then!"

We walked through the dome archway I'd correctly predicted would lead to his back patio.

I noticed additional potted shrubs, some of which were hanging and others that were placed on the ground. The patio was also fashioned in a Mediterranean style. There were two small tables, each complete with a red umbrella and four cushioned chairs, adjacent to a swimming pool and a small putting green. Beyond that was a generous view of the Pacific Ocean—the cherry on top for the quintessential A-lister home.

***

"Wow, so you basically became famous overnight!" I noted, adjusting my position on the cushioned seat.

Justin and I were bringing each other up to speed on the past thirteen years, with an occasional interjection from Olivia.

"Yep! Pretty much," Justin responded. "I was only eighteen years old and college-bound, so I never expected my life to change after that film."

"Well, I really enjoyed 'Midnight Club', even if it was originally made for TV," Olivia commented, swishing around the ice in her glass of iced tea. "The sequels were great, too, but they lost a bit of that low-budget charm the first one had."

I felt the cool ocean breeze brush against me as I took a sip from my glass. "I like your patio design, by the way," I said. "It almost feels like I'm on vacation. Well, vacationing out of California, I mean."

"I know! This place is gorgeous!" Olivia remarked.

"Oh, thanks," Justin said. "The layout was mostly Erica's idea."

"Your girlfriend, Erica Rhode, right?" Olivia clarified.

"Yep," Justin confirmed, glancing off to the side, at the aqua-blue pool. Now, I was curious. "How did you two meet?"

"They were co-stars in 'Midnight Club'," Olivia explained. "They've been dating since filming the sequel, so that's eight years now. Is that right?"

"Uh-huh," Justin answered quickly, seemingly uncomfortable.

"So, are you guys going on any vacations this summer?" Olivia rested her chin on her hand, elbow propped up on the table, and continued, "Must be nice to be able to travel anywhere! I can only dream."

He shook his head. "No, our schedules are both pretty tight. Haven't been on an actual vacation together in a couple years."

"Aww, that's too bad."

Justin gestured toward Olivia and me with his index finger. "What about you two? Are you seeing anyone?"

Olivia sighed. "It's complicated."

He looked at me in anticipation. The midday sun began to feel like a spotlight, beating down on my shoulders. "I'm not seeing anyone," I quickly answered him.

Out of the blue, I felt the urge to elaborate further. "Yeah, I don't do casual dating. I prefer remaining single over settling into a half-hearted relationship. It'd just be a waste of time for both of us. A relationship requires some effort, in my opinion."

Justin looked down for a moment; a serious expression crossed his face. He then returned his attention to me, proceeding to change the subject. "How's your family doing, Natalie?"

Crap. I overshared, didn't I?!! That's why he'd changed the subject—after a moment of awkward silence. I tried to keep calm and not reveal my regret.

"My mom's doing well," I responded. "She's still living with my grandma in Montana, not too far from Kalispell. She's working as an administrator again for an elementary school. They're actually in town right now—in San Diego. They came for my med school graduation."

"Good to hear. I'm glad they could come for that. That's an amazing accomplishment! I mean, you were always at the top of our class, so it makes sense you're a doctor now. Still amazing." Justin cleared his throat. "So, do your other relatives also live in Montana?"

"No, just my mom and grandma. I'm currently living with my aunt and uncle, who are also in San Diego. I'll be looking for a place of my own once I begin my residency. How is your family?"

He adjusted the umbrella pole in the center of our table. "They're alright. My parents split a few years into my high school. My mom remarried about five years ago."

"I'm so sorry to hear that. Do they live nearby?"

"Relatively—except for my dad. He's still in Ville du Lac, I believe, at a different house. My parents sold our old home when they divorced. My mom and stepdad live in Pasadena. She's working in finance now, at a software company, I think. I forget what my stepdad does. Kyle lives in

Orange County, finishing school. I believe this is his last year. He's changed his major a couple times. I think he's studying computer science now. Haven't talked with them in a little while. But it sounds like they're all doing well."

As we continued to share more about our families, I still couldn't ignore my regret for speaking so rashly about relationships. I wanted to apologize, but I was unable to find an opportunity where it wouldn't come off as awkward. I'd done enough damage in the awkward category for the day.

***

After some time of chatting, Justin checked the time on his smartphone. "Wow, has it already been more than two hours? Damn. Almost lost track of time! Well, I should probably start getting ready for my press conference that's happening soon. I'll walk you both out to the front again."

We got up from our chairs, returning to the line of parked cars in the front courtyard.

"Thank you for inviting us over, Justin!" I said. "I'm so glad we had a chance to catch up! It's been a long time."

"Same here!" Justin agreed as he took out his phone. "Would you like to exchange numbers? Probably shouldn't wait for another thirteen years to talk again!"

He let out a small chuckle.

"Yeah, totally!" Olivia whipped out her phone.

"I trust you'll keep it to yourselves?" he asked pensively.

Olivia nodded assuredly.

"I promise," I told him.

After we exchanged phone numbers, Justin proceeded to give both of us a hug. I was thrown off-guard for a moment as he wrapped his arms around my upper back, my chest lightly pressing up against his. He had a subtle, fresh scent of pine. I steadied myself.

"It was so awesome meeting you!" Olivia enthused as we climbed back into my car.

"You as well, Olivia. Hope you and Natalie have a safe drive back," Justin responded with a smile and wave.

"Thank you. I hope your press conference goes well!" I said.

"Thanks!"

As Olivia and I drove onto the main road, I was still in disbelief that the past few hours had actually happened. I never would've imagined reuniting with Justin—a movie star, no less. The time we'd spent at his house seemed to have flown by.

At the end of it all, I'd received Justin's phone number—yet I didn't know the proper protocol. Is it ever acceptable to contact a celebrity directly? If so, is it okay to text Justin and ask about his day like I would with any other friend? Or should I wait for him to reach out to me, given his busy schedule? Even though he was no resident doctor, I'd imagine the work demands of an A-list actor to be quite taxing.

Chapter Six

"**N**atalie, do you mind moving this frame to that corner over there?" Mom asked me, gesturing to the right-hand corner of my uncle and aunt's family room.

"Sure," I replied, as my mom handed me an unused 11×14 wooden photo frame. I gently placed it in the corner of the room, per her request.

"Thanks, Honey."

I rejoined my family in the center of the room, continuing to dig through a large cardboard box—a box with my dad's belongings. Within its confines, I retrieved a smaller, sealed white box. I sat down on the carpeted floor to inspect it further.

"Still can't believe we missed this! It got lost within the mess of your old hobbies," Uncle Chris said to my aunt. "That top shelf needs to be cleaned. You can't find anything in that closet of yours!"

"My closet? It's just as much yours as it is mine! Besides, at least my sewing proved to be a fairly useful hobby," Aunt Liz stated, defending herself. "As for you, when was the last time you've gone paddleboarding? That board is taking up more space in the garage than all my sewing materials combined!"

"It's not taking up that much space!"

She looked at my uncle doubtfully. "Really? So you're telling me there's enough room to finally park my car in the garage?"

"No. I never said that."

"Well, then. I bet once you move that paddleboard of yours, it'll be a very different story."

"Doubt it."

Aunt Liz stood up from her seat on the family room couch. "Let me see for myself. It's about time I decluttered the garage, anyway."

"Hold on, I'll help you! You shouldn't handle the board alone; it'll strain your back."

Uncle Chris quickly followed her into the back of the house, opening the door leading to the garage.

"That's marriage for you!" Grandma observed with a smile. "Always right until proven wrong."

I nodded in understanding. During most of my time in their residence, I observed my aunt's and uncle's relationship to be rather comical—almost like a sitcom, in a way. For a moment, I thought back to my parents' interactions with one another. Their marriage also proved to be relatively positive and playful—until my dad began to spend more hours at the hospital than at home.

"Natalie. I keep meaning to ask. How was your visit with Becky on Wednesday?" Mom questioned me. "She works at Ernst & Young now, right?"

"She's still at Deloitte. I had a good time visiting her," I lied.

I didn't inform my mom—or anyone, for that matter—about my adventures in meeting Justin. It was much easier to use the excuse of visiting one of my undergrad friends.

"Good. It's amazing Becky can still tolerate that LA culture," Mom continued. "I can't stand the glorification of celebrities! What losers—just a bunch of entitled divas who'll do anything for attention."

"Not all of them are like that," I pointed out. "I bet some are just trying to go about their day, like the rest of us."

"Ok, not all of them. But still, a pretty scummy lifestyle, if you ask me."

Mom continued to look through the larger box of my dad's items. "You, on the other hand, are actually doing something productive with your life. I still can't get over how proud I am of you. I know your father would be, too—graduating with the same specialty as him!"

"Thanks."

Noticing the small unopened box still in my hands, I reached for the scissors. I carefully cut through the tape and opened its flaps. I peered inside.

"Wow, these items are still in pristine condition," I noted.

"Your father was always very careful with his belongings," Mom said. "A little too careful, sometimes. I remember he wouldn't let me within a foot of his fishing pole. Probably because every time I'd try to handle it, the line would get tangled."

Grandma chuckled.

I suddenly felt a spark of curiosity. "Mom, can I ask you something?"

"Yes. Go ahead," she responded, pulling out a gold watch.

"Have you ever thought about returning to Ville du Lac? I know it's been a while. I thought maybe it'd be nice to revisit our old neighborhood and the lake sometime. Dad always loved North Idaho—and for good reason. It's beautiful up there."

"Honey, you know it's not easy for me—to dissociate that place with your father's death. It's too dark. It's too much." Mom sighed. "Sorting through his belongings is enough for me."

She drew her eyebrows together pensively. "Now, what prompted you to ask that in the first place?"

I shrugged. "Nothing in particular. Just going through Dad's stuff, I guess. It brings back memories."

"Do either of you ladies know where I can pour myself a glass of water?" Grandma wondered.

"I'll grab you some," Mom replied. "The filter on their fridge can be finicky."

"Nonsense. I can figure it out."

"No, Mom. The ice and water settings are in different places than you'd expect. I don't want you tripping over ice."

"I can handle myself. How tricky can a water filter be?"

Mom and Grandma headed into the kitchen as I continued looking through the small box. Most of the items were related to fishing in some way. As I dug deeper into the box, my hand brushed against a photo envelope. Opening its flap, I found a series of developed photos, along with their corresponding negatives haphazardly shoved into the back pocket. I took a few photos and studied them for a moment.

They were sunset landscapes of the east bank of the Atlas River. I turned one of the photos over in my hand. I noticed it had a date of 8/31/02 printed on its back—probably when the photo was developed.

That was when I realized—the printed date was the day after my father's death when his body was found on the west bank of the river. I checked all the other photos in the envelope. Each of them shared the same date of 8/31/02.

Something wasn't right...

"Find anything interesting?" Mom called out to me from the kitchen.

Without hesitation, I quickly put all the photos back into their envelope, stashing it in my backpack. I was zipping up my backpack when my mom and grandma returned to the family room.

"No. Mostly fishing gear," I answered her.

"I figured." Mom sat down next to me. "Well, I'm going to miss you. This past week has gone by too fast."

She reached over to hug me.

"I'll miss you too, Mom."

"You know, you can always visit us whenever your schedule allows," Grandma said. "We'll host you anytime!"

I nodded. "Thank you. I'll let you know."

I took a deep breath, redirecting my focus to the last of my dad's items—my nervous system going into overdrive. I'm overthinking the situation, I realized. I must be... Overthinking was always one of my greatest weaknesses. I need to calm down and give my mind a break. I took another deep breath for good measure. Jumping to conclusions would only generate unnecessary stress—something I could live without.

***

"So, how's your family?" Olivia asked me, scooping another bite of Pad Thai from her to-go container.

We were just finishing our takeout dinner that same evening and watching one of Olivia's current TV obsessions—our usual Monday routine.

"Good," I replied as I threw the rest of my meal into her trash bin. "My mom and grandma leave tomorrow, so I'm glad I got the chance to see them one more time."

"Awesome!" Olivia pushed her container to the side of her living room coffee table. She took a glimpse of my partially unzipped backpack—lying next to the armrest of her couch. "What's that?"

I gave her a puzzled look. "What's what?"

She proceeded to reach into my backpack, pulling out the envelope of my dad's sunset landscapes. "These."

"Oh. Those." My heart stopped. "They're photos of the Atlas River, where my dad used to go fishing—about a thirty-minute drive from our old house in Ville du Lac."

"Cool. Did he go there often?"

"Whenever he was off the clock. Not many people knew of that part of the river, and the waters were calm, so he liked to fish there. He'd simply drive to the turnout, park his car, and walk through the forest until he'd reach his fishing spot." I sighed heavily, my hands beginning to tremble.

"What's wrong?" Apparently, the trembling wasn't as subtle as I'd perceived.

"Well," I began, "the Atlas River consists of the east bank, where these photos were taken, and the west bank, where the waters were faster and more treacherous..." I paused, working up the nerve to continue. "When my dad died, his body was found on the west bank. We'd presumed he'd slipped while fishing, hitting his head on a rock—blunt force head trauma, according to the autopsy report. An accident. But these photos seem to suggest he was actually fishing on the east bank that day, at around sunset."

In that case, my dad had kept his promise to me all along—the promise that he'd never fish on the west bank.

Olivia looked at me questioningly. "How do you know that? That the photos were taken on the same day of his death?"

I turned one of the pictures to its back, revealing its development date.

"August 31st is the day he died?" Olivia asked.

"The day after," I clarified.

"What if those photos were taken on an earlier day and were developed later?"

"Probably not. During our last summer in Ville du Lac, my dad was swamped with work and had very little time for fishing—it takes a few hours, at least. If that were the case, they'd have to have been taken much earlier in the year. But that'd be around wintertime, so I'd expect to see some snow on the ground."

Or, maybe he did find another chance to go fishing in the summertime that I wasn't aware of. There was no way to know for sure. I was unnecessarily spinning myself in circles.

Olivia scratched the side of her head, intrigued. "Hmm. Is it easy to walk from the east bank to the west bank?"

"Not with fly-fishing gear in tow. It's pretty bulky, I recall. The same turnout can access both riverbanks, but with fishing gear and the sun setting, it would've been a difficult trip by foot. So, it wouldn't have been his choice to visit the west bank."

"Then whose was it?" Her eyes widened in suspense.

"Exactly."

At that moment, Olivia's cell phone rang. She picked it up, glancing at the screen. "Be right back."

I nodded, as she brought the phone to her ear and sauntered into her bedroom.

I took a deep breath, trying to calm my nerves. With a quick zip, I slipped my dad's landscape photos back into their envelope, returning them to the main compartment of my backpack.

I adjusted myself on Olivia's couch and looked up at the muted TV screen. It was displaying some celebrity gossip show. I continued to watch the program, as it showed footage of paparazzi overcrowding a celebrity couple who were exiting a restaurant.

Ugh! It must be so rough having virtually no privacy wherever you go! I wondered how Justin dealt with having such a public lifestyle. Personally, I would go insane.

"What are you watching?" I asked Olivia, once she returned to the couch. "This doesn't look like 'The Bachelorette'."

She took the remote lying on the coffee table, unmuting the TV. " 'Entertainment Tonight'. We've got a few minutes."

Coincidentally, the footage shifted to another famous couple—half of whom I knew quite well.

"Ooh! Perfect timing!" Olivia remarked excitedly, turning up the volume.

Under the headline 'Justin & Erica Breakup,' the program displayed a photo of my childhood friend and a young woman whom I didn't recognize—Erica, presumably. They were holding hands and walking along a beach. The program continued to show additional videos and snapshots of the couple at various public outings and events.

It seemed that Erica's favorite place in the world was by Justin's side—fondly holding onto his arm, affectionately whispering in his ear, and passionately kissing him with her arms wrapped around him like a Christmas gift, minus the bow.

As I watched the TV screen, I took a closer look at Erica. Her silky dark-brown hair rested on her shoulders, complementing her flawless olive skin. She wore a dazzling, confident smile in a league of its own—only rivaling Justin's. She seemed to radiate as if she were a Greek goddess. There was no doubt that she knew how to work the camera—and Justin's heart.

"We have just learned that 'Jerica' is no more," the news commentator began. *"Justin Anderson and Erica Rhode have officially ended their*

eight-year relationship as of yesterday. Sources of the former 'Midnight Club' co-stars state that both of them have drifted apart over the years and have amicably agreed to go their separate ways. What will become of their multi-million dollar Malibu estate? It is too soon to tell. We will continue to provide you with updates as this top story unfolds."

"Can you believe it?!" Olivia exclaimed as she turned down the volume. "This is totally a sign!"

"Of what?" I asked, taking a sip of water.

"That you and Justin are meant to be together!"

I almost spit out my water. "Me and Justin? That's ridiculous. You know, it was probably inevitable their relationship would end, as they haven't spent much time together in recent years."

"Well, that'd be a pretty big coincidence! I mean, they broke up right after we saw him. I bet Justin was the one who broke up with Erica. That way, he could have a chance with you!"

I shook my head, half-laughing. "Try not to get your hopes up too much. It's only Monday. We've still got the rest of the week ahead of us."

As Olivia switched the channel to her program, I couldn't help but wonder: Did my visit with Justin have any bearing on his relationship with Erica? More specifically, did my off-hand comment about relationships rub him the wrong way? I tried not to overthink the situation. I'd done enough of that on the drive home.

Now that I have Justin's phone number, would it be understandable to text him and see how he's doing? Or would he need some time to recover from the breakup? Even if it were his doing, I'd imagine he'd like a break from people in general. Eight years would definitely require some grieving time.

He also had my number—if he really wanted to get a hold of me, I was a simple call or text message away.

Not like that would happen, though. The fact that we even met up at all was a miracle. I wouldn't expect to see or talk with Justin Anderson anytime soon.

Chapter Seven

"Crap!" I groaned.

I knelt to pick up the mess of coffee lids scattered on the floor. For some reason, I was struggling to finish my shift at the Coffee Bean. With only a half hour left, I was more than ready to return home for dinner. *I bet I could close shop early—no one usually stops by at this hour, anyway.*

I heard the jingle of the front door. *Well, so much for leaving early.* I sighed as I picked up the last lid.

"Hey! I think you missed one," a male voice said, handing me a lid.

"Thanks." I stood up, meeting the eyes of the customer.

It was Justin. He was partially incognito, wearing a baseball cap and a zip-up hoodie. I could see some of his hair peeking out from his cap, and I noticed a bit of stubble along his jawline.

"Oh, hi, Justin! I wasn't expecting you!" I abruptly waved to him—my hand knocking over the straws in the self-serve area. "Ugh! Not again!"

Today is not my day.

"Is this a bad time?" Justin wondered. "I don't wanna be an inconvenience."

"No, you're all good! It's been like this all day for me."

He grabbed a handful of fallen straws. "Here, let me help you with that."

"Don't worry about it. I'll clean up later."

"It's not a problem. I wanna help."

I paused, taken aback by his offer. "Oh. Well, thank you!"

I threw away a fistful of straws. "Would you like anything to drink? We have teas, lattes, macchiatos ... We have this concoction called 'Malibu Dream' that'd be right up your alley!"

Justin laughed. "I think I'm good, but I appreciate the offer! I actually came by to see you."

My heart skipped a beat. I wasn't expecting him to say that out loud. "How'd you know which Coffee Bean I work at?"

"Olivia."

Of course.

"Well, I'm glad you found the time out of your busy schedule," I said, sitting at one of the circular tables. "I know the drive from LA is not an easy one!"

Justin took the chair across from me. "I didn't mind. I had the afternoon off today."

"By the way, Olivia and I saw 'The Dalí Effect'."

He gave me an amused look. "Oh, you did?! I'm sorry!"

"For what?"

"It was generic and overhyped. Not my best work—not by a long shot."

"No, I really enjoyed it! The story was intriguing. Dreams have always fascinated me ever since I was little. I also thought the thesis advisor character was hilarious—how she tried to keep you from graduating. I'm glad she finally got fired at the end!"

Justin chuckled, leaning back in his seat. "So am I! Between you and me, Carly is not the easiest actress to work with."

"That's karma, alright! How were the rest of your press conferences and interviews, by the way?"

"Good, but exhausting." He unzipped his jacket, stretching his toned arms. "Not too much to say on that end. I'm just relieved to be done for a little while!"

"I bet!" I crossed my legs, propping my elbow on the table. "Do you have another movie lined up for the future?"

"Yep. Filming begins in August, so I'll be traveling to New Zealand for that."

"New Zealand?! That's amazing! How long will you be there for?"

"We'll be on location for a couple months."

"Cool!"

"When does your residency program begin? You're staying in San Diego, correct?"

"Yes. That'll begin in a few weeks."

"How are you feeling about it?"

I shrugged. "Not sure. I mean, at least med school's out of the way."

"Yeah, for sure. Hopefully, you didn't have any evil thesis advisors."

"Nope, no evil advisors!" I giggled. "But I will be both overworked and underpaid."

Justin gave me a small smile. "Well, I totally understand the former."

I took a deep breath, remembering my misstatement from the other day. "Justin, I need to apologize for what I said at your house—about relationships. I never meant to criticize you or your relationship with Erica. I'm sorry for being insensitive. I heard about your breakup, and I hope you're doing ok."

He shook his head. "Natalie, there's nothing to apologize for. Our breakup was overdue. We haven't been close in years. I appreciate your honesty, though. I've always admired that about you when we were kids."

I nervously twisted the ends of my hair. "Oh, thanks. I'm really grateful for our friendship, too. Things were much simpler back then."

"Yeah. I miss that."

"Me too."

Justin reached a hand in my direction. "I never really had a chance to offer my condolences. I'm so sorry to hear about your father. I can't imagine the hardship you and your family must've gone through."

"I appreciate it, Justin."

My hands began to shake as I was suddenly reminded of my dad's old photos. The east bank photos. I grew quiet for a moment.

"Are you alright?" Justin asked with concern.

"Yeah, it's nothing."

"You sure?"

I nodded. "I was just thinking."

He leaned toward me. "About what?"

"Well, it's kind of a long story."

"I'm listening."

I proceeded to tell Justin about my discovery of my dad's photos and the implications behind them.

"So now, I'm starting to wonder, you know ... if everything isn't as it seemed," I said.

Justin drew his eyebrows together in contemplation. "What—you think his death wasn't an accident?"

"Possibly. I'm probably jumping to conclusions, though."

"I don't think so. Sounds like you have a valid cause for concern."

"Forensics already closed the case over a decade ago. Even if there were an actual concern, there'd be no way to prove it. Unless ... somehow, I was able to return to Ville du Lac and investigate it further." I laughed it off.

"But that'd be close to impossible—in a few weeks, I'll be swearing off all my free time for the foreseeable future."

"Then now'd be the perfect time to go!"

I almost fell backward in my chair. "Now?!"

Justin shrugged casually. "Yeah, why not? Your residency doesn't begin for another few weeks, right? So you've got time."

"But I don't have money. Med school debt is no joke!"

"I've got that covered if you'll have me—on your trip, I mean." He looked down, blushing.

"You cannot be serious."

"Hey, I don't have any commitments until I begin filming in New Zealand."

I gave him a sideways glance.

"Or important ones, anyway," he clarified. "I have a second home in Ville du Lac where we could stay."

"Really?"

"Yup. I guess you could say I never really left Ville du Lac. I like to visit during the summers whenever I have a free week here or there."

"That's great! I haven't been back since moving to Montana. Has it changed much since we were kids?"

Justin took off his hat, smoothing out his hair. It looked like he'd gotten a haircut recently. "That'd be for you to find out!"

I laughed. "Ah, I see what you're doing there! Oh, alright! What the heck? As long as this trip wouldn't be a burden for you."

"Not at all. Yeah, I've been meaning to go for a long drive at some point."

"Well, this will be over twenty hours of driving, so I'd consider that a pretty long drive! Wouldn't a flight be easier?"

Justin shook his head. "No, driving would be much easier. I'd need a bigger security team for air travel."

Oh, yeah. Right. He's a celebrity.

"No problem. If you're concerned about security, we could switch off with the driving, so that we don't need to find a hotel—if you're ok with me driving your car."

He nodded. "Sure, I'm good with that."

"Would we be traveling with any bodyguards?"

"I don't think that'll be necessary. I'll have my security team on standby, just in case. I plan to keep a low profile, so hopefully, there shouldn't be any encounters with the press, crazed fans, or anyone like that. It's pretty easy to stay out of the public eye in Ville du Lac."

"That's a relief."

As Justin and I continued to discuss the logistics of our trip, I began to wonder: Would I be putting the two of us in danger by further investigating my father's death? I mean, his death was determined to be an accident—so, theoretically, we wouldn't be walking onto a crime scene. We probably wouldn't find any leads at all.

However, the truth behind my father's passing wasn't my only uncertainty. I'd be spending over a week with Justin. Without a doubt, I was looking forward to some quality time with him in our hometown—just like the way things used to be. But, at the same time, I was afraid. Afraid of opening up and being vulnerable with someone—susceptible to potential hurt, just like the last time I was in Ville du Lac.

I knew what I had to do.

"Uh, Justin? I do have one more request for you—if it isn't too much trouble," I said.

"Sure, Natalie. What's up?"

"I was wondering if we could add another investigator to our team ... an investigator by the name of Olivia McKenzie."

Chapter Eight

"Home sweet home," Justin yawned as he, Olivia, and I drove up to the gated entrance of his Ville du Lac residence.

Sighing, I took a sip from my disposable coffee cup. After a long night of driving with minimal sleep, even a double-shot Caramello Latte couldn't pull me out of my fatigue. I didn't mind the slight detour to a drive-thru coffee shop, though.

After Justin disarmed the security gates, we continued down the private road leading to his house, and he parked his Audi in the driveway. We climbed out of the car.

"Sweet digs!" Olivia remarked, pulling her bulky suitcase behind her.

I studied Justin's craftsman-style home for a moment. Judging by the number of windows, the house appeared decent-sized but not extravagant—five bedrooms, I estimated. There was a three-car garage off to the side, and the front entrance was designed with earthy tiles that gave it a rustic appearance. Three stone steps led to the porch, wrapping around the front of the house. Dark wooden pillars framed the front door—glass window panes carved above the handle. On the right side, I noticed a porch swing daybed. Very quaint.

"I'll meet you guys inside," Olivia said. "I need to make a quick call."

"Let me guess: Derek?" I asked, smirking at her.

She smiled slyly. "Maybe! I haven't talked with him in four days—before I even knew of this trip!"

I turned to Justin. "That won't be quick! We should probably get ourselves settled in the meantime."

"Sounds good," he replied, disabling the house alarm.

Stepping inside, the home's interior reminded me of a mountain lodge but with a modern flair. As with the house's exterior, dark wood and earthy tiles were prevalent. The ceilings were high-vaulted, and the layout consisted of two floors—a winding staircase leading to an open balcony, giving the home a spacious yet comfy vibe. The interior was immaculate. Housekeeping probably stopped by just before we arrived, I assumed. House cleaning was never an inconvenience for the rich and famous.

Justin proceeded to give me a quick tour of the first floor. We passed the living room and kitchen, both of which utilized the open floor plan. We then came to one of the rooms—one of the few rooms on the first floor.

"Here you are," Justin said, opening the door.

As I peeked inside, I observed a rather large bedroom—the bed itself was almost double the size of my bed back in San Diego.

I instantly felt a rush of nerves. "Uh, isn't this the main bedroom?"

He shook his head. "No, this is one of the guest rooms. There's more upstairs, too. I figured you'd like the biggest one before Olivia gets her pick."

"Oh, right! I don't think she'll mind. Thanks so much!"

I followed Justin to the kitchen, and he opened the sliding glass door for me. I stepped onto his uncovered back patio, passing by a cushioned sofa sectional surrounding a stone fire pit. Past the sofa, I noticed a grassy lawn that offered a generous view of Lake Awl. Off to the side was a small gate leading to some stairs, presumably to the lakeshore. Beyond the property, on the other side of the lake, numerous pine trees offered plenty of seclusion.

Suddenly, a wave of sadness hit me; thirteen years ago, the last time I was in Ville du Lac was almost half my life. Nearly half my life spent without my father. I swallowed the knot in my throat.

"Everything alright?" Justin asked.

I took a deep breath. "Yep. All good. I just need some time to rest. I'm not used to long car rides."

"Of course. Take as much time as you need. If you need anything at all, just let me know."

"Thanks, will do."

I returned to the guest bedroom, moving my suitcase to the side. Exhausted, I plopped onto the bed, a comforter pillow nestled underneath my head—Savasana—the final resting pose of any given yoga practice. Much to Olivia's dismay, I was not experienced in the art of yoga, but mental rest was exactly what I needed. A system reboot, where I could simply turn off my mind for a little bit. A novelty for me.

***

"There it is! On your right," I said to Justin from the passenger seat.

In response, he steered his car to the turnout and put it into park—the mid-morning sun streaking across the windshield. Although it was a new day, my energy level was still not at its peak—blinding sunlight was the last thing I needed.

I glanced at the car dashboard—10:47 am. We'd been driving for about a half-hour by that point. Seemed about right.

"You sure this is the right turnout?" Justin asked as the three of us stepped out of his car.

I nodded. "I remember it was next to a meadow with a dirt trail."

"Isn't that the same for every turnout in this area?" Olivia remarked, smoothing out her skirt.

"This one's different! I can tell," I said.

At least, I thought so ... I'd only fished with my dad a handful of times.

Justin adjusted his baseball cap. "Ok, then. You lead the way."

We trekked into the forest, coming across a riverbank a few minutes later—a rush of white-water channeling downstream.

"This must be the west bank," I figured as we walked closer to the river's edge.

Justin grabbed a fallen branch and dropped it into the water. Almost instantly, the current carried it downstream toward the rapids. "Damn, that current is strong!"

"Yeah, it is! But it's early summer, so the snow from the mountains likely hasn't completely melted. The water flow in late August is probably lighter."

Olivia raised her index finger. "Oh, yeah. They get snow here, don't they? Dude, I wouldn't wanna be here in the winter! No shoveling driveways for me, thank you very much!"

"It's not too bad." Justin shrugged. "But it's been a while. Probably need to reacclimate to the cold."

"Still warmer than Montana!" I pointed out. "But, yeah. This is still a risky place for fishing, no matter what time of year."

As we headed down the riverbank, I studied the surrounding area closely. It seemed treacherous for anyone to venture into these waters—even someone with as much fly-fishing proficiency as my dad.

However, I still couldn't rule out the possibility that he'd fished on the west bank. I'd need actual tangible proof.

Olivia snapped photos of the river with her smartphone, offering it to Justin and me. "Selfie?"

I shook my head. "Not now. Maybe later. I'd like to check out the east bank while we're out—if you're both good with that."

"Sure! Sounds good to me," Justin replied.

"Yeah, what he said!" Olivia agreed.

We walked back to the turnout. Justin unlocked his car to retrieve his aviator sunglasses, closing the door behind him. He slid his sunglasses onto his face as he casually walked away from his silver Audi—locking it remotely with a simple beep of a button.

I was instantly reminded of a scene from 'Double Blind'—a big-budget action flick, one of my so-called "homework assignments" from Olivia: Justin's character, Jeremy, nonchalantly walks away from an exploding car—slipping on his sunglasses with one hand, holding his leading lady's hand in the other. As the ashes and debris fall from the sky like snowflakes behind him, he turns to her and remarks, "This is why we can't have nice things."

So cool.

As I gazed over at Justin, I tripped over Olivia, consequently sending us both barreling to the dirt ground, a sea of dust surrounding us.

So not cool.

"You alright?" Justin wondered.

He turned around to find us lying on the ground, our limbs sprawled in different directions—as if we were amid a game of Twister. One hand over his mouth, trying not to laugh, he extended the other to us.

I took his hand, scrambling myself up to a standing position. "Yup! All good!"

Except for my self-esteem.

"Easy for you to say!" Olivia quipped lightheartedly. "You're not wearing a skirt!"

Justin and I both offered her a hand, which she accepted.

We trekked through the forest to the east bank of the river. I unzipped my backpack, taking out my dad's photos. I walked up the riverbank and compared his photos with the terrain. Other than a few new shrubs that'd sprouted since then, it was mostly unchanged. The waters were much gentler than on the west bank. They appeared to be shallower, too—if I wore a swimsuit, I'd consider going for a swim.

I stashed the photos away, returning to where I left my friends. As I half-expected, Olivia was taking selfies on the top of a boulder, surrounded by a bed of wildflowers. She was fluffing up her blond hair and teasing her phone with surprised yet seductive poses. I rolled my eyes. This is why you couldn't pay me to use social media!

Splash! I looked over my shoulder, noticing a series of ripples along the water's surface. Justin was skipping rocks.

"Find anything interesting?" he asked me as he reached for a small rock on the shoreline.

"No, nothing new. But this definitely seems like a safer area to fish."

Justin tossed the rock into the river. It skipped four times before sinking. "Yeah, your dad took Kyle and me fishing here once. I remember he kept getting annoyed with me 'cause I was skipping stones upstream. He thought I was scaring the fish away. That's probably why he didn't invite me to join him again!"

I laughed, picking up a stone of my own. "Yup. Sounds like my dad!"

I threw the stone into the river, attempting to skip. Instead, it landed in the water with a single plop.

Justin shook his head, amused. "You might wanna brush up on your technique, Natalie!"

"What's wrong with my technique?!" I joked. "All you're doing is throwing a rock into the river, right?!"

"Not exactly." He picked up a flat stone, holding it between his fingers and thumb. "Mind if I show you?"

"Sure."

Justin demonstrated the arm motion for me—without actually tossing the stone into the water. He then handed it to me.

I attempted to mimic his arm motion. I watched the stone fall directly into the water with another audible plop.

Strike two.

He grabbed another stone. "Let's try it again. I can guide you if you're down."

I nodded.

Justin handed me the stone and stepped behind me. He rested his warm hand on my arm as he provided the proper skipping motion. Goosebumps suddenly shot up my arm.

I tossed the stone, watching it skip across the water three times.

"That's perfect! Good job!" he said, his hand still touching my arm.

"Thanks!"

I turned my gaze back to the riverbank. Olivia was standing a few feet away from us, grinning from ear to ear.

Justin abruptly let go of my arm.

"Oh! Uh, do you guys mind looking over the photos before we go?" I asked, slightly disoriented. "You're basically looking for any inconsistencies."

"Sure thing!" Justin agreed.

I handed him the photos from my backpack. He reviewed them for a moment and shook his head. "Nothing I can see. Olivia?"

Justin gave the photos to Olivia, who then studied them intently, bringing them closer to her face. She bit her lip in concentration.

"Well?" I leaned over her shoulder.

"Yeah, I see something here!" Olivia observed.

"Ok, great! What is it?"

"A beautiful shade of yellow-green. Not sure what kind of tree it is, but it'd complement your skin tone well. In the fall, you should really consider getting some portraits taken over there! Maybe Justin could get some headshots, too—they'd look great on your IMDb page!"

I groaned, planting my head into my palm. "Olivia, that's not helping!"

Justin looked down, seemingly pensive. "Wait a minute ... you might be onto something. Olivia, can I see that photo real quick?"

"Yeah, totally!" she replied, handing him the photo.

Justin wandered downstream, studying the photo in his hand. "That tree over there—the leaves are green. But in this photo, they're beginning to turn yellow, which means this photo was taken just before autumn."

"August 30th," I said, in realization of his logic.

"Cool! Glad I could help!" Olivia affirmed.

"Yes, thank you, Olivia. I'm sorry for doubting you earlier," I apologized.

"No offense taken! So, what do we do now—knowing these photos were taken on the same day of your dad's death?"

"I'm not sure."

"Well, we could always return tomorrow," Justin suggested. "Maybe we'll find something, then."

I nodded in agreement. "Yeah, it'd be good to relax. I'm still exhausted from yesterday's drive."

The three of us headed back to the car. I adjusted the straps of my backpack, feeling hopeful. It appeared we were headed in the right direction. My intuition didn't lead me astray—for now. Only time would tell.

***

A knock on the door woke me up that same evening.

Wiping the drool off my cheek, I rolled over to the side of the guest bed, checking the time on my phone. It was just before 9 pm.

Dang. I must've fallen asleep while watching TV—that was unlike me.

I reached for the remote, turning off the TV.

"Come in!" I called out, groggy.

The door opened, and Olivia stepped inside, beaming—her default expression.

"Were you sleeping?" she wondered, closing the door behind her.

"Unintentionally," I answered, smoothing out my messy hair.

"Well, you need to wake up and smell the Syringa! That's the state flower here, right?"

I rolled my eyes. "Yes. But what's your point?"

I was too groggy to play guessing games with Olivia right then and there.

She sat on the side of my bed with a spark in her blue-green eyes. "We need to talk about you and Justin!"

I chuckled. Of course, she would say that. "What about? I understand your theory behind his breakup with Erica, but seriously, nothing is going on between us!"

"Oh, don't you play dumb with me!" she teased. "We both know you're too smart for that, Dr. Baker!"

I sighed. "No, really! Can't two friends just visit their hometown together?"

"Not when one of them is Justin Anderson!" Olivia lay on my bed, extending her arms out in a T-position. "Oh, Natalie. I know you're into him—even if you don't realize it yet."

She brought her arms into her chest. "When you tripped into me earlier, I saw you admiring him. No shame in that! After all, he's been voted Top 10 for the Sexiest Man Alive for a while now!"

"I was not admiring him!" I stated. "I was simply ... admiring the surrounding forest. There's so much green up here, I'd almost forgotten."

"Sure, you were! And those stones you tossed—you just 'happened' to need his help, right? Hah, that's one of the oldest tricks in the book!"

I shook my head. "I'm not trying to date Justin. I'm just trying to get some peace of mind before my residency begins. I doubt he's even interested in a relationship at this time."

Olivia rolled up to a seated position. "Well, you're wrong about that."

I yawned. "You know, I should really get some rest now."

"Ok, ok. I'll leave."

Olivia sauntered over to the door. "Let me know once you've professed your love to each other!" she teased, batting her long eyelashes at me.

"Will do!" I replied sarcastically.

As she closed the door, I turned on the TV once again. I flipped a few times until I came across the E! Channel, which coincidentally displayed footage of Justin and Erica together.

Intrigued, I turned up the volume.

"After Erica Rhode's breakup with Justin Anderson, it appears she has found a new leading man in her life," the news commentator announced. "Rhode has now been linked to actor Chad Johnson in recent weeks. The two were spotted together on several occasions—most notably, an LA

Dodgers game and the premiere of Rhode's latest flick, 'The Perfect Catch'. Meanwhile, Justin Anderson is nowhere to be seen. His rep has stated that Anderson has 'some family matters to attend to and would appreciate some privacy during this time.' It isn't certain if Anderson is still grieving over the end of his eight-year relationship with Rhode, or maybe he has found a leading lady of his own."

I turned off the TV, sighing to myself. I clearly understood that Justin's lifestyle was vastly different from mine. Very cognizant of that fact. So then, why did it frustrate me so much—that we'd be returning home at the end? I almost wished there was another option ... an option where our homes weren't separated by security cameras and press reporters.

I dismissed the thought. *Olivia's comments are getting to my head. I need to stop—before I give myself a headache.*

Even if I were to develop feelings for Justin, it'd be very unlikely that a relationship between us would last. With his fame and massive fanbase—women constantly throwing themselves at him daily—it'd even be a miracle if our friendship would last.

Fame is a fickle thing.

Chapter Nine

"Damn. My house hasn't changed a bit," Justin observed.

I rested my hand against my forehead, shading my face from the mid-morning sun. "Neither has mine."

Of course, there were a few minor changes to our former homes. For instance, the front yard of Justin's now consisted of more shrubbery than grass, and my house now included fencing with a beige color instead of white. But I still noticed the same two maple trees framing the front porch steps—the exact steps I remembered hopping down, waving goodbye to my father for the last time.

A lump suddenly formed in my throat as I thought back to that fateful evening thirteen years ago...

***

Riiing! I heard the extended sound of our cordless landline resting upon the kitchen countertop.

"I'll get it!" I called out, scooting my chair away from the table.

My parents and I had just finished our dinner that evening—the aroma of sweet potatoes and bacon still lingering in the kitchen.

I eagerly made my way over to the phone, pushing away the generous stack of unread mail sitting out in front. "Hello?"

"Hey Natalie!" a pubescent male voice said—a voice I'd heard many times before.

My stomach fluttered.

"Hey, Justin!" I responded, walking into the family room, trying to get some semblance of privacy from my parents. "Did you eat dinner yet?"

"Yep, just me and Kyle. My parents went to a work event. They probably won't be back until late, as usual. You?"

"Yeah, we just ate."

"Wanna go swimming at the lake for a bit?"

I looked out the front window. It was mostly sunny outside, but I could see an influx of darker clouds in the distance. We both knew we had a short window of time to spend outside.

"Sure!" I replied.

On the other line, I thought I heard Kyle call out to Justin, but the receiver could not pick up any audible words.

"Quit it! You know that's not true!" Justin responded to his brother as I heard the sudden slam of a door on his end.

"Sorry, Kyle's being a pest again!" he apologized. "Does ten minutes work for you?"

"Yeah, I can meet you out front."

"Awesome!"

"See you soon!"

I returned to the kitchen, placing the phone back in its holder.

"Can I go to the lake with Justin?" I asked my parents.

Mom glanced out the kitchen window, raising her eyebrows in concern. "There's a thunderstorm forecasted for tonight. Can you please make sure you're back before dark?"

I nodded. "Yes, Mom."

She sighed in exhaustion. "Good! I've got enough on my mind already."

I went over to the mirror in our family room, fixing my slightly frayed ponytail in its reflection.

"Donna, remember how we said we'd leave our work at the office?" Dad reminded her, resting a hand on her shoulder. "That includes worrying, too."

"Yes, but the students' schedules need to be finalized before Tuesday. They won't print themselves out! The entire admin is running on fumes."

"Well, that's a concern for tomorrow. For tonight, why don't you do something relaxing? Maybe join Natalie and Justin for a swim?" Dad winked at me.

I rolled my eyes. As a fourteen-year-old girl, the last person I'd like to join me and my friend-turned-crush was my mom.

"No, that's ok," Mom said. "I think I'll watch a movie. I need something mindless."

"I know! How about one of Natalie's chick flicks?" Dad offered.

He then sorted through our extensive collection of DVDs, neatly organized on our bookshelf by the TV—alphabetized by yours truly.

"Let's see here..." Dad searched the bookshelf, pulling out two DVD cases. "Does either 'Clueless' or 'The Princess Diaries' sound good to you?"

"Dad, please don't!" I pleaded, embarrassed.

"That's ok, John," Mom said. "I think I'll watch some TV. Maybe there's something dumb on, like a celebrity gossip show. That's as mindless as you can get."

Mom headed into the bathroom, closing the door behind her.

Dad reached for his fishing pole and tackle box. "You're not the only one embarking on a high-water excursion this evening!"

"Hopefully not fishing on the west bank. My teacher told me at least one person drowns there every summer," I said.

He shook his head. "Absolutely not. I'll be on the east bank. I gave you my word, didn't I?"

"Yes, you did. Can I ask you a quick question?"

"Sure! Fire away."

"With school starting soon, I was thinking about joining one of the clubs there. What would you say is a good club to join?"

"Great question, Nat! Hmm ... good club to join..." Dad adjusted his wire-rimmed glasses, pondering. "Ah ha! I've got it! How about the drama club? It'd be a good way for you to get out of your shell and meet some new friends, too. A two-for-one!"

I raised an eyebrow at him. "Really? Drama club? I've never really acted before, just a couple Christmas plays in elementary school. I doubt a dancing snowman qualifies as true acting experience!"

"You'd learn." Dad gently tapped my nose with his hand. "In fact, I think you'd catch on relatively quickly. You've always been receptive to learning new skills."

"Academic skills, not creative skills."

"Why don't you ask one of your friends to join you? Like maybe Justin?"

I shrugged. "Sure, maybe. If he's open to it."

"I think he'd try it out with you. Besides, even if you later decide this club isn't for you, you can always try a different activity. I recall high schools have plenty of clubs to choose from. I'm assuming Hillview High is no different?"

"I think so."

Mom returned to the kitchen as Dad checked the time on his gold watch.

"Oh! Didn't realize how late it's getting!" he observed, swiping a strand of his gray-blond hair to the side. "It always takes some extra time driving to the river. As the saying goes, 'good things come to those who wait.'"

"There's also a saying about 'early to bed, early to rise,'" Mom pointed out. "Why don't you go fishing tomorrow morning instead?"

Dad shook his head. "Can't. Have a scheduled Cesarean for 9 am."

Mom sighed. "Another one?! Geez! It seems like every other woman here is pregnant! What's in the water?"

Simultaneously, the two of them looked over in my direction. I was buckling my sandals by the doorway—the halter strings of my bikini top peeking from underneath my green tee. With an amused expression, my parents returned their focus to each other—as if they were about to bust at the seams in laughter.

"Sorry, Nat! You should be fine at the lake," Dad reassured me in a joking manner. "Don't pay any attention to your mother's comment!"

"Noted," I said.

He didn't have to tell me twice.

I grabbed the beach towel hanging on the coat rack and opened the front door.

"Natalie heads up!" Dad tossed me another towel—the soft fabric hitting me square in the face.

"Oomph!" I sounded.

"Say hello to Justin for me!"

I chuckled, folding the towel underneath my arm. "Will do. Have fun catching cutthroats!"

"I'll certainly try!" Dad smiled, waving to me.

***

I swallowed the large lump in my throat as Justin, Olivia, and I continued our walk.

"Still feels like yesterday, you know—when you and I ran up and down these streets," I reminisced.

"Yeah. Doesn't feel that long ago," Justin agreed, fixing his baseball cap.

"Such a cute neighborhood!" Olivia noted as she snapped a few photos of the tree-lined streets. "Where'd you say you went to school again?"

"Riverstone Charter," I responded.

"Right! Is it near here?"

"Only a few minutes by car. We normally walked to school."

"Cool! It's a small school, right?"

"Relatively. I personally liked having a smaller class size."

"Yeah, except there were a couple kids I couldn't wait to get away from!" Justin said.

I looked at him curiously. "Really? Like who?"

"Like Jeff Davis. Remember him?"

"Oh, yeah. I recall he wasn't very nice to you."

Justin shook his head. "Not at all. He and his friends liked to pick on me before I hit my growth spurt. But I appreciated the times when you stood up for me. Like that one time in fourth grade, at recess."

"What happened then?" Olivia wondered.

"Natalie and I were playing tetherball," he began. "Jeff and his friends came up to us and started teasing me—saying something dumb about the two of us playing together. I told them to leave us alone, but they didn't listen."

"Then Jeff said something mean to you, and without thinking, I remember hitting the tetherball directly at his crotch area," I added, smirking.

Olivia began to laugh. "Are you serious?! Oh man, I'd love to have seen that!"

"Your aim was pretty spot-on!" Justin said. "He was too embarrassed to say anything afterward."

I nodded. "He threatened to tell on me, but instead, they all just ran away."

"They'd have better run away! Didn't they know who they were messing with?" Olivia remarked. "They'd be begging for forgiveness now if they ever saw you again."

"Yep, never liked them. At least they weren't vicious like the middle school girls," Justin pointed out.

I sighed. "Yeah, I was trying to forget about those times."

"Oh, sorry."

I waved him off. "No worries! My friends were being unreasonable, like all middle schoolers."

"If you're ok with sharing, what happened?" Olivia wondered.

I took a deep breath. "Well, at one point in eighth grade, my friends Megan and Christina decided I wasn't cool enough to stay in their group. They laughed at me whenever I wasn't around—making fun of my appearance. Of course, they didn't tell me any of this—I learned about this secondhand from a girl named Nikki, who didn't like me either."

"What bitches!" Olivia said.

"I was very grateful Justin and his friends invited me to sit with them at lunch. Literally, none of the girls wanted to be friends with me during that time."

Justin nodded. "Of course."

"My friends eventually apologized, and I rejoined their group, but still ... I never felt truly comfortable with them after that. That's probably why I spent so much time at the treehouse."

"That's right ... the treehouse." A small smile crept across Justin's face.

Olivia clasped her hands together enthusiastically. "Ooh, I wanna see it! Is it nearby?"

"Yeah, about a block away, if I recall correctly—across from the lake," I remembered.

"Then what are we waiting for?!" Olivia exclaimed.

We walked over to the adjacent street, coming across an empty lot instead of the treehouse. I read the sign planted in its stead—a permit for a future housing development. No surprise there.

"Really?" I remarked. "That's so sad! And let me guess: these are gonna be apartments with inflated rent because of the lake view."

"Sounds about right. Well, I guess it was a matter of time before the land would be developed," Justin figured.

"Why can't the developers just build another treehouse in its place?" Olivia said.

I gave her an amused look. "Another treehouse?"

"Yeah! Like a rental treehouse, where you could cook meals and spend the night and stuff. Like a cabin, in a way," she explained.

"But who'd buy this so-called rental treehouse?"

"I would! Wouldn't you, if you weren't swimming in debt?"

I shrugged. "Possibly."

"So then, what would your perfect treehouse look like?"

I thought for a moment, observing the empty lot. "Well, first thing, it'd have sable wood, like the original. There'd be a fire pit and cushioned chairs on the ground level. The staircase would wrap around the tree trunk—maybe with some lights. The next floor would probably include an open kitchen and a separate space for the bathroom. The top floor would be the bedroom, surrounded by wide windows—with drapes, of course.

On the roof, there'd be some hanging lights. That way, there'd always be stars, no matter the weather."

"Wow, you really put a lot of thought into this!" Justin said, intrigued.

I shook my head. "No, I came up with this all right now."

"Really? That's impressive."

"Thanks."

Olivia glanced over at the lake across the street. "Wanna go swimming?"

"I'm not wearing a swimsuit, but I'd like to see the lake," I replied.

"Not down for diving with your clothes on?" Justin joked, immediately turning his face away, blushing. "I mean, wearing normal clothes instead of a swimsuit."

Olivia giggled, bringing a hand to her mouth.

"I knew what you meant," I told him. "Another day, we can go swimming."

"So, this is Lake Owl, right?" Olivia asked as we started crossing the street.

"Awl," I corrected her. "It's a tool that pierces leather."

"Oh. Never heard of an 'awl' before."

"I think we learned about it in school once," Justin recalled. "Do you remember, Natalie?"

"Yep, in third grade," I confirmed.

Once we reached the lakeshore, I took off my sandals, letting my feet sink into the warm sand. A light wind ruffled the bottom seam of my flowered sundress. I turned my gaze to the vast lake, with its crystal-clear waters—tiny white waves breaking onto the shoreline. Its edges were bordered by evergreens, with a series of mountains jutting from the horizon. A crisp, woodsy scent wafted through the gentle breeze from the lake.

I lifted my gaze, observing a small peninsula off to the side—Mudgy Hill. I felt my throat tighten, remembering the last time I'd hiked there—when my dad was with me...

It was a sunny Sunday afternoon. I was hoping to take a dip into one of the swimming holes. It was a fairly warm day, so all the swimming holes were occupied. My dad, noticing my disappointment, calmly told me it wasn't our time. I asked him what he meant by that, to which he responded that everything happens for a reason—where we find ourselves, who we run into, what chance events occur. It's not our job to try to control the process or predict the outcome, he told me. All we can do is trust in the bigger picture, God's greater plan. That particular afternoon, it wasn't our time to enjoy the cool of the lake. The moment belonged to those already there, whom each had a story to tell: the family of five who packed a light picnic in their cooler along with a blanket and Frisbee; the older gentleman who desired to paint a landscape—one that his grandkids could remember him by every time they walked past the living room; the young couple, arms wrapped around each other's shoulders, admiring the beauty of the lake—hoping to spend the rest of their lives together, immersed in many more moments of warmth and comfort like this one...

I let out an audible exhale.

"Gorgeous. Absolutely gorgeous," Olivia said in awe. "Yup, I could see myself living here!"

"Even in the winter?" I asked.

"No, only in the warmer months. I'd have a second home, like Justin. If I won the lottery!" She giggled.

"I'm glad you suggested this walk, Justin," I said, fastening my sandals. "It was nice seeing our old neighborhood again."

"Of course! Glad you enjoyed it," Justin acknowledged with a nod.

We continued to walk until we reached the car.

"So, back to the river like yesterday?" Olivia inquired as she climbed into the backseat—my turn to ride shotgun.

"Sure," Justin said, sliding into the driver's seat.

I crouched down to sit in the passenger seat—I was still not used to the low seating of his high-performance Audi. The seating arrangement of my Volvo at home felt much more natural.

As we drove into the backcountry, I observed a sign along the side of the road—a sign I'd missed yesterday.

"Can we take a quick detour to Bayview State Park?" I asked. "Maybe they'll have some information on the park visitors—like from the day of my dad's death. The river's only a few miles from here—so who knows? Maybe that'll give us a lead of some sort."

"Yeah, that's fine with me," Justin replied. "But where would we get that kind of info? Like, what—the visitors center?"

"Yeah, there's probably one there. I bet state parks normally record their attendance. Hopefully, they still have the records from that day."

"Makes sense. Might as well check it out."

Maybe a visit to this park was just what we needed, I thought. Perhaps it'd lead us one more step in the right direction. Worst-case scenario: I'd be visiting a nice scenic park with my friends.

Then again, I might've not even considered that a worst-case scenario.

Chapter Ten

"We'd like to buy a day pass, please!" Olivia said from the driver's seat, upon pulling up to the wooden kiosk marking the entrance to Bayview State Park.

"Of course!" the receptionist—a lady with blond hair and round glasses—replied. "May I see some ID first?"

"Sure! Here you go." Olivia handed her ID to the receptionist. From the passenger seat, I saw her nametag read "Lauren."

"So, California, huh?" Lauren inquired, as she continued to inspect Olivia's ID card.

"San Diego. Born and raised," Olivia stated confidently. "Well, I'm from San Diego. These two are originally from Idaho but later moved to California when... OW!"

I dug my elbow deep into Olivia's side, trying to quiet her down. Justin slouched down further in the backseat, pulling down the visor of his baseball cap. Maybe it wasn't the best idea to have Olivia and Justin switch driving positions.

Lauren returned Olivia's ID card. "You're not the first. Seems like every other car here has a California license plate. Well, summer's definitely the time to visit, as long as they all return home after their visit! Of course, we all know that isn't the case!"

She chuckled.

"Oh, tell me about it!" Olivia remarked with a laugh. "Those ridiculous Californians, buying up all your precious property. They should all just go back to where they came from! They've got their Silicon Valley startups and Hollywood movie studios. What else do they need?"

I cleared my throat audibly. "How much is the day pass?"

"Five dollars," Lauren answered.

Before Olivia had a chance to add to her mindless tangent, I fished in my backpack for some cash and handed Olivia a five-dollar bill to give to Lauren.

"Thank you!" Lauren said as she received the cash, and in exchange, handed us a map of the park. "The visitor center is right down that road to the left. They have a nice museum and cafe there as well. Enjoy your visit!"

My body sprung forward as Olivia pressed a bit too firmly on the accelerator, steering us onto the main road. I was surprised the receptionist didn't recognize Justin—after all the damage Olivia had done. His hat and sunglasses must be doing the trick.

A minute later, Olivia abruptly braked next to a brick building—the visitor center. "Dude, this car is awesome! Thanks for letting me drive, Justin!"

I looked behind my shoulder. Justin had a somewhat bewildered expression on his face. "Uh, sure. Just try to take it easy around those turns next time."

"Oh, totally! At least I didn't get myself a speeding ticket on the way up here!" she reminded him lightheartedly.

Justin turned his gaze down. "So, what's the plan exactly?"

"We ask to speak with one of the managers, and then we request to see the visitor stats if they're available," I explained.

"I'm not sure if I should go in there," he said. "I'll have to remove my sunglasses to be inconspicuous."

"Don't worry about it! There are only a few cars here, so you should be fine," Olivia reassured him.

Justin shook his head. "I just don't wanna cause a scene. There's been enough of those incidents at home."

"It's up to you, but I doubt people care about pop culture here," I pointed out to him. "We're in a remote area, downtown's a good distance away."

"Well, if you're sure." Justin adjusted his hat.

We exited the car and made our way to the visitor center entrance. Justin pulled open the door to let Olivia and me through.

"Thanks," I said.

"No problem," Justin replied, taking off his sunglasses.

Once inside, I took a glimpse around the room. Its layout resembled that of a small retailer, with some clothing and outdoorsy merchandise on display. On the other side of the room, there were two additional doorways—leading to the museum and cafe, I would presume. Toward the front, there was a desk with a collection of maps and pamphlets on a stand. I didn't see a receptionist present, but I did notice a metallic call bell resting on the countertop.

We waited until the older couple, browsing through the maps, walked away before approaching the desk. I tapped the bell with a simple ding.

A moment later, a stocky middle-aged man with a full beard emerged from the other side.

"Yes, can I help you?" he bluntly questioned us. He was wearing a nametag that read "Mitch."

"Hi, Mitch! We'd like to take a look at your past visitor information, please," Olivia requested.

"Are you the auditors? Thought they weren't supposed to come for another month," Mitch grumbled. "The June bank statements aren't available yet."

"He was an auditor once!" Olivia pointed to Justin.

Without hesitation, Justin turned his focus to the floor.

I looked at Olivia sideways, perplexed at her comment. "We're not the auditors. We were hoping to view some stats on the guests who visited the park thirteen years ago. Is that possible?"

Mitch shook his head. "I'm sorry, but visitors are not authorized to view these types of records. Unless you have a financial interest in the Parks & Rec Department, I cannot grant you access to confidential information."

"We understand. Thank you for your time," I said.

I sighed as Mitch returned to the back of the room, out of sight.

"An auditor?! Why'd you say that?!" I asked Olivia.

"Because it's true!" she replied. "He was an auditor for one of his previous roles."

I turned to face Justin, trying not to laugh. "Really?!"

He nodded. "Yeah, it was for 'Enron Empire'. Let's just say we weren't the good guys."

"Looks like we missed a flick, Natalie!" Olivia said.

Justin gave us a confused glance.

"It's nothing," I told him.

I would spare him the details of our Justin-Anderson-movie-marathon, I decided. I couldn't imagine his reaction if he knew, especially the rom-coms. I cringed at the thought.

My eyes swept across the room. Other than the older couple, we were alone. Maybe there's additional staff in the museum we could talk with.

Returning my focus to the main desk, a young woman with long brown hair headed over to us, carrying a large stack of folders and loose paperwork. Her nametag read "Katie."

As she caught a glimpse of us, her eyes widened in shock, her paperwork plummeting to the floor—sans a few airborne papers.

"Justin Anderson? Is that you?" Katie exclaimed. "Oh my God! I am a huge fan! Love your movies! 'Midnight Club' is my favorite, of course. Team Andrew, all the way! I even watched your TV guest roles from before you were famous—when you were on 'The OC' and 'Stargate.' Never thought I'd ever meet you! Well, here you are, at my work! Crazy, right? What can I do for you?"

Justin glanced over his shoulder nervously. The older couple briefly looked at us as they walked into another room. Luckily for him, it appeared the damage was minimal.

"Hi, Katie! We'd like to see some of your past visitor information, please," Olivia requested.

"Like the attendance stats? You'll find them under our website's 'Park Information' section," Katie informed us proudly.

"We'd actually like to view more intricate information on the specific guests who visited the park," I explained. "In particular, we'd like info on August 30, 2002, if you still have those records available."

Katie sighed, disappointed. "I wish I could help, but it's unfortunately against our policy. Our board members would have a fit. I'm so sorry!"

Olivia's face suddenly brightened up. "Totally understand! Rules and regulations, right? That's pretty standard for Justin's line of work, as well. He can barely interact with his fans, even when he wants to. Just smile and wave—that's about it. Photo ops are almost always out of the question. Right, Justin?"

I looked over at Justin, who initially appeared puzzled. His expression then changed to serious—catching onto Olivia's plan. "Oh, yes. Normally out of the question. But I'd be willing to bend the rules a bit for you, if you could do the same for us. Would you like a photo together?"

He immediately took off his hat and swished his hair to one side. Very smooth.

Katie squealed with delight. "Oh my God! Yes, I'd love that! I'll make a quick copy of those records before Mitch returns. August 30, 2002, correct?"

"Correct," Justin confirmed.

"Great! Just give me a few minutes, and I'll be back. Please keep these records confidential and shred them as soon as you're done with them."

"Will do," I agreed as Katie headed into the back room.

I smirked at Justin. "How often do you use that hair trick of yours?"

"Not much. Only sometimes," he replied nonchalantly, with a sly smile.

About a minute later, Katie returned with the visitor records, handing them to me. "Here you guys go!"

"Thank you!" I said.

She directed her attention toward Justin. "Now, I believe we have a photoshoot awaiting us!"

Katie handed Olivia her smartphone as she eagerly scooted around the desk, meeting us on the other side. She stood next to Justin, his arm lightly slung around her shoulders. Olivia snapped multiple photos of the two of them together at a state park visitor center of all places. Not quite the same spectacle as a red-carpet premiere.

Olivia then returned the phone to Katie, and the two of them reviewed the snapshots, heads close together, giggling loudly. I wasn't taken aback by the sight—Olivia could make friends with almost anybody.

"So, what do you think?" Justin asked me, removing a women's straw sunhat off one of the merchandise hooks.

"Definitely inconspicuous!" I joked. "It really compliments your polo shirt."

He laughed, shaking his head. "Not me! You!"

"Me?! I don't know, it looks too much like one of those fancy hats you see at the horse races."

"Not necessarily. I think it'd look nice on you."

"Oh, really? You think I'm fancy enough? Even with my Teva sandals?" I gestured toward the sporty sandals strapped around my feet.

Justin smiled. "Especially with your Teva sandals."

I glanced over my shoulder. Katie and Olivia watched us with fascination—they appeared to have finished gushing over their snapshots.

"Thank you so much!" Katie said, turning to me. "So, are you family? Friend?"

"Friend. Family friend. Visiting our hometown," I responded awkwardly.

Katie studied Justin and me briefly as a grin crept across her face. "Oh, I see! Don't you worry, your secret's safe with me! I know there are people who'd love to make a pretty penny on the inside scoop on celebrity relationships, but I'm not one of them. You two need your privacy, I totally get it!"

"We appreciate it. Thanks for all your help!" Justin said.

"Yeah, you're awesome!" Olivia added. "Just text me if you'd ever like to meet up sometime!"

"Sounds good! It was great meeting you all! And thanks again for the photo!" Katie called out to us, as we exited the building.

"So, I'd say that was successful!" Olivia noted.

Justin nodded, as he slipped on his hat and sunglasses, unlocking his car from a few feet away.

As we climbed inside, I couldn't help but remember Katie's remark. Did Justin and I appear as a couple? Did Katie see something between him and me that I wasn't seeing? My bigger question, however, was why Justin didn't correct her on her assumption. But then again, why didn't I?

I stopped myself from overthinking the situation. The visitor center was probably not a convenient place to clarify our intentions. Still, I wondered why Katie would believe that Justin and I were together—even with Olivia there. That was very odd to me.

***

"Would you mind handing me that piece of paper?" I asked Justin, signaling to a sheet of paper on his left side.

"Sure thing," he replied, reaching down to retrieve it. "Here you go!"

"Thanks!"

I brought the spreadsheet closer to the lampshade—the dim, soft lighting added a tranquil aesthetic to Justin's living room. I examined the various names and addresses on the spreadsheet, hoping to find something suspicious or peculiar. Unfortunately, no such luck.

"Well, that's the last of it." I sighed. "Apparently, Olivia didn't miss much."

"Is she still on the phone?" Justin wondered.

"Probably. She's talking with Derek. They're back together again."

"Oh. Is that new?"

I chuckled. "Your guess is as good as mine!"

I knelt to gather the visitor records scattered on the rug next to the fireplace.

"Did you check that one yet?" Justin pointed to a lone piece of paper underneath the leather couch.

I reached over to grab it. "I believe so, but I'll take a look, just in case."

I studied the spreadsheet closely. After a few minutes, it was obvious there were no inconsistencies to be found. However, I did find one name that struck me by surprise. "Wait, isn't that your dad? Rob Sanders?"

I gave Justin the piece of paper. He glanced at it for a moment, his eyebrows scrunching together. "Yup, that's him. I know he liked to hike there, at Bayview. He'd usually go in the mornings before work."

"Did you guys go hiking as a family much?" I asked.

"Not really. We did when Kyle and I were younger before my dad's landscaping business took off. We barely did anything together, he and my mom were too busy with their jobs once I was in the seventh grade, I believe."

I nodded, organizing the visitor records into a neat pile. "Yeah, my dad was also super swamped with work. He'd sometimes come home after I'd gone to bed. Most of my family dinners were just me and my mom."

"That must've been hard for you."

I shrugged. "I got used to it after a while."

"Well, dinnertime at my house definitely wasn't better." Justin took a deep breath. "When I was in high school, my parents would normally argue at the dinner table, in front of me and Kyle. It was frustrating. Honestly, I would've rather eaten alone than dealt with their constant bickering."

He shook his head. "Yeah, at that point, I knew their marriage wasn't gonna last, even before they separated."

"Was that why your mom moved you and Kyle to LA? So she could have a new start after the divorce?"

"Yep, pretty much. She doesn't talk about my dad. He and I have lost contact over the years—we've had a couple phone calls, but that's about it. Sometimes, I wonder if my mom used my acting career as an out. She was the one who pushed for Anderson as a screen name. She said it was more marketable. I don't think that was her only reason ... but that's none of my business."

"I'm sorry to hear that." I pushed the stack of visitor records aside. "My mom also pressured me to pursue a medical career. After my dad died, she encouraged me to focus heavily on my studies. She told me how important it was to make a name for myself, so it was the logical conclusion that I'd follow in my dad's footsteps. My mom was thrilled about that, of course."

Justin looked at me with concern. "You know you don't have to do that. What you do with your life is up to you."

"I wish it was that easy. I wish time could just slow down." I let out a long sigh.

"I agree. The years have gotten away from us, haven't they?"

"Yeah, for sure."

He briefly glanced over at his phone. "Speaking of which, I didn't realize how late it's getting."

"How late?"

"Almost ten."

"Wow! That's later than I thought."

Justin yawned, stretching. "Well, there were plenty of names to review. Glad we got through them all."

"Yeah, but we didn't find anything significant."

"We've still got more time. I wouldn't worry about it. We should probably get some rest in the meantime."

He pushed himself up from his spot on the rug. He offered a hand to me, to which I accepted.

"I hope you sleep well," I said, smoothing out my sundress.

Justin gave me a small smile. "You too."

I watched as he walked down the hall and into the main bedroom, closing the door behind him. For a moment, I wondered: What was Justin's bedroom like, beyond the closed door? Or better yet, how did he rest his weary head at the end of the day? Did his bed have an array of pillows like mine did at home? Or a series of blankets? Did he lull himself to sleep with the TV chatter or the sound of a music speaker? Did he ever find himself alone, awake at night, wondering if someone else was thinking about him? And the dreams themselves—what sort of visions captivated his mind during the night?

For some reason, as I made my way to the guest room, my mind pondered these curiosities. I realized they were far from the most pressing questions of my day, as my dad's case was still unresolved. We still had time, as Justin pointed out—five more days in Ville du Lac. Anything could happen during that time ... for all we knew, the truth could be right under our noses.

Chapter Eleven

Alone in the house, I peeked out the front door, taking a quick sweep left and right. *Where were Justin and Olivia this morning?* Maybe Justin was still on his run, I thought—he'd usually run earlier in the morning, but perhaps he got off to a late start. As for Olivia, who knew? Spontaneous was her middle name, after all.

I closed the front door, almost tripping over Justin's Adidas running shoes—socks still inside, oddly enough. Where could he be?

I went out to the back patio. As I checked the lawn, I observed something below—something shiny. A small metallic dock with a boat, partially hidden by some pines along the lakeshore. Looking over my right shoulder, I noticed the gate leading to the stairway was ajar.

Closing the gate, I descended the stairs. At the bottom, I was met with a blue-and-white speedboat tied to the dock. I caught motion within the boat.

"Morning, Natalie!" Justin called out. I could only make out his white T-shirt, as his head was down. He was diligently searching for something within the boat.

"Are we taking a boat to the river?" I asked, half-joking.

"Nah! I thought it'd be nice for us to take a break and enjoy some time on the lake. As long as you're good with that!"

Justin's head popped into view, as he stood up, holding two life vests. In one swift motion, he dangled his legs along the boat's edge, as his sandals made contact with the rocky shoreline. He made his way over to me, dressed in a Muse T-shirt and swim trunks.

"Sure! Where's Olivia?" I wondered.

"She's visiting downtown with Katie—the lady from the visitor center, I believe, from two days ago," he responded.

"Are you serious? When did she leave?"

Justin handed me a life vest. "About ten minutes ago. She told me not to wait on her, as she's unsure when she'll return."

Olivia had a long history of absent-mindedness. But to completely blow me off—to leave without a simple text or goodbye—was unlike her. I knew there must be a reason for her madness... a very attractive reason, who was, at this moment, offering me a life vest.

"Oh, ok," I said. "It's a beautiful day for a boat ride!"

"Awesome! Let me double-check the safety equipment, and then we'll be good to go!" Justin said as he pushed himself back up, climbing into the boat.

"Can you give me a few minutes? I need to change into my swimsuit real quick."

"No problem! Take your time."

I returned to the house, heading into the guest bedroom, a surge of energy running through my body. I hadn't even had my morning cup of coffee, yet I could barely keep my hands still enough to tie the strings of my bikini top. I then slipped on a sleeveless sundress over my swimsuit.

I turned into the adjacent bathroom, taking a quick glance at myself in the panoramic mirror. I didn't find any major issues with my appearance—my brown hair seemed to be obeying itself, and the mascara outlining my hazel eyes was still intact. The pesky freckles sprinkled across my cheeks and nose were also adequately concealed.

Yet, my hands were still shaking. *Why am I so jittery this morning?* Without further self-reflection, I knew it wasn't the speedboat causing this abrupt rush of nerves.

***

"Wow! I didn't know this corner of Lake Awl existed," I said as Justin turned off the boat's engine.

"Not many people do," he said, taking off his hat. "Yeah, I like coming out here whenever I get the chance. It's nice that it's secluded."

I nodded, admiring the view before us. The sky was a clear azure, reflected in the rippled waters of the lake. Along the surface, the mid-morning sunlight glistened like a collection of crystals. Across the way, distant evergreen-laden mountains lined the horizon.

A gust of wind suddenly blew a lock of hair into my face. Sweeping it aside, I looked at Justin—his wavy hair tousled by the wind. He brushed his hair away from his eyes. His notable blue eyes. My heart began racing as I felt the short, strong pulses within my chest.

"Thanks for bringing me out here!" I said. "The last time I was on a boat was with my dad when we went lake fishing."

"Of course! I remember Kyle and I joining you guys once for that. I must've really enjoyed myself, 'cause I remember asking my parents for a boat afterwards!" Justin laughed.

I sighed. "If only pursuing hobbies was that easy."

"It can be if you're willing to push fear aside—like when you asked me to join the drama club with you."

"Yeah, but that was my dad's idea originally. And I never got around to joining the drama club. At least it paid off well for you. Very well. Now, you're living the dream."

"Supposedly," Justin said, looking down for a moment. He seemed doubtful.

"You don't sound too thrilled about being famous and admired by everyone."

"That's the problem."

"Really? I always thought the admiration of adoring fans was the selling point."

He shook his head. "Anything but. They always expect me to act a certain way and deliver on certain promises. I'm always on my A-game, no matter where I go. So, let's say you're having a bad day, and you're a bit short with the cashier at the store. For the average person, that'd cause some mild annoyance on the cashier's end. For me, that'd mean a front-cover headline on 'Us Weekly' announcing to the world how much of an asshole I am! No grace given whatsoever."

"Dang, I'm sorry. That sounds super inconvenient."

"Yep. Haven't had too much trouble with the fans themselves—my security team's been on top of things. But all my interactions with them are shallow and one-sided. Basically, tell them what they wanna hear. After a repeat of the same conversation, day after day, it gets old. Real quick." Justin sighed deeply. "But what about you? Do you have a dream job?"

"Kind of. I wouldn't call it a dream job, exactly."

"What is it?"

I took a deep breath as I looked out at the horizon. "It's a bit complicated, but I'd love to own a coffee shop and bakery with a shared workspace.

Coffee shops have always had a special place in my heart. When I was in high school, my grandma and I often stopped by this one coffee shop near the park. It was one of my fondest memories of Montana after my dad died. So, you can probably guess my first job in college. Yeah, during my Coffee Bean shifts, I'd normally see a handful of customers working remotely on their laptops. They didn't typically engage in conversation with any of the other regulars. So, I thought: why not create an environment where self-employed individuals can come together while enjoying a cup of coffee?"

I giggled. "I know! Silly, right?"

"No, not at all!" Justin said. "That's a brilliant idea."

I looked at him in disbelief. "Really?"

"Yeah, really. Why didn't you consider it as an option before?"

"Well, I was convinced I'd be letting my family down, especially since I wouldn't be using my college degree. They've always emphasized the importance of higher education, so owning a small business would've been frowned upon. And, of course, I was afraid of investing time and money in a business that could possibly fail. There's that, too."

"Well, you'll never know unless you try. But I get it. I'm assuming you don't find the medical path fulfilling?"

"Not really."

"May not be easy, but you could always change your career path down the road."

I nodded, adjusting the straps of my life vest.

Justin reached for his aviator sunglasses. "Shall we go for a swim?"

"Swim? Here? Don't we need to tie up the boat before we do that?"

"Not necessarily. I've got an anchor. We could swim closer to the shore if you'd like." He gestured to the lakeshore about a half-mile away from us.

"Sure, sounds good!"

Justin turned on the engine, his hands guiding the steering wheel, as the boat progressed. Approaching the lakeshore, I watched the hypnotic motion of the small white waves lapping onto the sandy shoreline. *I could get used to this! Just give me a book and an iced caramel macchiato, and I'm set for the rest of time!* The soothing sound of the crashing waves had put me in a trance—so mesmerized that I didn't even notice Justin anchoring the boat.

Without warning, he removed his life vest and T-shirt underneath—revealing his toned chest and abs. *Holy crap, he's been working out!* Trying not to stare, I felt my body temperature rise.

The next thing I knew, Justin scooted over to the boat's stern and jumped into the lake with a splash. "Come on in! The water's nice!"

I sat along the stern, allowing my legs to dangle in the water. *Geez, the lake is cold!* Much colder than I'd expect for a warm summer day.

"You know, I think I'm good!" I replied. "My legs are in, at least."

Justin splashed the upper half of my body.

"Hey!" I exclaimed.

"Now, you'll have no other choice!" he teased, laughing.

Shaking my head, I removed my life vest and sundress and slipped into the water. Shivering slightly, my body was shocked by the chilly temperature of the lake. After a few minutes of treading water, the shock eventually wore off. In fact, the cool water had a calming effect on me. Therapeutic, even.

"Water feels better now, huh?" Justin said as he floated on his back, reaching his arms toward the sky.

"Yeah, it does," I said. "Wouldn't you say the same?"

Before he could answer, I splashed him in the face.

"Hey! Uncool!" he joked.

I smirked at him. "Now, we're even!"

"Not for long!" Justin dove into the water for a moment and resurfaced on my other side, splashing me almost immediately. He gave me a smug smile.

"Well, two can play that game!" I quickly swam to his other side and splashed him, giggling.

"Aren't you glad you joined me in the lake after all?" Justin said.

"I don't know about that!" I quipped. "That's a lot of cold water thrown in my face!"

"That's what towels are for!"

I splashed him once more. "Well, you're gonna need a bigger towel!"

It'd been quite a while since I'd allowed some spontaneity in my life, I realized—probably not since my last summer in Ville du Lac with Justin. And, as with the cool of the lake, it felt nice.

Very nice.

Chapter Twelve

"**M**an, these s'mores brownies are killer!" Justin remarked, grabbing another piece.

"Shouldn't we save some for Olivia?" I wondered.

"Nah! She decided to go on the dinner cruise, so she's made her choice."

I moved the plate of brownies to the other end of the dining room table, out of Justin's reach—not without taking another piece of my own. He wasn't the only one enticed by the comforting aroma of melted chocolatey goodness.

"I'm glad the meal turned out all right," I said, biting into my brownie. "It's always a risk cooking up some decent tacos outside California! Thanks for your help!"

I took a quick glimpse out the dining room window. The rain was finally beginning to subside—tiny water droplets covering the back patio, a sharp contrast to the weather earlier in the day.

"No problem! Did your parents like to cook?" Justin asked.

"Yeah, my mom did. She taught me how to cook when I was younger. After my dad died, she took control of all the cooking in our house. She doesn't really allow me to help much, in general."

"Sounds like she didn't let herself grieve enough."

"Yeah, I think so, too." I took a deep breath. "If I'm being real here, I don't think I allowed myself to grieve either. I was expected to move on from tragedy and stay strong for our family. Survivalism, in a nutshell. That was when I developed the self-sufficient mindset—I learned to rely on myself and avoid asking for help whenever possible. It was easier that way."

"I wouldn't call that easier."

"No, not at all. In college, I continued to push forward with this mindset until it led to burnout. I was in my fourth year, with a full course load and no time to breathe. My anxiety was through the roof, and I eventually caved into the pressure of it all—the perfect grades, the perfect MCAT scores, the perfect everything. I was forced to slow down, look at my life, and decide what was truly important. After some counseling and prayer, I decided to take a break from my studies, allowing myself the extra time to graduate and prepare for medical school."

I took a sip of water. "I haven't told my family about this. It's like there's a wedge between them and me. Higher education is everything to them—more than it is to me, the resident doctor. I often feel excluded from them, like I'm in middle school all over again. I guess I've never really fit in with anyone..."

I pushed my dinner plate away from me. "I'm sorry if that's too somber. I don't wanna bring the mood down."

Justin shook his head. "You're fine, Natalie. You never need to apologize for opening up. That must've been so rough, not having the emotional support of your family."

He sighed. "Yeah, my family hasn't been available either; to the point when I was struggling with substance abuse, I couldn't confide in them at all."

"If you don't mind me asking, what did you struggle with?" I asked.

"Alcoholism. It was a couple years after the 'Midnight Club' series ended when I was struggling to find the right roles. I had a bit of success with the following two films, but after that, I hit a wall. My mind became my own worst enemy, and I sunk into a depression. With no one to turn to, I began to self-medicate. Over time, I found myself drifting further into the drug and party scene, my only real key to connection."

Wow. I had no idea. "I'm so sorry to hear that. Did you end up getting help?"

"Yes. It was at my lowest point. I'd dug myself into a deeper hole. I looked forward to the end of the day more than my work. Escapism was the only way to numb the pain of my failed career and life, I thought. I refused to believe there was another option. But I was wrong. I found a way out of my mess. I chose to be persistent in my recovery efforts, even when the temptation to relapse was knocking on my door. It wasn't easy."

Justin brushed his hair out of his face. "That was over two years ago. Sometimes, I wish I'd known better, so I could've avoided falling into a downward spiral and losing myself. But, at the same time, I was found by someone who knows me better than I know myself."

I nodded in understanding. "I'm glad you found hope at the end of it all."

"Erica was supportive, too, on my path to sobriety. I still feel guilty about us—prolonging our relationship when I knew it wasn't going anywhere. I wish I'd had the courage to end it sooner than I did. I wasn't fair to her."

"It sounds like you were going through a lot of change at the time, and you didn't have the hindsight you have now. You don't have to be so hard on yourself."

Justin nodded. "Thank you for your support, for listening, all of it. I hadn't opened up about this with anyone before—not on this level. It means a lot to me."

"Same here. I really appreciate confiding in you. I'm so used to doing life alone."

He looked at me with intent, his blue eyes expressing concern. Deep, genuine concern. "You don't have to do life alone."

The possibility of Justin's romantic interest in me suddenly crossed my mind. I learned that he was the one who'd ended his previous relationship. At that moment, with that smoldering look of his, it seemed like he wanted to say something more. *I'm almost certainly overreading the situation again.* I'm pretty good at that.

To combat my nerves, I glanced around the house. I noticed an acoustic guitar resting on its stand in the living room, not too far from the fireplace. "Do you play? Guitar, I mean?"

"Uh, yeah. I do. In my free time," Justin replied.

"That's great! When did you learn?"

"It was actually for one of my roles, the rock musical 'Rockin' the Paradise'. The film sparked my interest in classic rock, and I began trying to learn some of those songs on guitar."

Justin smiled at me sheepishly. "I'm not very good, though."

"Oh, come on! You're probably way better than I am. I took a guitar class in college, and I still can't strum a chord to save my life! I'd love to hear you play one of your favorite songs."

He went to the living room and took the guitar off its stand. "Well, are you down for some mediocre music?"

"Why, yes. I am!" I quipped.

I joined Justin on the leather couch. He began to strum and sing 'Sunshine On My Shoulders.' Over the course of the song, I found myself mesmerized by his vocals and instrumentation—the softness of his voice complemented by the soothing chords of the guitar. There was something about it—music, that is... the way it could speak to you on a level spoken words couldn't. It never really crossed my mind until that point.

"That was really good!" I said after Justin had finished the song. "That wasn't mediocre at all! I also never knew you could sing."

"Oh, thanks." He looked down, seemingly embarrassed.

"Have you ever considered using your musical skills in a part-time gig?"

"Like a band?"

"Yeah, or some other job involving music. I think you'd be great at it!"

"I hadn't given it any thought before. I'd say my current line of work keeps me pretty busy!"

"Maybe after you retire at some point?"

Justin shrugged with a half-smile. "Maybe."

He then handed the guitar to me.

"Me?! Play?!" I laughed. "Ok, I hope you like broken chords."

"Well, I'm here to help you unbreak the chords."

Holding the neck of the guitar with my left hand, I extended my fingers to the appropriate strings and pressed down, attempting to strum one of the chords I'd learned in my college class—C major, I think. As expected, the sound didn't come through correctly.

"I warned you," I said, grimacing.

"That's ok. It takes time and muscle memory. Can I show you what helped me?"

"Sure."

Justin moved behind me, assisting me with my grip and finger alignment. I felt his hand gently touching mine as I noticed our proximity, his warm breath tickling the nape of my neck. My stomach did a backflip.

"So now, try again. Just keep your fingers curved and press the strings with your fingertips," he calmly instructed.

I played the same chord once again. This time, the sound came out clean.

"See, I knew you could do it!" Justin said reassuringly. "Now, you're one step closer to joining my retirement band!"

I giggled. "Yeah, in that case, I'll stick with the triangle!"

"Ah, that's not rock! Not even bass guitar?"

"How about an electric triangle? I bet I could do a mean solo! Just give me a stage and a single spotlight!"

Justin busted up laughing, which caused me to laugh alongside him, my sides aching. I'd forgotten about that sensation.

As he continued to play additional chords and songs for me, I couldn't help but appreciate the warmth and comfort of that evening. I wish I could enjoy more moments like this, I thought. Simple yet intimate—unplugged, so to speak. A time to be myself. It was then that I realized how much I'd missed my hometown.

Even more so, I realized how much I'd missed Justin.

Chapter Thirteen

"Well, where do we go from here?" I sighed, staring into the rocky waters of the Atlas River.

"We could always review your dad's photos again," Olivia offered. "Or what about the visitor files?"

"But we've already double and triple-checked those records. And the landscapes—that's all they are: landscapes of the river. No people, vehicles, place names. Otherwise, forensics would've gotten involved after the photos were developed," I pointed out.

"I'd say maybe sleep on it. A clear mind may help," Justin suggested.

I nodded, "Yeah. It's just disappointing, you know? All this time, I thought we'd find something. I'm not sure if it was worth our time—traveling all the way up here."

"'Course it was worth it!" Olivia exclaimed, "We got a vacation, didn't we? I sure as hell needed one! And so did you! Justin too!"

She let out a long sigh. "Ugh! I'm so not looking forward to returning to work on Monday. A micromanaging office is not a happy office, let me tell ya."

"Yep, you did. For half the drive up here!" I remarked with a laugh.

"Still better than listening to Justin's progressive stuff. I swear, those songs go on forever! They need more lyrics."

Justin shook his head, amused. "That's not the point of progressive rock. And if you think my music is hard to listen to, you haven't met my brother yet!"

Olivia giggled as she took out her phone, swiping through her text messages.

I continued to fix my gaze on the river.

"Hey, I'm sorry things didn't work out how you'd hoped," Justin said, picking up a small stone. "Why don't you explore some sights while we're here? We've got until Thursday."

"Haven't we been doing that already?"

Justin tossed the stone across the river's surface as I watched it skip four times. "You haven't been to the city yet."

"As in downtown? I didn't think that was possible. Aren't you trying to keep a low profile?"

He took off his baseball cap, smoothing out his hair. "Yeah, but I'll be on some work calls this afternoon. You and Olivia should go."

"Oh my God, yes! That'd be amazing!" Olivia enthused. "Think of all the shopping we can do!"

I shook my head. "I'm not looking to add credit card debt to the mix."

"Did I mention there's coffee? Multiple coffee shops within a one-block radius." She smiled smugly at me as if she'd just checkmated me in a metaphorical chess match.

"Yes, yes. We can go. But we'll need a car—Justin's house is not within walking distance. Maybe Uber?"

"Feel free to take my car," Justin offered. "I'll be staying at home."

"Awesome!" Olivia rubbed her hands together excitedly. "I can't wait to get behind the wheel again! That engine is so powerful, it's seriously addicting!"

He picked up a new stone, looking doubtful. "Um, yeah ... about that. Would you mind if maybe Natalie drove this time around?"

"Natalie?! Oh, ok. Guess I can allow her to give it a spin," Olivia joked.

"You're ok with that?" I asked him.

Justin skipped the stone across the river. "Yeah. You drove it part of the way up here, so I trust you won't run over any banana peels."

He smiled slyly at me, referencing our childhood Mario Kart competitions. Needless to say, I was never the victor.

Blasted banana peels!

"Oh, well, thank you. You can trust I won't get any speeding tickets, either!" I returned the same sly smile to him.

"Hey! I thought we weren't bringing that up anymore!" Justin said in a playful tone.

I shrugged, picking up my own stone and rubbing it between my thumb and index finger. "It's been a while since I've visited downtown. I wonder if that floating boardwalk is still there."

"Yup, you can't miss it," Olivia affirmed. "Katie and I went there yesterday."

I tossed the stone across the river, watching it skip three times. "Hey, I think I'm getting the hang of this!"

"Awesome! You wanna know what the next step is?" Justin asked.

"What? Skipping two stones simultaneously?"

He grabbed two stones from the riverbank, handing me one. "A faceoff."

"Ooh... a faceoff!" Olivia said in an intrigued tone.

I shook my head, half-laughing. "Uh, a competition? I think I'll pass."

"Oh, really? Not even best two out of three?" Justin wondered.

I sighed. "All right. But only two out of three—even if we tie."

Like that's possible, given my minimal experience with skipping stones.

He nodded. "Deal! Ladies first."

Olivia chuckled.

Oh, God! What did I get myself into?

I initiated our so-called friendly competition by tossing my stone with a quick flick of the wrist. I watched it skip across the river two times. Only two times.

Darn!

"Do we really have to do this? You're probably gonna crush me now," I said.

"Yup, but you never know, you could always come back," Justin said as he tossed his stone, skipping four times—the corners of his mouth curving into a small smile.

Yeah, right! I'm most certainly out of this game!

"Round two." He handed me another stone.

"You know, I'm gonna pick my own this time," I said as I reached for a new stone. "I think yours are loaded. That's why you're doing so much better!"

Justin shrugged. "Suit yourself."

I proceeded to toss my stone, which skipped four times. My own personal record!

"That's more like it!" I remarked.

He tossed his stone, which skipped three times.

"You did it, Natalie! You won this round," Olivia said.

I nodded as I grabbed two stones from the riverbank, handing one to Justin. "Now, it's my turn to give you a stone. That'll make it even!"

"If you say so!" he teased.

I tossed my last stone into the river, which skipped five times. Even better! "Your turn!"

Justin tossed his last stone. I watched as it skipped a total of four times.

"And the winner is ... Natalie!" Olivia cheered.

"You sure about that?" Justin quipped.

"Yep. I believe five skips is greater than four," I explained as a matter of fact.

"I also had five. The last one was hard to see, but I counted the ripples."

"I wouldn't rely on that! Ripples can be deceiving, especially as they spread out."

"C'mon! Is a tie really that bad?"

"It is when you're trying to win!" I smirked at Justin.

"Well, well. Looks like you've got a competitive streak, after all! We'll just have to plan a rematch, then!"

He smirked back at me, retrieving his hat by the riverbank. "Good game!"

Olivia eyed me with curiosity. "Good game, indeed!"

As the three of us returned to the car, I felt a sense of disappointment. Not so much due to the inconclusiveness of my father's case—instead, the approaching end of our trip in only a matter of days. After that, I'd be back in San Diego, preparing for my residency.

Away from Justin.

***

"Thank you!" I said to the barista as I grabbed my Huckleberry White Mocha at the pickup bar, fastening the lid with a simple push.

"Dude, can you ever go one day without having coffee?" Olivia asked rhetorically.

I grabbed a cup sleeve. "Can you go a day without your phone?"

She shook her head. "That's not fair, everything's on my phone! I don't think I even know your phone number by heart!"

"Well, you better start learning," I said as we exited the coffee shop.

Downtown Ville du Lac was surprisingly pleasant. I was expecting more crowds and grime—typical characteristics of a downtown district—but Ville du Lac was rather quaint in comparison. There were plenty of restaurants and shops, some scenic parks, and walking paths, all with a generous view of the lake. The best of both worlds, you could say.

"I remember the boardwalk was down the street, by the boat launching area," I recalled as we approached a street corner.

"Yeah, it's pretty awesome!" Olivia remarked. "Wanna check it out?"

"Sure!"

We headed down the street toward the lake. Before we knew it, we approached the entrance to a wooden dock—boats of varying sizes parked along its sides—the floating boardwalk. As I remembered from childhood, the U-shaped walkway was fairly long, extending at least a half-mile from one side to the other—ending next to a grassy park shaded by several large trees. I didn't recall that in addition to boating ports, it also hosted a cafe, gift shop, and lounging tables and chairs. A floating mini-mall. Were those always there?

"Quite the place!" I observed.

As we strolled along the boardwalk, we passed by a sizable number of couples in both directions, mostly hand-in-hand—a few locking arms or smiling together for a lakeside photo.

"So, you and Justin..." Olivia questioned.

Apparently, I wasn't the only one who'd been people-watching.

"What about us?" I wondered.

"You know, for someone with a medical degree, you'd think you'd pick up on the symptoms right away."

"Symptoms?" I rolled my eyes.

She had to bring out the medical metaphors. Of course, she did!

"Yeah, you're lovesick," Olivia clarified.

I gave her a confused look. She was really stretching out those metaphors—so much that she wasn't even making sense anymore.

"Do I even need to explain?" She moved a strand of her hair behind her ear. "Seriously, Natalie. I've seen you around Justin enough to know there's something there. Even from the beginning, back in Hollywood, at the movie premiere. But definitely, since we've been in Ville du Lac. I mean, even Katie picked up on the two of you."

I shook my head. "She was mistaken."

"I wouldn't say that. More like she was stating the obvious—that you two are fond of each other."

I stopped to appreciate the view beyond the boardwalk. The mountains along the horizon were reflected in the lake's clear blue waters. Puffy white clouds floated across the sky as a cool breeze gently blew my hair—almost reminiscent of my boat ride with Justin the other day.

"What are you thinking about?" Olivia asked as I'd grown quiet.

"Just remembering," I responded.

"Remembering what?"

"Yesterday, when Justin and I went boating."

Olivia grinned. "Ah, that's right! Sounded like you had quite the adventure—sailing the high seas with a mega-hunk at your side. How breathtaking!"

I took a sip from my coffee cup. "A speedboat, not a sailboat. And this is a lake, not the ocean."

She shrugged casually. "Same difference! But you enjoyed the view, right?"

"Of the lake? Definitely!"

"And of Justin? Shirtless?"

I laughed nervously. "Olivia, come on! Do we really have to do this?"

She concentrated her focus on me, her blue-green eyes unflinching. "Yes, we do! Tell me, Natalie, how were you really feeling out on that boat?"

I sighed heavily. My patience with Olivia—and myself, to a greater extent—had run dry.

"You want the truth? Well, then. Yes! I do find Justin very attractive! Happy now?"

Suddenly, it was as if a light switch had turned on in my mind as I found myself venturing into its crevices for the first time in a long time.

The truth was, I wasn't only admiring the lake on our boat ride.

I was also admiring Justin. All of him, really. His wavy brown hair was always so perfectly tousled, framing his genuine wide smile. A smile that made me feel right at home, where I felt understood, cherished—truly mattering to him. And, of course, his sky-blue eyes. Even more stunning than the reflections of blue in the lake. I could bask in them all day long.

Olivia raised a finger. "Ah ha! Knew it!"

"But that doesn't mean anything," I said. "Everyone thinks he's hot. You think he's hot. That's a celebrity crush for you."

"Not to the same extent as you. I mean, putting physical attraction aside, you two have some serious chemistry together. Good looks can only take you so far."

I sipped my coffee, surrendering to my unfiltered caffeinated thoughts. "Yeah. He's gorgeous, all-around..."

The most amazing thing was, he was never trying to be. What I loved most about Justin was that he was incredibly humble and down-to-earth despite his fame and fortune. He carried charm and humor up his sleeve but never sacrificed his kindness or sincerity.

"… just like I remember him to be." I sighed yearningly.

I stopped myself mid-thought and, consequently, mid-step as I stopped along the boardwalk. "Wait. What am I saying? I can't be falling for Justin."

"Why not?" Olivia wondered.

"Well, for one thing, I've already headed in that direction before—when I was fourteen, after our first kiss. And how did that work out for me? Oh yeah, that's right. We didn't talk for thirteen years. Not so great, then."

"But that wasn't your choice—or his. You lost contact, simple as that. That happens. Life happens. So now, you're basically picking up from where you left off when there was some sweet lip action. Add all the time you've spent together on this trip, and boom! There you have it: a match made in heaven!"

We exited the boardwalk, heading down the shaded pathway through the park. With each sip of my coffee, I allowed my thoughts to wander deeper…

Justin never ceased to amaze me. His spontaneity was alluring, and he could turn a boat ride into a journey or an adventure—or a simple interest like skipping stones into a passion. He had that way about him … that mysteriously irresistible way. I thought back to the night he played the guitar for me. I was not only enthralled by his instrumentation and vocals but also by his laughter. His loud, iconic laugh—a laugh that was an octave higher than his normal speaking voice and could quickly fill a room. It was music to my ears. His zeal for life dews infectious, and I could see no cure.

"I'm in love with Justin," I whispered to myself.

"What was that?" Olivia asked, confused.

"Me and Justin. You're right. I do care about him." I took a deep breath. "But I doubt he feels the same."

Why would he?

He was a celebrity, after all. He could have any girl of his choice.

Why would he ever want me?

I wasn't a supermodel by any means. I'd never acted in films, participated in televised interviews, or attended premieres or award shows. Heck, I'd never once spoken into a camera that wasn't connected to our home VCR back in the day. I was just plain Natalie Baker—the girl who'd lived across the street from Justin Anderson at one point.

"Oh, there's a lot you don't see!" Olivia said as we continued our stroll through the park. "He's definitely interested, trust me. The way he looks at you, smiles at you, talks with you, laughs with you, asks about you when you're not around—all signs. I mean, this morning, at the river, when he was teasing you about a rematch—dead giveaway. Back at the Coffee Bean, when he came in for a surprise visit—that was straight out of a scene from 'Notting Hill'. The list goes on. Girl, the boy is smitten. Hopelessly so."

I took a moment to process this new information. Was I that dense—oblivious to the signals Justin was communicating to me the whole time?

"Yeah, but even if that is the case—if he's somehow interested in me—I don't see a relationship lasting," I said. "He's leaving the country in August for his new film. Who knows how long that'll take. Besides, I'll be too busy with my residency program to have the time to spend with him, even if he wasn't filming. And let's not forget the nature of celebrity relationships—where they either fizzle out over time or end abruptly. There's no third outcome."

"But what if there was?! What if you're the exception? I mean, look at your friendship. It's still strong, even after a decade of lost contact. That's gotta count for something!"

"Yeah, and that's another thing. I wouldn't wanna risk ruining our friendship over the possibility of a relationship."

"Natalie." Olivia supportively placed a hand on my shoulder. "From all the years I've known you—back to college orientation—I've never known you to stray away from the sidewalk, to take any risk. Every decision you make is based on deep analysis. Well, I'm telling you now to quit overthinking for once and take the risk! Let me put it this way: would you rather be upfront with Justin, at the expense of your friendship, than live another decade or more with regret?"

I stopped momentarily, Olivia's prior statement resonated in my ears. I looked across the spacious lawn before me. Off to the side, I saw a playground—a wooden play structure nestled amongst the trees. Its design resembled a sort of castle or fort. Treehouse.

"Yes. I can talk to Justin." I tossed my empty coffee cup into the nearby trash bin. "I can tell him how I feel."

Olivia hugged me, exhilarated. "Yay! It's about time!"

"Now, the only question is, when?"

"Oh, I wouldn't worry about that. I've got a plan!"

I raised an eyebrow at her. "Now, where've I heard that one before?"

"But when have I ever failed you?"

As I opened my mouth to respond, Olivia cut me off, finishing her sentence. "...with anything related to Justin?"

I shook my head.

"Then trust me." She crossed her arms confidently. "By tomorrow, you'll be more than just the girl next door to him. Oh, yeah! He'll be your biggest fan!"

Chapter Fourteen

"Wow! That's beautiful!" I observed, admiring the landscape beyond Justin's backyard.

"No doubt about that! Olivia's missing out—again." Justin leaned his back against the sidewall. "Is a night on the town worth missing this?"

I'd informed him about Olivia's interest in experiencing the downtown Ville du Lac nightlife with Katie. I'd failed to explain her sudden interest—all according to plan.

The sun was edging closer to the horizon as the setting sun's golden rays illuminated the clouds over the lake.

"You could almost camp out here if you wanted to," I said. "Just pitch a tent in the grass over there, and you'll get a nice lake ambiance."

"Yeah, I've done that before," Justin said.

"Really? Camped in your own backyard?"

"Not intentionally." He laughed. "I fell asleep while reading a book once. Don't remember much about it. Apparently, it wasn't very interesting!"

I giggled. "Well, I've definitely fallen asleep to some of my college textbooks—especially in med school."

He shook his head. "It's amazing you could even read through those books. Don't think I'd make it past the first page!"

"Yeah, they weren't beach reads, that's for sure!"

I suddenly remembered my plan from earlier: to come clean about my feelings for Justin. To do so, I'd need to organize the appropriate setting first.

"Would you like to sit on the back lawn?" I asked. "I'd love to get a closer view of the sunset!"

"Sure! I was thinking the same thing."

As we headed to the lawn, Justin casually ran a hand through his hair. My body temperature rose sharply as I felt the sudden desire to kiss him—right then and there. *Get a grip, Natalie. You're not a teenager anymore!*

"I have to apologize," he said as we sat on the grass. "Didn't realize how long work would take. I would've waited to eat dinner with you, but I skipped lunch and ended up having an early dinner instead."

I extended my legs and crossed them, adjusting the waist of my skinny jeans. My most flattering pair. "No worries! Were you able to get it all done?"

"Yeah. Pretty much. There's just a lot of moving pieces, you know. It's sometimes hard to keep up with everything." Justin tugged on a few strands of grass. "And there's also the house sale stuff—mine and Erica's old house."

I nodded. "Oh, I'm sorry. That sounds complicated. Do you plan to move into another house after the sale?"

"Not currently. I'm thinking about holding off until I finish the film shoot."

"The one in New Zealand?"

"Yep. I'll still own this house, so it could be my primary US residence overseas."

"That sounds like a good idea."

I directed my focus onto the lake. The clouds above were beginning to transition to hues of pink as evening twilight was on its way. The watercolor-esque cloudscape was reflected upon the lake, giving it a dynamic yet serene appearance.

"Gotta love these sunsets." Justin reclined on the grass, resting on his elbows. "I'd forgotten how much better they are here than in California."

"You think so?"

"Absolutely! You can watch the sunrise here, too, depending on which side of the lake you're facing."

"True. I haven't watched a sunrise before. Have you?"

"I tried to once. Over the ocean."

"The Pacific Ocean?!" I put my hand over my mouth, trying not to laugh.

"Yep." Justin looked down, half-amused. "On one of my first dates with Erica. I thought I was being smooth—picking up breakfast, bringing her to my favorite beach spot, and watching the sunrise together. After some time, she asks, 'What are we waiting for?' 'The sunrise, of course,' I tell her. 'You mean that sun over there—that's already risen in the other direction?' Well, damn it!"

I couldn't contain my laughter anymore. He watched me lose control of my sanity, my head hanging low as my body shook with uncontrollable laughter. God, I love his sense of humor!

"You ok over there?!" Justin began cracking up.

I raised my index finger in the midst of my laughing storm. "Yeah, give me a minute!"

This was the appropriate moment, I realized, while my nerves were at bay.

"This has all been so amazing, Justin," I began once I'd calmed down. "Being back here, in Ville du Lac, with you. Thanks for coming on this trip with me and opening up your house. You've been so helpful along the way. I've really enjoyed our daily adventures to the lake and whatnot!"

He smiled at me. "Of course! Likewise. I'm glad we got a chance to get away."

I took a deep breath. "There was something that came to mind earlier that I'd like to talk to you about. If you're ok with it."

"Yeah, I'm listening."

"So, earlier, I realized that–"

At that moment, Justin's cell phone rang. He picked it up and briefly studied the screen. He canceled the call and returned his phone to the grass, screen face-down.

Of course, something had to come and wreck my plans!

"Sorry about that," Justin apologized. "It's my agent again. He's in the process of setting me up for a spot on 'The Tonight Show'. I'm not a fan of the late-night talk shows, to be honest—my PR team keeps urging me on, saying it'll be good for my image and all that smoke-and-mirrors crap. Very annoying."

"No problem! That does sound annoying."

"So, what was that you were saying?"

I froze in fear as I tried to resume my previous line of thought. His call reminded me of the significant differences between our lifestyles. *I'm being idealistic.* There's no way a relationship between Justin and me would work out—a famous actor and a resident doctor. It's much safer to remain friends.

I quickly thought of something to replace the void in my prior statement. "I was saying I realized that when we return home, it'd be inconvenient for you to drop us off in San Diego and then drive back up to LA. Olivia and I could split an Uber or take a train from LA to San Diego."

Justin shook his head. "Not an inconvenience, Natalie. The longer I can avoid returning to LA, the better. Plus, driving at night will be better with less traffic."

"Oh, ok. Thanks so much!"

"You're welcome!"

I sighed, still disappointed with myself. "Well, I should probably start settling in for the night. I'm pretty tired."

Justin checked the time on his phone. "Wow! Almost 9:30. I forgot how late the sun sets here! Yeah, I should probably do the same."

He pushed himself up from the grass, extending a hand to me.

"Thanks!" I said as I stood up.

We returned to the sliding glass door. For a moment, I'd considered retrying my previous conversation, but that was before I realized I had no willpower left in me.

"Hope you can get some rest," Justin said.

"You too," I replied.

Maybe rest is what I need at this point, I thought as I retreated to my bedroom in defeat. Maybe I'll be able to make better sense of things in the morning. I could only hope.

***

I was unable to sleep that night. My frustration from earlier was keeping my mind from being at peace, thus preventing me from falling asleep.

After a considerable period of tossing and turning, I eventually gave up, pulling off the covers. I placed my feet on the floor, stood up, and stretched my arms. *I think some fresh air will help me clear my head.*

Exhausted but not sleepy, I slid open the glass door to the back patio.

I wasn't expecting to find Justin sitting on the sofa facing the lit fire pit. He was wearing a zip-up hoodie and flannel pants. His hair was a little messy, but I still found him incredibly handsome at that moment.

Our eyes met as I entered the patio.

Immediately, I felt self-conscious. I was in my pajamas and had removed all traces of my usual makeup. I hadn't even thought about brushing my hair. I might as well be wearing scrubs at that point.

"You're up pretty late," I noted, sitting next to him.

"Couldn't sleep," Justin said. "You?"

"Same."

"Is there something on your mind?"

I smoothed out my hair with a hand. "A lot, actually. I wish my mind would just slow down for once."

He nodded in understanding. "I feel ya. Thoughts have been keeping me up at night lately. It's been a while since I've slept well."

"I'm sorry to hear that."

I looked up at the clear ebony sky. I noticed the stars were shining oddly bright for some reason. There must be less light pollution at this late hour, I figured. Beyond the patio, I observed the fullness of the moonglow as it rested peacefully on the lake's surface.

Much to my surprise, the scenery at night was even more spectacular than at sunset. The vibrant orange blaze of the fire pit, along with its profoundly woodsy aroma, also didn't hurt—adding to the cozy ambiance of the back patio.

Suddenly, I began to shiver, realizing I'd forgotten to put on a jacket. Besides my striped pajama pants, I only wore a short-sleeved UCSD T-shirt. It was deceptive how much colder it was here at night, even when the days were warmer.

In response, Justin took off his sweatshirt and offered it to me. "Here you go. This should keep you warm."

"What about you?" I asked. "You're only wearing a T-shirt."

"I'll be fine. With the fire going, I'm actually a bit too warm for my liking."

"Thanks!" I said as I slipped on his sweatshirt, zipping it up the middle. It was much too big on me. It went below my hips, and I couldn't see my fingers beyond the sleeves. It was warm inside and had a subtle masculine scent of pine that reminded me of Justin—my little cocoon. It was perfect.

"So, what's going on?" Justin wondered, looking at me intently.

"With what?" I didn't quite understand his question.

"The things on your mind. I'm here to listen if that'll help."

Oh, right. My love for Justin—the reason for my madness. My hopeless, irrevocable madness.

Well, I guess there's no running away now. I didn't know if it was my physical exhaustion or illogical infatuation to blame, but as I released my breath, I released my inhibitions along with it.

"Sure. So, uh, where to begin? Well, ever since we've reconnected these past few weeks, I keep thinking back to the last time we saw each other—at the treehouse when we kissed. To be honest, I had feelings for you then. Much more than a friend." I blushed. "The grieving process ended up preoccupying my mind, so I lost focus of you and me. But now, after spending all this time with you, in the hometown you and I both love, those feelings have returned. But even more so. I ... I can't explain it. Everything about you ... your charisma, kindness. How you can be silly one moment and sincere the next ... it bewilders me. I don't know how you do it, Justin. But I know I'm captivated by it ... by you."

I sat in silence for a moment, staring at the glowing fire pit. I snuck a peek at Justin. He was looking downward, expressionless.

Oh, shit! I've just ruined our friendship! I might as well start apologizing now.

"Justin, I'm so sorry for what I just said! I never meant to make things awkward, bet–"

Justin interrupted me mid-sentence. "–Natalie, I've always loved you, even before our kiss. You were my first kiss, too, and I couldn't stop thinking about you after that. So, I found it very difficult to move on after you left Ville du Lac. I had no way to contact you. I thought maybe I'd hear from you again, or maybe you'd visit in the future. I don't know. That's part of why I decided on a second home here—hoping I might run into you again by chance. When I saw you at my premiere, it truly meant the world to me. Nat, you're beautiful. You were always beautiful. Brilliant, too, I mean, you're a frickin doctor! And don't get me started on your sense of humor—hell, if I laughed any harder, I'd break a rib! I can't keep up."

He lifted his eyes and reached out his hand, lightly wrapping it around mine. "I know you think you have to build up these walls—to keep yourself safe from the outside world. But you don't have to do that with me."

I held his gaze, lacing my fingers between his. "I know. You've always had a skill in scaling walls. We had a treehouse, after all!"

Justin let out a small chuckle. He leaned in closer to me, tucking a lock of my hair behind my ear. I closed my eyes as I felt his lips gently press up against mine. Time suddenly slowed down.

While absorbing the warm sensation of our lips touching, I gradually began to sink my lips further into his. In response, he wrapped his arms around me, drawing me closer to him. I felt our torsos touch. His chest's soft rising and falling synchronized with mine as we breathed in unison. I melted deeper into him.

Ever so slightly, we pulled apart. I paused, breathing in the sweet space between us. I opened my eyes to look upon Justin and his remarkable blue eyes. He smiled at me, stroking my cheek with the back of his hand. I leaned into his caress and slowly ran a hand through his hair. His soft, wavy hair.

Justin was indeed an expert at the art of physical affection. He certainly had ample practice from his past film productions. I'd watched through most of them, and his roles were very compelling. I could see why so many girls would swoon at the sight of him.

At that point, though, I didn't mind. As he held me close, his lips finding mine once again, I knew his physical response to me was beyond that of a movie script.

It was something better...

Chapter Fifteen

- -

I woke up to the morning sunlight shining across my face. Still in a daze, I tried to think back to the previous night—when Justin told me he loved me. Was that all a dream? It seemed too good to be true.

I opened my eyes, taking a glance around me. I was not in the guest room bed, as would be expected. No, I was on the back patio, lying across the sofa. The fire pit was no longer burning, but I could see remnants of a previous flame from not long ago. I looked down, noticing that I was still wearing Justin's oversized gray sweatshirt and a wool blanket covering my legs.

I rolled over to find Justin lying next to me on his side—the same wool blanket covering his flannels and the bottom half of his black Queen T-shirt. He was fast asleep, snoring softly, his wavy hair resting on his face.

I realized then that the previous night's events were not a dream. They were real. Very real. I remembered us kissing for quite some time and eventually resting on the sofa together, looking up at the countless stars in all their beauty. I couldn't recall anything else, as I must've fallen asleep shortly after that. In Justin's arms, apparently.

Gingerly, I pulled off the blanket, sitting up from the sofa, trying not to wake him. Unzipping the sweatshirt, I slipped it off and lightly draped it across Justin's torso as a makeshift blanket.

I admired him for a moment as he continued to sleep soundly. It was hard to believe he shared the same feelings for me. I never would've expected that.

But I was elated by the fact. Very much so.

Judging by the temperature and the sun's orientation, I predicted it was around mid-morning by that point. *I should probably get dressed and make some breakfast.*

Groggily, I slid open the glass door to the kitchen. I felt like I was in slow motion—as if I were moving in water. I wasn't used to waking up this late ... or waking up in a man's arms, for that matter.

Well, my grogginess isn't a problem that a quick cup of coffee can't fix.

***

I'd just finished preparing our breakfast when Justin woke up. Convenient timing. Guys and food, I'm telling you, they must have a sixth sense.

"Good morning!" I greeted him as I brought two full plates of food to the patio.

Justin pushed himself up from the sofa, yawning. "Morning, Nat! That looks delicious. Is that a scramble?"

I smiled. Maybe a nickname isn't so bad after all. "Uh-huh. Essentially, it is an amalgamation of eggs and other ingredients from your fridge. Hopefully, it doesn't taste too weird!"

"Doubt it. Everything you've cooked so far has been amazing. Thanks for making breakfast!"

"No problem!"

Justin stretched his arms above his head. "How long have I been out?"

I peeked at the microwave clock through the glass door. "It's 10:14 now."

"Really? Damn, that's late!"

"Well, you must've needed the extra rest. A lot's happened lately." I paused awkwardly.

He nodded as if he'd understood what I meant. "Yeah, for sure."

I wasn't quite sure of his interpretation of the previous night. I was immensely curious how he'd respond to me at that moment. I might as well find out.

I carefully placed our plates onto the sofa, turning around to face Justin. He met my gaze as he gently embraced me. I rested my head on his shoulder, wrapping my arms around him and relaxing into his chest. I exhaled heavily, feeling his rapidly beating heart against mine.

I heard the slight squeaking of the sliding glass door. "Oh, man! Who's ready for some breakfast? This hangover is the worst, I–"

Olivia stopped mid-sentence to observe the two of us, with a plate of food in one hand and a fork and knife in the other. She grinned, her eyes widening with excitement.

"Oh! I'm just gonna go back and get us something to drink."

She took her plate and utensils and scurried back into the house, sliding the door behind her. She didn't need to ask questions—our actions indeed spoke louder than words.

***

"I believe this way brings us to the top." Justin gestured to the dirt path on our right.

We'd decided to hike one of the nearby hills after breakfast. At that point, we'd reached a fork in the road—as with the metaphorical fork in my life.

I stopped to catch my breath. "Can we take a water break first?"

Justin nodded. "Sure thing."

"It's probably good Olivia decided to stay behind."

"Yeah, hangovers are rough. She needs to stay hydrated."

We scooted to a corner that overlooked the valley of green flora below us.

I popped open my water bottle and began to drink from it—the cool, refreshing water trickling down my throat. After quenching my thirst, I realized I was still unsatisfied.

"Everything ok?" Justin asked, taking a sip from his Yeti water bottle.

"Yep," I quickly answered. I wasn't about to converse about my frustration with my future.

"Doesn't sound like it. Seriously, Nat. What's wrong?"

"Well," I sighed. "I'm sad our trip is coming to an end. I mean, we just got here, and now, we're expected to pack our bags and leave tomorrow? I just wish we could stay here longer, together."

Justin stashed away his water bottle into his backpack, draping his arm over my shoulders. "I know. Me too. What if we left a day or two later? I know your residency begins on Monday, so we could get you and Olivia home by Sunday at the latest. I'm good with that if you are."

I shook my head. "Yeah, theoretically, we could do that, but that wouldn't make much difference. You're returning to a life of fame, and I'm returning to a life that's not my own."

We both paused, staring off at the plethora of evergreens and shrubs. Eventually, Justin spoke. "What if you did something different with your life? Like the idea you told me on the boat?"

"You're not talking about the hybrid coffee shop-workspace thing? Yeah, right!" I laughed. "Like I'd throw away all the time and money I'd spent on my medical career for a startup business that may not even take off."

"But you'd enjoy it, right?"

I shrugged. "Sure. I mean, I'd find it interesting. But 'interesting' doesn't pay the bills. Ideas are only useful if they're put into action—like real, tangible plans. I have no course of action with this idea."

"But you could if you really wanted to. You, of all people, would be able to make it work. I believe it."

"Me?"

"Yes, you." Justin pointed at me. "You're the girl who'd alphabetize the bookshelf in our classroom. Every single time I'd return a book there, I swear it'd be in a different place by the end of the day."

"The right place," I corrected him. I had a duty, after all.

"Don't think I haven't noticed you rearranging the fridge, too," he playfully teased. "I've never seen a fridge organized by food groups before. Except, maybe, at the grocery store!"

Darn, I was caught. "Thought I was being stealthy!"

"But that's what I mean. You have a skill."

"With what? Organizing the dairy products from the vegetables?"

I was playing dumb at this point. Not that I cared. This whole line of thought was rather ridiculous.

"Organizing a business."

I unzipped my backpack, pulling out my sunglasses. "We should continue our hike before it gets too warm."

"Yeah, sure."

As we resumed our ascent, I noticed Justin's demeanor was a bit solemn—as if he were disappointed that I'd dismissed his idea. Starting a new business isn't practical. There's no conceivable way I could turn that dream into a reality – even if I really wanted to.

***

"Finally!" I said, relieved, as we'd reached the summit.

Justin took a swig from his water bottle and took off his baseball cap. I pulled out my phone to check the total elevation gain of our hike.

"That's a sweet view!" he observed, looking at the vast water below us.

I'd forgotten about the massive size of Lake Awl. It was asymmetrical, as the lake seemed to funnel into a curve as it reached the southern end—mountain ridges bordering its sides. Without a doubt, it was a beautiful sight to behold.

"Well, that's a 700-foot elevation gain," I said. "I think we've successfully burned off those brownies!"

Justin chuckled as I took out my phone and took photos of the lake.

"Would you mind if I took one of us?" I asked.

He nodded. "Allow me."

I gave Justin my phone as he proceeded to snap some selfies of the two of us, our arms wrapped around each other, facing away from the lake. He then handed the phone back to me.

I was surprised that each photo was perfectly aligned—Lake Awl shimmering behind us. No one's face was partially cut off, like with my selfies—the reason why I don't typically take selfies in the first place.

"Dang! Your photos are perfect! How'd you do that?" I wondered.

"Practice. Lots of it," Justin replied.

Makes sense. Everyone and their mothers would love to take a selfie with Justin Anderson.

"Fascinating, isn't it?" I said. "Lake Awl in its entirety. I'm so used to seeing only one piece of it at a time ... as with life."

"And now, you're faced with a choice, but you see only one viable option," Justin added. "Am I right?"

I took a deep breath. "You really wanna know my biggest problem with changing my vocation? It's the debt. It's crippling. I used to pride myself on having no loans as an undergrad—only to have that carpet ripped out from underneath me as a medical student. I know, eventually, I'll pay them off when I'm more established. But in the meantime, I'm supposed to stick it out and wait for my life to begin someday."

"I'm sorry you've had to go through this," Justin sympathized. "That sucks, for sure. Suppose, hypothetically, your debt was taken care of. No more loans. Would that change things at all?"

"Yeah. I mean, I'd have more financial freedom and peace of mind." I studied him, perplexed. "What are you getting at?"

"Would you consider a new career path if debt was out of the equation?"

"Oh, we're back to the coffee shop idea again? Uh, I don't know. I mean, there are other issues besides debt, like starting a new business from the ground up. There's probably lots of paperwork involved, and complicated taxes, too. But my loans are definitely the biggest hurdle."

"Then consider it done."

I paused briefly. As I comprehended Justin's implication, I stumbled backward, astounded. "Wait. You're gonna pay off my loans? All of them?"

"Yup."

"But that's a lot—a lot of money." My vocabulary had been reduced to a three-year-old's level from the sudden shock of the situation.

"I'm aware." Justin's expression remained unfazed.

"But you earned that money. I wasn't proactive enough with scholarships and financial aid."

"You're probably much more proactive than you give yourself credit for. I wouldn't have a better use of the funds, anyway. They'd probably go towards another car."

Try two. Med school debt is insane!

"Yes. And we both know you're done collecting cars for the foreseeable future." I raised an eyebrow at him.

"Am I, though?" Justin joked.

I playfully messed up his hair.

"Hey!" he exclaimed lightheartedly.

"Well, thank you! I do appreciate your offer! But I don't know if I'm willing to start a brand-new career like that. It's a bit rash, don't you think? My residency begins in less than a week."

"Why don't you give it some thought over the next day or so? You could make your final decision then."

"Possibly. It's just so soon, you know?"

"Tell you what." Justin picked up his hat, spinning it around his index finger. "Regardless of your decision, I'll take care of the loans."

"Are you serious?"

"Dead serious. As of tonight, you'll be debt-free. Well, as long as you have your login info."

"Yes, I do. But, wow! How can I ever thank you enough for that?"

Justin pulled his baseball cap onto his head. "Nah, don't worry about it. Just promise me one thing, ok?"

"Yeah. What is it?"

"Take some time to think it over—your career path."

I nodded. "I can do that."

He sighed deeply. "Thank you."

"But what's in it for you?" I glanced over at him, intrigued. "Why are you so relieved? You're not the one having a quarter-life crisis here."

Justin smiled slyly at me. "No. But I'm crazy about the one who is."

Entirely enamored, I moved in closer to him. I took off his hat, freely tossing it to the side. In return, he cupped my face with his hands. I caressed the side of his face—his gorgeous face. I felt our lips meet, his upper lip brushing against mine as he slowly pressed the rest of his mouth onto mine. I put my hands through his hair and drew him close, inhaling his sweet, alluring scent.

Looks like his craziness was contagious.

Chapter Sixteen

"I need to get myself a porch swing!" Olivia decided, sitting next to me. She pushed her feet off the ground; giving momentum to Justin's swing.

"Imagine: a porch swing by the sea, waves crashing along the shore, a light ocean breeze, sun glistening on the water—as you kick up your feet, sipping a piña colada." She closed her eyes, visualizing the scene. "Ah, that'd be the life!"

I inhaled deeply, taking in the fresh pine aroma and the morning coolness. The air was crisp as the sunlight was still in its early stages—lightly illuminating the sky but not abrasively warm.

"I like the terrain here better," I said. "Plants actually grow here, for one. There are evergreen forests, winding rivers, and scenic mountaintops. Plus, it's nice having a break from the high-rise buildings and strip malls."

"But you don't have the beach," Olivia pointed out, extending her legs as we continued to swing.

"There are beaches here—lake beaches."

Olivia brought a hand to her chin in thought. "Hmm ... that's true."

"They're a lot less crowded than the beaches at home. Yeah, I'm gonna miss it here."

I then remembered the choice I was facing—the choice involving my future. Today was the day we'd originally planned to leave Ville du Lac—before I'd fallen for Justin and subsequently rethought all my life's aspirations.

"Is everything ok?" Olivia asked.

I nodded. "I'm considering changing my career path."

"Really? To what?"

I skidded the swing to a stop. "To my own business."

"You mean the coffee shop?"

"Yeah."

Olivia looked at me with widened eyes. "Wow!"

"I'm being too hasty, aren't I?"

"No, sounds awesome! I just never thought you were serious."

I sighed. "Neither did I, to be honest. I'm still not sure if it's the right thing to do."

Olivia turned around to face me. "Girl, whenever you're faced with a decision, don't think of it in terms of 'shoulds' and 'should nots.' It all comes down to want. Do you want to do something? If so, go for it! Otherwise, don't do that thing. It's that simple!"

"I wish! I just don't wanna be wasting my life, you know. Turning down my degree is not something to take lightly."

"Well, I think you're finally living your life! First Justin, now your own coffee shop. You're on a roll!"

A grin swept across her face. "Speaking of Justin, how have we not talked about this already? I'm dying here! Oh my God, you two are an item now!"

Olivia nudged me with a hand. "Tell me everything! How did it all happen? Did you tell him at sunset, like we planned?"

"Not quite. We both sort of mutually expressed interest later that night. Well, technically, it was me first, but Justin immediately followed. Apparently, he's had feelings for me all along, when I was still living in Idaho. And I was his first kiss, too."

As I thought about our night on the back patio, a warming numbness suddenly spread across my body. It was hard to believe Justin and I were now in a relationship—I was still getting used to the concept of a friendship with him, a celebrity. Of course, I had no objections to the progression of our relationship. None whatsoever. Our trip felt almost surreal but in the best possible way. I wished it wouldn't end!

"Aww, that's so sweet! He's such a softie. I love it!" Olivia folded her legs underneath her, sitting on top of them. "So, tell me—honestly. Does he kiss as well as he does in the movies?"

I felt my cheeks run hot as I hid my face from her. "Even better!"

She squealed in delight. "So excited for you! I can't believe it! My best friend is dating a movie star! Can it get any better than that?"

"If you could please keep this to yourself, I'd appreciate it. I don't want the paparazzi knocking on my door tomorrow."

Olivia nodded. "Oh, of course! Totally! No one will ever know."

"Know about what?" Justin wondered, walking up the porch steps, having just returned from his morning run. He was holding his water bottle in one hand and baseball cap in the other. Even with the extra perspiration and wind-blown hair, he looked mighty fine.

"Oh, nothing," Olivia replied casually.

Justin nodded as he began to drink intensely from his Yeti bottle.

"Looks like you've had quite the workout," I observed.

"Yeah. Had to take a slight detour." Justin grabbed the hand towel draped along the side, patting his face dry. "Took the route up the hill, away from the park. Didn't want to put myself in danger."

"Did you see a moose?" Olivia guessed.

"No, worse. Girls. Teenage girls."

Olivia and I giggled in unison. That could've been lethal.

"Well, I'm glad you're alive!" I joked. "I would've missed you. Though, at least I'd be off the hook for our stone-skipping rematch!"

"Hey! You're not getting off that easy!" Justin teased. "We had a tie, remember?"

I playfully rolled my eyes as I scooted closer to Olivia, making room for Justin on the swing. He set his towel on the porch steps and sat next to me.

"So, what have you ladies been up to?" Justin asked, resting his arm around my shoulders.

"Not much. Just relaxing," I replied. "A few deer passed through your yard earlier."

"Oh yeah?"

"They're gone now, but they were surprisingly close to us."

"Never underestimate the wildlife here."

"Or the fangirls, apparently!"

He laughed, shaking his head. "You have no idea! Consider yourself lucky."

"I'll keep that in mind."

"So, did you give more thought to your coffee shop idea?"

"I did."

Justin looked at me curiously. "And?"

I was now at the point of no return—where I couldn't put off my future any longer. It was time to decide once and for all.

I took a deep breath. "And I've decided to go through with it."

"Yes!" Olivia cheered. "It's about time you took your life back!"

"Yeah, but now, the question is, how does one start a new business?" I wondered. "I have virtually no business experience. I don't even know where to begin."

"Well, I happen to know someone who could help," Justin offered.

"Really?"

He traced his fingers along the armrest of the swing. "Yup. An old college friend who's launched a few startups since then."

"Wait. You went to college? But how?" Olivia questioned him. "How could you attend a lecture hall without being spotted?"

"I was already accepted into UCLA when 'Midnight Club' was released," Justin explained. "I attended as a commuter student for my first year when I was lesser known. I completed some classes online the second year, as we filmed the sequel."

"Wow, that's great! Did you end up graduating?" I asked him.

He shook his head. "No. My schedule got too busy. I was set to major in business economics but never took any of the Upper Divs. But my friend Blake is a pro at any business-related venture. You give him the details and financial parameters, and he'll give you the roadmap to a legit startup."

"Thanks! I could always use the help!"

"So, when do you plan to tell your family about your new coffee shop?" Olivia asked me.

A lump immediately formed in my throat. "As late as possible, especially my mom!"

"How come?"

"Well, she probably won't take the news well. I mean, she's the one who keeps emphasizing the prestige of a medical career—to an obsessive degree. She bought me a diploma frame before I stepped onto the graduation stage. So, the later she knows, the better."

The porch became silent as Olivia appeared to be deep in thought. She was conjuring up one of her so-called brilliant ideas again, I was almost sure of it.

"Olivia? What are you thinking?" I waved a hand in front of her, bracing myself for an outlandish response.

"Oh, nothing. Just that we should visit your mom and grandma this summer," Olivia replied nonchalantly, flipping her hair over her shoulder.

And the award for the Most Outlandish Response goes to ... Olivia McKenzie. "Oh, really? And why would we do that?" I half-laughed.

"Well, maybe your mom will be more receptive to the news in person instead of on the phone. Also, you're in Idaho, so Montana is pretty close, right?"

"If a four-hour drive through the backcountry is considered 'pretty close,' then yes."

"Great!" Olivia looked over at Justin. "And you—what about your family? Your mom and brother, maybe you could invite them to stay with us here, in Ville du Lac."

Justin shook his head. "Not a simple request."

"Olivia, most people can't just pack up their suitcases and travel halfway across the country on such short notice," I pointed out to her.

"Still no harm in asking! Maybe you could set them up with some round-trip, first-class flights," Olivia suggested. "I'd travel anywhere just to fly first class!"

"Yeah, sure," Justin responded dubiously.

I then realized a vital question was left unanswered. "Speaking of traveling, where would I even establish this new business?"

"How about in Ville du Lac?" he offered.

"Here? Why here?"

"I can list several reasons: more affordable, lower taxes, a growing population—more demand for your business—your familiarity with the city's culture and layout." Justin counted off with his fingers.

I took a moment to ponder his points. "Well, if I did decide to move out here, I'd need to drive back to San Diego, say goodbye to my aunt and uncle, and pack up all my belongings. The latter is not an easy feat."

"Well, I could help you with that, filming doesn't begin until mid-August."

"Yeah, me too!" Olivia chimed in. "Together, the three of us could begin setting up your shop over the next month. Then, we drive back to California and move you out."

I laughed in disbelief. Olivia made the process sound so simple. Revamping my life was a bit more complicated than updating a patio or kitchen.

"Wait a minute. Aren't you supposed to resume work on Monday?" I questioned her. "I doubt your marketing firm would allow a month-long vacation."

"Sure, I can! You don't believe someone can travel halfway across the country on short notice? Well, then, watch me!"

Olivia unraveled her legs excitedly, springing up from her spot on the swing. She immediately stumbled onto the floor—her legs apparently still asleep from sitting on them. Unfazed, she climbed to a standing position, shaking her legs awake, as she proceeded into the house, closing the door behind her.

"Well, that's Olivia for you!" I laughed as I laid my head on Justin's shoulder—my favorite pillow.

"Yup," he said, leaning his head on mine. "You know, you can always stay here, at my house as you set up the new coffee shop."

I sighed. "No. I can't."

"Why not?"

"You've already paid off my loans. I can't burden you any more than I already have. I need to make my own way at some point."

"You're not a burden, Nat. You're my girlfriend." Justin paused to process his prior statement. "Wow. Still not used to saying that."

He cleared his throat. "But, how about this: you could stay here until you've decided on your own place. But, seriously. Take as much time as you need."

As I glanced around the porch, observing my surroundings once more, I came to the conclusion: Ville du Lac had always been my home. I just hadn't realized it until that point—until after more than a decade of living elsewhere. It was time to return home.

"I can't believe I'm saying this, but that all sounds like a plan." I lifted my head, turning to face Justin in gratitude. "Thank you! For everything! I still can't believe it's been thirteen years! I've missed you."

Justin smiled at me. "Me too. Uh ... I mean, I've missed you too. Obviously, I don't miss me. That'd be lame, for sure."

He looked down, seemingly embarrassed.

I giggled. Justin could be such a dork sometimes. It made him seem all the more adorable. "No, you're all good!"

"You sure about that? Even with yesterday's dinner?"

I held back a chuckle. Justin cooking the meal entirely on his own was certainly an experience, to say the least. "Well, you've learned from it ... like how to drain the pasta before adding the sauce!"

"Hey! Never in the instructions did it say to drain the pasta beforehand," Justin defended himself.

"Yeah, because it's common sense!"

"Maybe to those who don't have someone else cooking for them."

He did have a point there.

"Well, then. Now's your chance to learn, Justin Daniel. By next month, you'll be cooking me a three-course meal."

He rubbed his stubbled chin pensively. "Will I? Is that a challenge?"

"Maybe." I gave him a smirk.

"Challenge accepted!"

"Well, it looks like we've both got some challenges ahead of us!"

Justin looked at me with fascination. "Hold on, are you trying to summarize our whole conversation?"

I shrugged. "Possibly. And what's wrong with that?"

"Nothing. It's just cute—how you neatly tie everything together. You should try stand-up comedy sometime!"

"Oh really? So that I can hear the lovely sound of crickets coming from the audience?"

"I'd laugh."

"Laugh at how no one else is laughing? Wow, thanks a lot!" I shoved him playfully.

"No. Laughing with you."

"Uh-huh. But I'm not laughing."

Justin began cracking up in response. Despite my greatest efforts, I eventually followed in line.

"See? Now you are!" He pointed at me as if to prove his point.

"That's not fair! You intentionally caused me to laugh!"

"Didn't specify who'd start laughing first."

"No. But I can decide who'll stop first."

I focused on the driveway beyond the porch, trying to keep a straight face. In the corner of my eye, I saw Justin getting up to grab his baseball cap. He then curled his wrist toward his body, preparing to throw the hat like a Frisbee—obviously trying to invoke a response from me.

"Guess who's moving to Ville du Lac, guys? Me! I did it! I quit my job!" Olivia exclaimed as the front door swung wide open.

Her face was met with the visor of Justin's hat. "Ow! What are you doing?" She giggled.

I lost it.

"Trying to make Natalie laugh, which I believe was a success!" Justin quipped.

"Well done!" Olivia returned his hat, high-fiving him. "Nice aim! Do you play?"

"With hats? No." He chuckled. "Disc golf, sometimes."

"What are you doing?" I asked Olivia. "Quitting your job out of the blue like that?"

"Supporting your new business." Olivia placed a hand on her hip confidently. "Say hello to your newest marketing manager!"

Chapter Seventeen

I t turned out I was wrong—wrong in that a family visit was not an outlandish idea.

I called my mom the next morning to ask about a possible visit in the coming weeks. As expected, she and my grandma were thrilled to open their home to the three of us. After some prompting on my part, I was able to convince Justin to reach out to his mom. Despite my prodding, he didn't provide me with much of an explanation after his call—other than his family was doing well and would like to visit us.

At the end of it all, I'd compiled the following facts regarding our families' visitation plans:

For me:

Justin, Olivia, and I would be visiting my mom and grandma.

We'd be driving through the rugged terrain of Montana for about four hours one way.

Our trip would last about five days. I told my mom I had some time off work (not a lie, as I'm self-employed, after all).

We'd leave for Montana in a little over two weeks, in mid-July.

My mom and grandma knew I had a boyfriend, but no further details other than that.

Neither of them knew I'd quit my residency program so that I could start my own coffee shop business in Ville du Lac.

For Justin:

Justin's family would like to visit us sometime in the foreseeable future.

***

So, you can see my astonishment when I heard a knock on the front door—one week later.

I opened the door to find three people on the other side: a petite middle-aged woman with wavy blond hair, a tall, middle-aged man with gray-brown hair, and a slender young man with light-brown hair and square-rimmed glasses. The trio had their suitcases in tow, wearing an assortment of North Face apparel. They looked like they were ready for a hike.

"Natalie! It's been too long!" the woman exclaimed, throwing her arms around me for a hug. "You've grown beautifully! No wonder my son's so head-over-heels for you!"

That was when it clicked: Justin's family was visiting us today. Here. Now.

I smoothed my hair back with both hands, flustered. I was styling an oversized UCSD T-shirt, striped pajama bottoms, and half-brushed hair—not expecting any guests that morning.

Why the hell didn't Justin tell me they'd be visiting us today? The day before, his housekeeper had stopped by, but I'd figured that was because his house needed tidying. Not because we were about to host his family for the next week.

"Oh! Did Justin forget to tell you we were coming?" his mom wondered, noticing my confusion. "Doesn't surprise me."

Before I could answer, Justin walked up behind me, draping his arm over my shoulders. I observed he was clean-shaven—no light stubble like usual—and was wearing one of his nicer polos and tailored jeans. It was evident he was expecting them.

"Sorry, Nat! Thought I mentioned it to you," he apologized.

Nope, not at all. "Oh, that's ok!" I said, trying to mitigate the already-awkward situation. "It's great to see you all! How was the trip up here?"

"Good. Mostly," Justin's mom replied. "Except for the drive from the airport."

"Traffic?" I wondered.

"No. Kyle here decided to give us a sample of his current playlist. What on God's earth do you even call that type of music?"

"Progressive technical death metal," Kyle, the young man, informed them proudly.

Justin laughed at his brother's statement.

"Right. I'll just call it 'death' for short!" their mom quipped.

Kyle shook his head, amused. "Philistines. The flight was awesome, by the way! Justin set us up with some sweet first-class tickets. Thanks again!"

"No problem," Justin said with a nod.

"Glad I suggested it!" Olivia squeezed into the doorway next to me. Hand on her hip, she was fresh from her yoga mat—dressed in leopard-print yoga pants and a sports bra. Suddenly, I didn't feel so underdressed anymore.

"Ah! You must be Justin's family!" Olivia exclaimed.

Enthusiastically, she hugged his mom. "Oh my God, you must be so proud! I mean, how many people can point to the big screen and proclaim, 'Yup, that's my son up there'!"

I rolled my eyes. I could feel Justin shifting uncomfortably behind me.

"And you are?" His mom gave Olivia a baffled look.

"Olivia! Olivia McKenzie. Best friend and former college roommate of Natalie's," she replied, extending her hand to Kyle.

"Hmm. Justin didn't mention you at all, but it's great to meet you, regardless!" his mom said. "By the way, this is my husband, Dale. You haven't met Natalie yet."

"Nice to meet you!" Dale said as we shook hands. His grasp was firm, as would be expected for someone with his muscular build.

"And, of course, you remember Kyle, but it's been a while."

Kyle reached out to shake my hand. "Good to see you again!"

"You too!" I replied. "I believe the last time I saw you, you were a foot shorter, and your voice was an octave higher."

"Or two!" Justin added.

"Well, at least I've grown a foot since then! You're still waiting on your growth spurt," Kyle joked, focusing his gaze on his brother. "You're not even five-nine!"

"Yes, I am!" Justin lightheartedly shoved him with his free arm.

"Some things never change!" Their mom laughed. "Oh! You can call me Jen, by the way. No need for 'Mrs. Hillard' or any formalities like that. We're family here!"

Jen dropped her suitcase to her side and gestured over to Justin. "Speaking of family, a mother would like to hug her son."

Justin abruptly let go of my shoulders to initiate a hug with his mom. "Sorry about that."

"Now, I know you can't get enough of your lovely girlfriend, but there'll be plenty of time for that later!" Jen said with a chuckle. "How about a grand tour of the house, then? The outside is a sight to see, but surely, the inside is even more so! After all, we're not spending the night outside, are we?"

"Of course. Right this way," he said, opening the door widely as his family and Olivia shuffled inside. I moved out of the way to let them through.

Once they were out of earshot, I nudged Justin, still holding the door open. "Is your mom always this..." I whispered, not quite sure of the correct adjective in this context.

"Overbearing? Intrusive?" he quietly offered. "Yup. Pretty much."

Huh. I wasn't quite sure what he meant by that. Jen appeared to be a bit spunky but not forceful or outspoken. But, then again, I didn't converse too much with Justin's mom when I was younger—or his dad, for that matter.

Chapter Eighteen

"Pretty evergreens! We should absolutely hike this hill again before we leave," Jen said as the six of us continued our ascent.

Justin nodded. "This is one of our favorites." He sent a small smile in my direction.

"That's nice the trail's near your house," Dale commented. "Isn't there a river around here, too—where you can go fishing?"

My heart froze. I'd almost forgotten about the primary reason for our trip. "Um, yeah, the Atlas River. That's further into the backcountry but not too far of a drive from here," I told him, trying to keep my voice from wavering.

"Yeah, kind of reminds me of when we were kids," Kyle remembered. "Running off into the forests until dinnertime. Nowadays, I'm running through chaparral. Not as ideal."

"Oh! Do you like to run?" Olivia asked him.

He nodded. "Sometimes, I'll run 5Ks, but I'm normally not involved in races as much. More of a hobby than anything."

"He was on varsity cross-country and track for all of high school," Justin explained, adjusting his baseball cap.

"Really? I was on the track team, too!" Olivia enthused.

"Cool! Which events?" Kyle wondered.

"I ran the sprints: 100 and 200-meter. I usually faked an injury to get out of the 400-meter—I hated that race with a vengeance! What about you?"

"Long-distance. Primarily 1600 meters, but sometimes the 800 or 3200."

"He set some Top 10 records in high school," Justin added.

"Seriously?! That's awesome!" Olivia remarked, turning to Jen. "Damn, you must have some super genes in your family!"

"I still haven't figured that one out!" Jen laughed. "Yep, Kyle even missed his senior prom to compete in the track state finals."

"But he was invited as a junior, so he went anyway," Justin said.

"Yeah, but she only asked me out so she could meet you," Kyle pointed out. The last 'Midnight Club' was just released in theaters, so all the girls in school were talking about it."

"Did you meet his prom date?" I asked Justin, curious.

"Yep, after the dance," he replied.

Obviously. I couldn't imagine the chaos that would've ensued if he, Justin Anderson, happened to show up at the dance, all dressed up in a tux and bow tie—like in the prom scene from the third 'Midnight Club' flick.

"That was very nice of you!" I told him. "So, Kyle. Are you still taking college classes? Justin tells me you're studying computer science at Cal State Fullerton."

"Just graduated last month," Kyle said, straightening his glasses. "I'm beginning a new job at Sony PlayStation next month, in San Diego."

"PlayStation?! Wow!" Olivia exclaimed. "I've lived in San Diego my whole life. Natalie and I went to UCSD together."

"Really? That's cool," he said. "What did you both study there?"

"Communications," Olivia responded.

Kyle, Jen, and Dale looked at me, awaiting my answer. I knew this topic would be brought up eventually.

I sighed, bracing myself for the awkward conversation about to take place. "Biology."

"Did you go to grad school afterward?" Kyle asked me.

"Yes, I went to medical school there as well."

"Awesome! So you're a doctor."

I shook my head. "Not quite."

"Oh, yeah. You still need to complete your residency first, right?"

I moved over to the side of the trail. Everyone else followed in line. "Yes, but I've decided not to go down that path. Actually, I..."

I trailed off for a moment, taking a deep breath. "...I've left the medical industry entirely. I'm starting a new business. Here, in Ville du Lac."

I turned my gaze to the ground, avoiding eye contact. Justin slipped his hand into mine.

"Wow..." Jen began.

I squeezed his hand, still looking down, praying the conversation would end already.

"...I've underestimated you! You're phenomenal, you know that? That you can put your mind to something and not let the power of the paycheck stop you." She swiped a loose bang to the side of her forehead. "I knew my son had a good taste in women!"

I exhaled in relief. I didn't see that coming.

"What's your new business gonna be?" Kyle asked me.

"A coffee shop with a shared workspace," I answered him.

I proceeded to elaborate further on the establishment of my new coffee shop.

"Very cool!" Dale said. "So, do you have a site in mind—where the shop would be?"

"Yeah. We've checked out a few properties in the area. There's one in particular we're thinking about, not too far from downtown," I said. "It's an older brick building that used to be the Ville du Lac bank in the '20s. It's seen better days, but if we decide to purchase it, we'd hire a contractor to help with the renovation process—especially the roof. We'd also need a landscaper, as a few trees out in front need to be removed in case of a bad storm. The shop should hopefully be ready by early next year."

"Amazing! I like to hear that!" Jen said, turning her attention to Justin. "So, is that what's been keeping you busy since our last call? You'd think your cell service was down for that entire week."

Justin sighed, seemingly bothered by his mother's interrogation. "Yes. That and enjoying the sights of Ville du Lac."

And enjoying each other's company. I smiled to myself.

"Well, an occasional response to a text message wouldn't hurt, would it?" Jen pressed further.

Justin glanced down at his Adidas sneakers, furrowing his brows.

"Why don't we continue with our hike? If everyone's all ready to go, that is," I offered, changing the subject.

"Good idea," Justin said quickly.

"I'm ready," Kyle said.

The rest of them nodded in agreement as we resumed our ascent. Not too long into our hike, Justin's cell phone rang.

"Well, it looks like you do get cell coverage, after all!" Kyle joked.

Justin gave his brother an annoyed look as if to say, "Zip it!" He then took out his phone, putting it up to his ear.

"Yes?" he answered in a serious tone. "Oh, yes. Yep, I've got a couple minutes. Gimme just a sec."

Justin motioned to us with his index finger, as he moved further up the trail, phone still on his ear. He obviously wanted some privacy for his call, which was probably work-related.

"Hah! I've seen that look before," Kyle remarked.

"When was that?" Olivia wondered.

"When we were younger—when Justin would be on the phone with Natalie."

Suddenly, I was immensely curious. "What do you mean?"

"Well, Kyle here wasn't very respectful of his brother's privacy," Jen smirked. "He'd tease him and call you his girlfriend. Eventually, Justin would take the phone to his room and lock the door behind him."

My heart skipped a beat. "Really? Why'd you say that?"

"Because it was funny, at the time," Kyle said, "when he'd blush whenever you were on the other line."

I felt myself glowing at the thought. Looking back, I'd always considered myself the only hopelessly hormonal teenager in our friendship. It turned out I was mistaken. Before he knew it, Justin was already a skilled actor—before he'd even stepped foot into an audition room.

"Everything ok?" I asked Justin as he rejoined us, slipping his phone into his backpack.

He nodded. "Yep, just my agent."

"Oh! Any new gigs?" Kyle wondered.

"No. He's just giving me an update on the film production schedule," Justin explained. "It sounds like the New Zealand shooting's gonna take another one to two weeks. Just some minor delays. Pretty standard in the business."

"One to two weeks?!" Jen remarked. "Which one is it, one or two? They can't even give you that?"

He shrugged.

"Well, that's not a minor delay," Jen continued. "You might as well spend the rest of the year in a foreign country!"

"It's not up to me," Justin stated bluntly.

"Well, the allotted timeframe should be clearly outlined in your contract. Otherwise, the powers-that-be could keep tacking on delays. You've gotta pay attention to the fine print."

He clenched his jaw. "Yes, I know. Again, not my choice."

"But you can choose which projects you sign onto—those that won't keep you from your loved ones too long. Or something local, in LA. It'd be nice to celebrate Christmas with you, for once. Your grandparents would love to see you, too. They're getting up there, you know!"

Justin forcefully pulled off his hat. "You know what? I'm done with this shit! I'll meet you at the bottom."

He abruptly stormed off in a huff. Dumbfounded, the rest of us watched him in silence.

Finally, Jen moved forward—as if she were about to follow Justin in his descent. In response, I held my hand out in front of her.

"Maybe we should finish our hike and join him after we're done? Give him some time to cool off?" I suggested. "We're almost at the top, anyway."

"That works!" Dale agreed.

As we continued hiking, the mood lightened again as we dove into further detail about our vocations. Despite the current conversation, my focus was elsewhere.

Why was Justin so aggravated by his mom? I realized Jen was a handful, for sure. But it seemed Justin had very little interest in reconnecting with her. Something was bothering him—a roadblock between him and his mother.

However, I was even more troubled by the extension of Justin's film shooting. A long-distance relationship was already an unnerving concept for me. Now, I have to endure an additional one to two weeks of physical separation. If the New Zealand shooting were a one-time deal, that'd be one thing, I acknowledged. But a lifestyle of physical separation—a lifestyle of film projects, premieres, and press tours—was entirely different. A lifestyle, if I were being honest with myself, I was unsure about in the long run.

***

"Why does it bother you so much?" I asked Justin. "Watching yourself in one of your previous roles."

That same evening, he and I were able to catch a free moment for a walk. His family was watching TV in the living room—while unintentionally stumbling upon a scene from 'Flame in the Sky', starring, you guessed it.

"That's a loaded question." Justin breathed in deeply as we continued on the forested path toward the lakeshore, hand-in-hand. "Pretty much, it comes down to me being my own worst critic. I'm never convinced I've succeeded in my work. I can always find something wrong with my performance—a forced facial expression, flat dialogue, unnatural blocking. It's honestly painful to watch myself through a microscopic lens. That's why it's much easier to put my past projects on a shelf and move on. Out-of-sight, out-of-mind."

I nodded. "That sounds exhausting—always finding fault with yourself. You can give yourself some slack, you know. No one's perfect, and that's ok. And, for the record, you're a far better actor than you give yourself credit for. I think you're amazing!"

He smiled at me. "Thanks, Nat."

"I'm gonna miss you, by the way—when you begin filming in New Zealand," I said as we reached the sandy shoreline.

"I'll miss you too. I doubt I would've agreed to it if I'd known you'd reenter my life. It's a pretty hefty project—rebooting a beloved franchise is not a small undertaking. I knew that when I first signed onto the project. As pre-production is wrapping up, I have no choice but to move forward with it. I'm told the budget is one of the highest in the business."

I let out a nervous laugh. "Wow! No pressure, right?"

"But I don't wanna talk about work. I wanna spend time with you."

Justin let go of my hand, finding himself a spot along the shore to sit. He patted the space next to him. I sat down, unbuckling my sandals and extending my legs in front of me. I felt the cool sand massage the spaces between my toes. He wrapped his arm around me as I scooted closer to him.

"I'm sorry for snapping earlier on the hike," Justin apologized. "You did nothing wrong, and I hate that I put you in that uncomfortable position. My mom can really test my patience sometimes."

"It's ok. I know you're trying to figure out your relationship with your family," I said.

"What relationship? I don't even know my family—not even when I lived with them. My mom keeps on trying to pretend the past is behind us. She tries to force herself into my life, even when it's unwelcome. She's probably trying to combat her guilt for not being there when I was younger. But I wish she'd stop with this bullshit facade of us being a close-knit family that spends holidays together and makes impromptu phone calls for no fucking reason."

Justin took a moment to catch his breath. "Sorry, that was too much. Didn't mean to vent."

Sympathetically, I placed a hand on the top of his leg. "No, you're ok. I understand there's a lot of hurt there. It seems your mom wants to connect with you on a deeper level but doesn't know how. Suppose you spoke with her about your upbringing and resolved any hard feelings. Would you reconsider her invitation into your life then?"

"Why now? Why not five, ten, or even twenty years ago? How would investing time now make any bit of a difference? The past twenty-seven years showed a completely different story: where a boy longed for connection while his parents were God knows where. And, of course, the only thing worse than their physical distance was first-hand witnessing their argument matches—as if they didn't even give a shit that Kyle and I were present for it all. I know my mom wishes things were different, but she needs to wake up and realize that we can never be as close as she'd like us to be. No amount of reconciliation can ever make up for lost time."

I sighed, realizing that Justin establishing any connection with his mother was easier said than done. "I believe there's hope for you still, even if you don't. For tomorrow, why don't you and the guys do something together? Olivia and I could take your mom downtown to shop or something like that."

"If she'll allow it. She's made it abundantly clear that she needs more time with me."

"I can ask her. That way, it's coming from me."

Justin brought a finger to his chin as he pondered. "Hmm. Well, I've wanted to take them disc golfing. SoCal has fewer options."

"That sounds great! I bet they'd like that."

He nodded, gazing up at the evening sky. The stars were beginning to make their grand appearance, stretching their way across the ends of my field of vision.

"Impressive, huh?" Justin remarked as he reclined onto his back, resting his head on his bent arms. "Never realized what I was missing back in LA. The smog and lights blocked any real chance of seeing the stars. It's like they didn't exist over there."

I followed his posture, lying on my back next to him, arms cradling my head. "It's pretty astounding when you think about it—the universe, that is. Even tonight, we're only viewing a tiny smidge of it. There are countless stars we'll never get a chance to see—those that are billions of light-years away, or more."

"I have a difficult time wrapping my mind around that. It's almost scary sometimes—how we can't measure the massiveness of the universe."

"But we're not expected to. I guess that's the beauty of it, right? Accepting our limitations as humans and trusting in a greater power—the one who set it all into motion. At least, that's what helps me when I become overwhelmed by concepts far beyond my comprehension."

"Yeah, that makes sense."

We continued to relax along the shoreline, admiring the darkening sky together. Even though Justin's upcoming departure saddened me, I wanted to savor the time we could spend together fully. As time was our only nonrenewable resource, I wanted it to matter, to last—as much as it could in a 24-hour format.

Chapter Nineteen

"Ooh, a salad bar! Sounds scrumptious!" Jen said, studying the restaurant menu.

"It is! I've tried it," Olivia affirmed, glancing out the adjacent window overlooking the lake. "After all that shopping, we've worked ourselves an appetite! Except for Natalie here, who already ate."

Jen closed her menu. "Well, that bakery sure had some delicious cookies. I'm surprised you were able to eat the whole thing. You're so small!"

"Me too!" I closed my menu as well, reaching for my glass of water. I was already starting to regret my previous decision.

"I'm not! You're always baking something, it seems. But it's not like I've tried much of it—you and Justin keep eating it all!" Olivia laughed. "Then again, Baker is your last name!"

A young man who couldn't have been much older than twenty approached our table. Our waiter. "Are you ladies ready to order?"

"Yes, I'd like the clam chowder," Jen said.

"I'll do the salad bar – again!" Olivia replied.

"Good choice. They've just restocked the salad bar," the waiter said as he jotted down our orders.

"And for you?" He gestured over to me.

"I'll have the pork tacos," I said.

"I never would've guessed!" Olivia smirked at me.

I handed our menus to the waiter. "Could we also order the mac and cheese to-go, please?"

"Absolutely!" he replied, grabbing our menus. "We'll get those orders prepared right away for you."

"Thank you!"

"Who's the mac and cheese for?" Jen wondered after the waiter left our table.

"Justin. Anytime he tries a new restaurant, he likes to order the mac and cheese. He compares them with all the varieties he's eaten so far and rates them on a scale of one to ten," I explained.

She shook her head in disbelief. "He's still doing that? I swear, that boy's culinary tastes haven't changed since he was eight!"

"Yeah. Ironically, his favorite is from a local gastropub, not a Michelin-star restaurant."

"Too funny!" Jen took a sip of water. "You two are adorable together, I must say. Aww, it makes my heart melt!"

"I know! I'm obsessed!" Olivia giggled.

I draped my cloth napkin over my lap, directing my attention to Jen. "We really appreciate you coming up to visit us! I'm sorry Justin hasn't been in the best mood lately."

"I understand," Jen said with a nod. "That boy can be a mystery sometimes. I wish I could see him more. It's been nearly impossible to plan anything with his busy schedule. As I've mentioned, he's also not the best at responding. Maybe I've gone a bit too overboard with that!"

She chuckled.

"So, you told me you quit the real estate business after all that office drama," I said, changing the subject. "What's your new line of work like? In finance, right?"

"Accounting," she corrected me. "I do bank reconciliations, expense variance analysis, and commission accruals. But I'll spare you the details."

"And I'll also spare you mine from my OB clinical rotations."

"Yeah, no one wants to hear about that!" Olivia remarked.

Jen laughed loudly. Now, I saw where Justin had inherited his iconic laugh.

"I had a few days off for the 4th of July weekend, so I figured that'd be a better time than any for a visit," Jen said. "Month-end close can pose a challenge to work around. But this position certainly has its perks. I love having the weekends to myself, for once. I can finally set aside some time for writing my book."

"A book? That's so cool! I'm personally a fan of anything romance." Olivia grinned at me. "Natalie is, too! Aren't you?"

I shook my head. "No, I'm not!"

"But you do have a penchant for friends-to-lovers and celebrity-commoner tropes, am I right?"

I redirected my attention to Jen, trying to hide my blush. "What's your book about?"

"It's sort of a self-help book for those who'd like to heal from previous trauma," she replied. "It'll be a collection of stories from individuals who've experienced personal growth and healing. I've reached out to several experts and practitioners on this subject matter, and I've had some pretty insightful conversations already. Like how our mental, spiritual, and emotional health can all majorly impact our lives—whether we're aware of it or not. I still have a ways to go. I still need to compile and edit more stories before considering publishing options. But the process has been inspiring—eye-opening, for sure!"

"That's awesome!" Olivia said, pushing her chair away from the table. "If you guys don't mind, I'm gonna make my way to the salad bar—while all the fixings are still there."

I nodded. "Yeah, go for it."

Olivia sauntered over to the other side of the restaurant.

"I'll definitely read your book once it's published!" I told Jen, taking a sip of water.

"Thank you! I've wanted to do something useful for humanity," Jen said. "I don't want anyone to carry shame like I did for all those years, even after my trauma was over."

Her statement piqued my curiosity. "If you don't mind me asking, what kind of trauma did you go through?"

Jen sighed, tucking a blond curl behind her ear. "Domestic abuse. My marriage to Rob was not an easy one. We both had our fair share of personal baggage, true. But as time went on, it was obvious that only one of us was willing to grow. There's only so much you can do when blame and denial are at the forefront of your marriage."

"I'm so sorry you had to go through that. Does Justin or Kyle know? About the abuse?"

Jen shook her head. "No. I never wanted it to taint their relationship with their father. I thought maybe after our divorce, Rob would want to keep in touch with his sons. But that turned out to be wishful thinking on my part. Maybe now, if my sons asked about us, I'd tell them."

She took a deep breath and a sip from her water glass. "Yeah, I wish things could've been different when the boys were younger. I was distant during those years—trying to keep my head above water. When you're experiencing trauma, it's hard to think about anything else. Nowadays,

I wish there was a way to bridge that gap—connect with my sons more, especially Justin. In all honesty, it broke my heart when he announced he was checking himself into rehab. The fact that I learned this from a tabloid, not from my son, was a giant stab in the heart. I wish I could've helped him, you know? Walked alongside him and caught him when he fell—like I did all those years ago when he took his first steps. I seemed to have forgotten how to be a mother."

Jen lowered her gaze, resting her head on her hand, elbow propped on the table.

I nodded in understanding. "You haven't forgotten. You deeply care about your sons and want what's best for them—isn't that what being a mother is all about? And I believe Justin desires that deep connection as much as you do but doesn't realize it yet. He's so accustomed to keeping people at arm's length. I'm amazed I'm even in the picture—him allowing me into his private life like that."

"Well, I'm not surprised. You're a remarkable young woman with a tremendous heart! We need more people like you! I know my son is blessed to have you back in his life. Besides me, of course, you were always his biggest fan—way before any fangirls or fan sites were concerned. A true fan."

Speechless, I sipped some water from my glass, trying to hold back the lone tear nestled in the corner of my eye. I'd underestimated the impact of her kind words on me. Platonically, genuine praise was not something I'd received very often.

"So excited! I'm famished!" Olivia exclaimed, returning to our table with a full plate of food.

I pushed back the tear to its proper place, in the crevice behind my eye—where I stored all my almost tears. I'd conditioned those muscles quite well over the years.

As the three of us continued with our lunch, I couldn't shake the prior conversation with Jen from my mind—namely, her abuse.

Throughout my childhood, I'd never perceived Justin's dad, Rob, as the kind of person who'd do such a thing. He said very little and always seemed to be working—whether on-site with customers or on one of his home improvement projects. Soft-spoken and handy never implied abusive to me.

However, during my time with Justin's family, I'd seen something else I hadn't expected: a deep, unresolved tension boiling underneath the Sanders family structure. I was now left with the following question: should I tell Justin about the abuse? Even though I felt the overwhelming urge to bring such an injustice to light, I also knew it wasn't mine to tell. I wasn't a Sanders. I was a Baker—a family with its own set of problems and losses. I was better off keeping my focus on those for the time being.

Chapter Twenty

Before I knew it, we were bidding farewell to Justin's family—their suitcases packed tightly into the trunk of their rental car, GPS set for the airport, en route back to California. As I watched them drive out of sight, I sighed a breath of relief. Their visit turned out to be an overall positive experience, especially after my lunch with Jen—time apart seemed to alleviate the tension between Justin and his mom. By the end of it, however, I was emotionally exhausted—very much looking forward to some R&R.

***

Unfortunately, for me, my social hiatus was short-lived. Less than a week later, Olivia, Justin, and I packed our suitcases this time, driving to Montana. After a few hours on the road—watching the continuous slideshow of open blue skies and mountainous terrain through the passenger-side window—the landscape shifted to suburbia. We'd arrived at Fair Brooks. Eventually, I began to recognize the outline of a country-style cottage nestled behind some trees and shrubs of varying sizes.

My mom's house. Well, my grandma's house, to be fair. She bought the home a few years after my grandpa had passed from his stroke. She wanted to plant a garden by which she could remember him. Consequently, her home became commonly called the garden-with-the-cottage instead of the cottage-with-the-garden.

It was an older, single-story home; cozy and tranquil would be the most appropriate words to describe it. A simple white picket fence wrapped around the premises—a cobblestone pathway leading to the front door, framed by two vintage-style windows. Next to the pathway was an extensive garden of fragrant flora—lilacs, honeysuckle and lavender.

It'd been more than four years since my last visit. Too long, I'd realized, as we pulled into the driveway—also made of cobblestone. I glanced at the car dashboard—3:43 pm—a bit under four hours of driving. I wasn't surprised that our actual ETA was less than my original estimate. After all, Justin had offered to drive the entire way. That man could drive! He should've been cast in the 'Fast & Furious' films. They wouldn't even need to hire a stunt double, that way.

"Natalie! You're finally here! Welcome!" my grandma exclaimed, meeting me on the other side of her rosebed, with open arms.

Behind her marbled cat-eye glasses, her hazel eyes lit up with excitement, as I leaned into her arms for a hug. Her salt-and-pepper hair was fastened into a soft bun. I noticed a smidge of a green stain at the bottom seam of her pants. She'd presumably been gardening before our arrival.

"Good to see you, Grandma!" I said, grabbing my backpack from the passenger seat. "Thank you for having us!"

Justin climbed out of the driver's side, stretching his arms.

"And who might this young fellow be?" Grandma wondered.

"This is Justin, my boyfriend," I introduced him.

"Pleasure to meet you!" Justin said, extending his hand.

True to her nature, Grandma disregarded his offered handshake and wrapped her arms around him for a hug. Over her shoulder, Justin gave me a look of surprise and amusement. At least he wasn't scared off by my grandmother's audaciousness. For an older lady shy of eighty, she sure didn't act like it!

"Any friend of Natalie's is a friend of mine!" Grandma stated, with a smile, releasing him with a firm, friendly pat on the back.

"Oomph!" Justin sounded.

"Good to know! I, too, am a friend of Natalie's," Olivia commented as she climbed out of the backseat.

"Wonderful! You must be Olivia," Grandma said.

"That I am!" Olivia confirmed, the two hugging tightly as if they were long-time friends. Both Olivia and my grandmother had that kind of effect on people.

"Where's Mom?" I asked Grandma.

"She's inside, probably 'improving' the dinner I started preparing for us," she replied. "She's always updating my recipes whenever I turn my head away. Never seem perfect enough for her."

I sighed deeply. "Yep. That's Mom, all right."

Grandma gestured over to the flowerbeds. "So, I'd love to show you around the garden, but I see you've got some luggage to drop off. Why don't we take an inside tour first and say hello to your mother, while we're at it?"

"Sure!"

"Sounds good!" Justin agreed.

Grandma opened the door for us—Justin holding it open as we stepped inside.

"I like him already!" Grandma whispered to me.

Once inside, the first thing I noticed was the assortment of family photos lining the walls. I recognized most of them—my cousins and me swimming at the lake, my mom with her brother and sister playing in their backyard as kids, and my grandma and grandpa on their anniversary trip to the Swiss Alps.

As my grandma continued her tour of the house, I was struck by one photo in particular—in the living room, hanging over the piano, next to a wooden cross.

It was a framed photo of my dad and me when I was little. We were at the beach, on a trip to San Diego to visit my aunt and uncle. He was holding my hand, our feet planted in the sand, as we faced the foaming waves of the Pacific. He wore jeans and a T-shirt, and I was dressed in overalls. I couldn't remember the details of that specific day, as I was only around two or three years old. But I could remember the sensation of holding my father's hand—the warmth and security I felt while standing beside him. Even as tiny as I was, I felt safe by his side—by his presence.

My throat tightened as a single teardrop trickled down my cheek. I quickly brushed away the tear, before anyone could notice.

We ended our tour at the French Farmhouse style kitchen.

"Ah, here's my daughter! Cooking away, as usual!" Grandma said, motioning over to my mom, who was turned away from us, peeling some potatoes at the sink.

"Now, if you'll excuse me, I need to finish putting some sheets on the beds. Now, what kind of host would I be without making the beds?" She sighed, heading into the other room.

"Hi, Honey!" Mom greeted me as she placed the potatoes onto the cutting board. "Was the drive ok?"

"Yeah, pretty uneventful," I replied.

"Good, good!"

"Awesome seeing you again, Donna!" Olivia said as she walked toward the bathroom.

I took a deep breath, attempting to release my newfound nerves. "Mom, you remember Justin—from across the street, in Ville du Lac."

Mom turned around to face us. Her light-brown hair was styled away from her face, held in place by a considerate amount of hairspray. She was wearing a kitchen apron over her tunic top and jeans. As she took a closer look at Justin, her facial expression turned serious, her blue-green eyes narrowing.

"Yes, I remember," she said in a slightly flat tone. "You're an actor now, right?"

"Yep, but only in front of the cameras. I don't bring my work home with me," Justin said with a half-smile, trying to lighten up the mood.

Mom nodded. "Hmm, sounds familiar ... Natalie, would you mind finishing these sweet potatoes? They'll need to be baked shortly if we want dinner on time. I need a moment to myself."

"Sure, of course!" I replied as Mom pulled off her apron, sharply walking out of the kitchen.

"Is she all right?" Justin asked me after we heard the door closing.

"Yeah. She's probably just frazzled about hosting guests. She'd get this way anytime our relatives would visit for the holidays. She just needs some time to relax."

And a good meal, I thought, as I made my way over to the sweet potatoes. That should do the trick.

***

"Wow! Childhood friends! How wonderful!" Grandma remarked. "And to think you've stayed friends for all these years. Truly amazing!"

The five of us were eating dinner together in the dining room. Grandma, like Olivia, was doing what she did best: socializing. As for Mom, not so much, barely saying more than a few words at a time.

"Well, we did lose contact with each other for quite a while," I pointed out, taking another bite of the cheese-and-bacon-stuffed sweet potato on my plate—a Baker family staple.

"Aww, that's too bad," Grandma said. "When did you reconnect?"

"Fairly recently. Just over a month ago," I replied, reaching for my water glass.

"But you wouldn't know it by watching the two of them. They're inseparable!" Olivia added as she stood up from her seat, carrying her empty glass into the kitchen.

Grandma's eyes shifted from Justin to me. "Ah, I see. Well, I'm glad you've finally found a man! So, Justin, what do you do for a living?"

In response to my grandmother's nonchalant demeanor, I began to cough, accidentally swallowing my water down the wrong pipe.

"You ok?" Mom asked me, concerned.

"Yep. Water down the wrong tube," I answered once I'd gotten my coughing under control.

Grandma redirected her focus back to Justin.

"Oh! Uh, I'm an actor," Justin responded, obviously not used to being asked this type of question.

"An actor? Really?" Grandma said. "So, do you perform in the local plays down in San Diego? I really enjoyed the Old Globe Theater during my time there. Donna, do you remember the play we saw? Was it 'Much Ado About Nothing'?"

"Yes," Mom confirmed.

"Uh, actually. I'm a film actor," Justin clarified.

"He's famous," Mom explained.

Grandma took a moment to process this new information. Her eyes suddenly widened in astonishment. "Natalie, you didn't tell me you were seeing a movie star. How phenomenal! I knew you could always dream big!"

I nodded, not quite sure how to respond.

"That reminds me of a joke! Can I tell it to you?" Grandma asked eagerly, sitting on the edge of her chair.

"Go ahead," Mom sighed, exchanging a look with me as if to say, "Let's get this over with."

"So. Arnold Schwarzenegger, Mel Gibson, and Sylvester Stallone are deciding on their Halloween costumes for the year. Mel suggests, 'We should be music composers!' Sylvester says, 'Good idea! I'll be Beethoven.' Mel says, 'I'll be Mozart.' Arnold says, 'I'll be Bach!'"

Mom rolled her eyes, returning her attention to the parmesan zucchini on her plate.

After a moment of silence, Justin began to laugh. "That's a good one!"

"Well, I'm glad someone likes my jokes!" Grandma said in a playful tone. "Did I ever tell you about the time I met Robert Wagner?"

"Who's that?" Olivia wondered, returning to the table.

"An old-time actor. And yes, you did," Mom answered. "At your high school, right?"

Grandma nodded. "Yup. Robert was up-and-coming at the time. He was making his rounds through some of the high schools throughout the country."

"I don't think I've heard about this before," I realized. "Did you talk to him?"

"No, I just watched him from afar."

"So you didn't meet him," Mom stated.

Grandma pointed toward her face. "I met him with my eyes."

Mom shook her head. "Doesn't count."

"Well, my friend did. Oh, boy, was she lucky! She got to kiss him!"

I raised an eyebrow in disbelief.

"Oh my God! Really?!" Olivia exclaimed.

"On the cheek, much later in life—not too long after his wife died. She drowned, I believe. Oh, what was her name again ... of course! Natalie Wood, like my granddaughter!"

Justin looked at me with intrigue.

Mom abruptly set down her knife with a loud clang. "I'm sorry, but I need to excuse myself."

She stood up suddenly, placing her napkin on the table.

"Are you feeling all right?" Grandma wondered.

"Bad headache. I should get some rest now. Hopefully, it'll resolve itself by morning." Mom rushed to her bedroom, closing the door behind her.

Very odd. My mother was on edge that evening. For a split second, I wondered if she'd figured out I'd quit my residency. But how would she know that? I hadn't told anyone about my decision other than Olivia and Justin.

Maybe my mom's headache was indeed that debilitating. Hopefully, she'll feel better after a night of rest.

Chapter Twenty-One

"Beautiful! Just the way I remember it," Grandma remarked.

The five of us were taking a stroll through Klamath Park. We passed underneath the marble archway leading to an extensive rose garden at the top of the hill. Even though it was a new day, my mom was still quiet. Oddly quiet.

"Yeah, I remember playing hide-and-seek among the peonies," I said.

Grandma nodded, smiling. "This park certainly takes the cake for the best hiding spots. Just ask the bunnies!"

Olivia turned to look over both shoulders, puzzled. "Bunnies? I don't see any bunnies."

"Exactly! They're masters of camouflage. You'd never know there's at least a dozen hopping around here at any given time. They usually come out around dawn or dusk. We've seen a couple during the day. In fact, whenever Natalie and I would visit this park, we'd take a count of how many bunnies we could find."

"When I was in high school," I explained. "Afterwards, we'd visit the local bakery and split a chocolate chip muffin."

"Don't forget the coffee!" Grandma added.

"Yes. You introduced me to a caramel macchiato one day, and I haven't looked back since!"

Justin nodded as if he were internally connecting the dots. "Oh, now I see where it all started! Your addiction to bean water."

"Bean water? Haven't heard that one before!" Grandma laughed.

"Yup. There's beans and they're boiled in water. Not much to it," he said.

"Brewed," I corrected him.

"Same difference! It's gross, and I'll stick with tea."

"You know, Justin Daniel. Tea is essentially 'leaf water!'" I giggled. "You steep tea leaves in hot water, and voilà: leaf water!"

Olivia began cracking up.

Grandma shook her head. "Neither of these descriptions sounds appetizing. How about we talk about a nice meal we've had lately? Any favorites?"

"Well, I've actually taught Justin a thing or two about cooking," I mentioned. "He's now able to whip up some meals of his own. Though, I wouldn't consider your mac-and-cheese concoction an actual 'meal.'"

"It tastes good, and it isn't out of a box. That's a legit meal, in my book!" Justin stated.

"Those bacon bits and breadcrumbs you sprinkle on top are the bomb!" Olivia affirmed.

"Sometimes, we could all use some good ol' comfort food from time to time," Grandma agreed. "So, what about you, Natalie? Has Justin taught you any new skills or tricks?"

"Yeah. He's taught me how to play guitar," I told her. "Or rather, helped me relearn it. I'd forgotten everything I learned from my college class."

"Not everything. You picked up 'Blackbird' pretty quickly," Justin said. "You didn't even need the sheet music. I'd say you're getting pretty good at the guitar—almost ready to join my band."

"For real? You have a band?" Olivia asked him. "Can I join, too? I could do backup vocals. I've had plenty of practice singing along to 'Shake It Off'!"

"There's no band, Olivia. It's an inside joke," I explained to her.

She chuckled. "You and your inside jokes. You two could publish a book of them all!"

"Aww, how sweet!" Grandma commented, reaching over to side-hug me. "The two of you make me so happy! Donna, I'm surprised you've never mentioned anything about Justin or his family before."

Mom nodded as she directed her gaze toward the pathway. She was obviously not thrilled to be there. There was something wrong.

"Uh, Mom. Would you mind coming back to the car with me?" I asked her, hoping she'd take the bait. "I'd like to grab my jacket, in case we stop by the bakery for some coffee and muffins—if you're all ok with that, of course!"

"Totally! You had me at muffins." Olivia licked her lips in anticipation.

"Sure, Honey," Mom replied. "We'll be right back. Feel free to meander around the park in the meantime."

As my mom and I headed in the other direction, I sighed with relief. Finally, I can get some answers. "Are you doing ok? You've been very quiet."

"Yep. Just a lot on my mind," Mom quickly responded.

"Is something bothering you? Like, something I did?"

She shook her head. "No, Honey. You've done nothing wrong. I'm just surprised, that's all."

"Of what? Of me and Justin?"

"Yes—that you're dating a celebrity. Just seems unlike you, you know. Dating someone like that, with the big personality and reputation."

"Mom, Justin's still the same guy as when we were kids. He's very intentional about not letting the fame get to his head. He even asked for a speeding ticket once, as the cop was going to let him off with a warning. He didn't think it was fair to be given special treatment because of his fame."

I immediately caught myself before elaborating further—that this traffic citation happened to be issued on our drive up to Ville du Lac. At that point, we'd been able to keep our trip under wraps—amazingly so. As far as I knew, my mom and grandma believed we still lived in San Diego. I wasn't sure how long we'd be able to keep up this act—I planned to come clean eventually when I told my mom about my career change.

Mom nodded. "Yes, that is commendable. But you should still be careful. He's an entertainer, after all. That's what he does—entertains people for their pleasure and enjoyment. I don't want you to get caught up in his world and all the drama that comes along with it."

"I understand, Mom. But I'm also a big girl who needs to make her own decisions. You and Dad taught me that. And I ask you to trust me on this and give Justin a chance."

"Yes, I can do that," she agreed as we approached her SUV.

I should wait a bit longer before telling my mom about my new coffee shop. We still had a few days left of our visit. There was no rush to reveal the news at an inopportune time. As I'd learned during my first day of clinicals, timing was everything.

***

"So, here's the current score," Grandma announced, reading aloud from her pad of paper. "Natalie has 45 points, Justin has 38 points, Olivia has 54 points, and I have 41 points."

We were seated around the dining room table, engaged in a game of dominoes, a favorite family pastime. Technically, it was closer to a tournament than a singular game—after completing a round, we'd tally up our points and add them to our current score, then continue with the next round.

"Awesome! I'm in the lead!" Olivia exclaimed. "Not too shabby for my first time."

"Uh, no. You're not. It's scored like golf, where the lowest score wins," I explained to her, "which means you're currently in last place."

She sighed with disappointment. "Oh, really? Are you kidding me? So, that means Justin's winning? Of course, he is!"

Justin shrugged casually. "What can I say? The dominoes speak to me."

Olivia looked over at him suspiciously. "I bet he's cheating."

"He's not. He's just had good luck, putting down doubles almost every turn," I pointed out.

Without a poker face. You could tell Justin always had something brewing up his sleeve whenever we arrived at his turn—with that sly smile as he craftily plotted his plan of destruction.

Mom walked into the dining room, putting on her sweater. "Ready, Natalie?"

"Uh, yeah," I replied, pushing back my chair. "Sorry, guys, but I'll be ducking out early. We're gonna go for a walk."

"No need to apologize," Grandma said. "I hope you ladies have a nice walk!"

I grabbed my zip-up jacket by the front door and took a deep breath. Whether or not I was ready, it was time to tell my mom. As my closest immediate family, she had a right to know.

"I've always loved this time of day!" I commented as we stepped into the evening twilight. "A good excuse to take a breather. Olivia was starting to get a little competitive."

"Olivia sure is something," Mom remarked. "Is she still seeing that boyfriend of hers? Darren?"

"Oh, Derek?" I shook my head. "No, they broke up a few weeks ago—for good."

"For good? How can you be so sure?"

"Because she's moving away to Ville du Lac..."

I paused briefly before finishing my sentence. "...to help me with setting up my new coffee shop."

Mom gave me a perplexed look. "New coffee shop?"

I then elaborated on my decision to turn down my residency program, instead opting to open a coffee shop-shared workspace in Ville du Lac.

"This wasn't an easy decision to make," I concluded. "After considerable time and self-reflection, I realized the medical path wasn't how I wanted to spend my life. I felt obligated, in a way, to follow in Dad's footsteps. I never really gave any thought to my aspirations and desires."

Mom stared at me, emotionless. I knew this news wasn't something she'd take lightly. After a long moment of silence, she finally spoke. "Why? Why would you choose this? Why would you willingly throw away all your hard work and money—for some dime-a-dozen startup? That doesn't make sense. You're setting yourself up for an unstable life!"

"It's not unstable. We've already bought a building for my shop. The renovations are underway as we speak. Plus, Justin helped me pay off all my debt. I'd say my life is more stable now than ever."

She shook her head. "That's irrational. Your relationship with Justin is irrational. I don't like what he's been telling you."

I felt my cheeks flush in response to her sudden accusation. "He's not been telling me anything. He's been encouraging, supporting, listening to me—things I wish you'd do more often."

Mom sighed. "Honey, I know it feels real to you—this 'thing' you have with Justin. But listen to me: Hollywood actors, movie stars, celebrities—whatever you prefer to call them—are bad news. Look at the headlines. How many famous couples are still standing by the end of the decade? Or even the last five years? They don't commit, especially the men. I know the type—they only want one thing. And once they've gotten their fill, they're done—ready to move on to the next pretty lady who catches their eye. You and Justin were neighbors and played together as children, but you're not a child anymore. You've grown up, and so has he—he's no longer the little boy who lives on our block. He's corrupted. Hollywood will do that to you. He won't stick around."

I instantly felt my blood pressure boil over. My patience had run dry. "How can you say that? You don't know him! You've never even given him a chance! No, you've been nothing but standoffish to him ever since we've arrived. All Justin wants is to spend time with you and get to know you, but you blow him off—communicating that he's not worth your time. He didn't have to come here to visit you, but he chose to because he cares about me and my family. So then, why do you judge him so harshly? Don't you think he deserves better–"

"–Because I had an affair with his father!" Mom blurted out suddenly.

Chapter Twenty-Two

M y eyes widened as my jaw dropped open with immediate and utter shock. I could not believe my ears. My mom... and Justin's dad? Holy. Shit.

"It was our last spring in Idaho after the last freeze of the season." Mom took a deep breath as we stopped underneath a lamppost. "Your father and I hired Rob to fix our backyard. We wanted to remove the sod along the sides and replace it with some flower beds. Early afternoon, he'd work on our yard—when I was alone.

"At first, it was nothing—just simple small talk whenever Rob had a free moment or two. At the time, I was facing a breaking point in my marriage—growing tired of waiting for your father to come home. He no longer prioritized family time. Most of his waking hours were spent at the hospital, not with us. I can't tell you the last time we spent any real one-on-one time together. I found out Rob was in a similar situation. His wife, Jen, had a more significant relationship with her career than her family. Eventually, as we bonded over the absences of our spouses, one thing led to another, and an affair was born.

"The yard was completed in a matter of weeks, but we continued to see each other well into the summer. Admin was on break, Rob's schedule was fluid, and neither John nor Jen knew. Whenever I had a free moment to myself, when you were out of the house, that was when I invited him over.

"I soon realized the severity of my actions—my unfaithfulness towards your father. The last time I saw Rob, I told him we could no longer see each other—that I was wrong and should've never let our interactions get out of hand like that. At first, he tried to deny we did anything wrong—as if our marriages were irreparably broken, so we needed to find love in other avenues beyond conventional marriage. But after I told him I was planning to restore my relationship with John and attend counseling together, Rob responded manipulatively. He tried to convince me that counseling wouldn't work—that John was too invested in his career to care about me. When he realized I still wasn't budging, he became angry with me, trying to threaten me. I immediately demanded he get out of the house—ordering him to stay away from me and my daughter, or I would call the police."

Mom began to cry, bringing a hand to her face. "I'm sorry for being such a shitty mother—an even shittier wife! Every day, I blame myself for John's death. If I'd known better not to screw around with somebody else's husband, then maybe he'd still be with us today."

I placed a hand on her shoulder in consolation. "You don't have to take on that blame. Dad's death had nothing to do with you."

Mom shook her head. "No, Honey. You don't understand. When Rob said those statements, those threatening statements, they were directed at our family. I still remember it clearly: he said John didn't deserve me, and he, Rob, wouldn't allow him to hurt me again if it was the last thing he did."

She sighed deeply. "And I lied to you—not just about the affair. After we moved, I remember you wanting to call Justin, but I told you their number was no longer operational, so they must've changed it recently. You didn't believe me at first, so I dialed a fake number—to prove it to you. Same with the letter you wrote him."

"He never received the letter..." I realized, thinking back to the night on the patio—when Justin said he'd hoped to hear from me but never did.

"That's because it never made its way to the mailbox. I lied to protect you from Rob. I didn't want him having any way of getting a hold of us, of finding us. After John's death, I couldn't take any chances, even if that meant ending a friendship as strong as yours and Justin's."

Mom hung her head low as tears continued to stream down her cheeks.

I wrapped my arms around her. "Mom, I forgive you—for everything. I know Dad would've forgiven you, too. He wouldn't want you to carry shame."

"But the betrayal, the lies. It's wrecked you and our family—the Sanders family, as well. I can't live with myself after knowing the damage I've caused."

"You've made some mistakes. We all make mistakes, some worse than others. We'll continue to mess up—that's human nature. The important thing is that we learn from it and then move on with our lives. It's ok to let go of your guilt, Mom. You owe it to yourself."

Mom nodded, resting her head in the crevice of my neck and shoulder. At a loss for words, my mind in a stupor, I leaned my head against hers. Silence was the best remedy in this situation.

Chapter Twenty-Three

Nausea is all I felt—clutching my knotted stomach in the backseat of the Audi. The remainder of our Montana visit swept right past me as my mom's revelations lingered in the forefront of my mind: my mother and Rob, my mom's intentional dissolution of my friendship with Justin, and Rob's possible role in the death of my father. My mind had gone haywire—a jumble of questions flooding my head: Why would my mother willingly betray my father like that? Did she ever try talking to him about her concerns before cheating on him? Does Jen know about the affair? Did my mom ever plan to tell me that Justin was a movie star? Were Rob's threats deliberate? And the most pressing question of them all: did Rob kill my father? My world was unraveling, and there was no spool to wind the thread.

Justin and Olivia noticed my chronic discomfort, of course. I attributed it to my lack of proper rest. It was not a false statement, as the realization of my family's brokenness had an adverse effect on my sleep—just as much as it had on my waking hours. There was no escape from it.

***

"Ah! Home at last!" Olivia sighed, as we drove up to Justin's driveway. "I need some relief from that barren wasteland of a drive! Wanna join me downtown?"

"No thanks." Justin gestured to the hat and sunglasses propped on his face.

"Oh, yeah! Almost forgot." Olivia turned to me. "Natalie?"

I shook my head.

"Ah, you're no fun," she teased, as we dragged our luggage out of the car. "Justin, would you mind if I borrowed your car? Or, I could see about–"

"–Go ahead," Justin replied. "Just ... drive carefully, ok? Like you're not from California."

"Totally! You won't regret it! Thanks so much!"

He nodded, as he tossed his keys over to Olivia. She caught them in midair, sliding into the driver's seat. Swiftly, she started the ignition and swerved onto the private road—leaving Justin and me in the dust.

"Welp. Already starting to regret it," Justin laughed as he helped me with my suitcase.

I gave him a half-smile—the most I could manage at the time.

"Nat, what's going on?" he asked. "You've been silent the whole drive—most of yesterday, too. What is it?"

I sighed, as we headed inside the house. "Now's not a good time. We're both exhausted from the long drive. We can talk later."

Justin lightly touched my shoulder, his blue eyes reading me like a book. "You sure?"

Even though my emotional reserves were close to empty, I also felt a strong desire to confide in him about everything I'd learned from my mom. Maybe talking about it would help alleviate some of my nausea and pent-up frustration. *I can trust him. He's my boyfriend, after all.*

So I did just that—telling Justin about the affair, Rob's threats, the phone number mixup—not a single detail was left behind.

"I know this is a lot to swallow," I said, "but it does concern me about what my mom said about your dad. I think he may have been involved in my dad's death, in some way."

Justin remained silent, as he got up from the couch. He began to pace around the living room, gaze toward the floor, eyebrows furrowing together—deep in thought. After a long moment, he let out an audible sigh. "Wow. Just wow. Your mom told you this?"

"Yes."

"Well, I appreciate the honesty. I do think you're jumping to conclusions about my dad. We have no evidence at this time to make such an accusation."

I stood up from my seat, laying a hand on the couch. "It's not an accusation, per se. More like an observation of your dad's mental instability, which could be a cause for concern."

Justin took a deep breath. "Yeah, I'm not sure what went down between my dad and your mom. We can't just assume her word over his—that he's the one with the mental problems. I haven't seen him since the divorce, but that isn't enough of a reason to accuse him of murdering someone."

I shook my head. "I never said he murdered anyone. I just wanted you to hear the truth."

"But that's not the truth. That's you overanalyzing the situation again. That doesn't help anyone."

"Overanalyzing?" I was caught off-guard by his tactless assertion. I felt my voice waver, as I fought to keep my breath under control. "I-I happen to be doing you a favor—keeping you in the loop about your family. You barely keep in contact with them, so you're clueless about what's happening behind the scenes—and I'm not talking about a movie set."

"Oh, is that right?" he retorted sarcastically. "Like what?"

"Like your dad abusing your mom, just before they divorced." I blurted impulsively. There was no turning back now, I realized. "In fact, that's the reason for their divorce, according to your mother."

Justin's body tensed up, his lips tightening. "My mother? Since when have you been talking behind my back with my mother?"

"Two weeks ago, when she was in town." My heart rapidly pulsated, and I released my shaky palm from the couch. "And no, we were not talking behind your back."

"I wasn't present for this conversation. I'd prefer you didn't talk about me or my family without me."

"Why not?" I jeered.

He scowled. "Because it's none of your damn business!"

"But if you have it your way, you'll never have this conversation with your mom! You rarely speak to her, as it is. It's been years since she's been able to spend any real quality time with you."

"Oh, did she tell you that, too?" Justin huffed, hardening his eyes.

I stood up straight. "Yes! She did! Because she loves you and misses you! But she can never get a hold of you, since you never answer your damn phone! You don't talk with people—that's your problem! I mean, she learned about your stint in rehab from TMZ, of all places!"

He creased his forehead, tensing his jaw. "Well, at least my relationship with my mom is nothing like yours with your mom—where she constantly berates you and destroys your self-confidence! Not even giving a shit that you're miserable in the life she's chosen for you! But you tolerate this, this borderline abuse—allowing her to fuck up your life more than she needs to!"

I threw my hands into the air. "So, this is what I get for trying to help! I get chastised by you and my mom—undeservedly, I might add! All because you two don't have your shit together, so now it's my problem!"

"No, your problem is you butting into our business when it's unwelcome! You never seem to take the hint!"

Adrenaline pumping through my veins, I jabbed a finger toward Justin. "You want a hint? Well, here's one: maybe I should've done us all a favor by not coming on this fucking trip!"

Before he could say anything, I stormed into the guest bedroom, forcefully slamming the door behind me. With my whole life caught up in a whirlwind of confusion, I had but one certainty: I got the last word. I sure as hell deserved it!

Chapter Twenty-Four

Still fuming, I pressed my palms together, hoping to find some semblance of peace. Cheeks flushed, arms trembling. Completely and utterly alone. *This is what I get for allowing people into my life!* It was easier when I didn't have to rely on anyone—I only had to answer to myself. That way, at least, I'd be protected from the hurt. Numb but unscathed.

As I struggled to catch my breath, I sat on the side of the guest bed. Next to me, on top of the nightstand, I noticed the envelope of developed landscapes from the Atlas River. Those photos were the catalyst for all my current problems and frustrations. At that moment, I didn't care whether or not they belonged to my father. I wanted nothing to do with them. I was done.

In one swift motion, I seized the envelope and vigorously flung it across the room. As it bounced off the closet door with a thud, it landed on the floor. I watched as several photos fell out of the envelope, along with their negatives.

As my breath began to calm, I observed something else. Another envelope—a tiny, white envelope, lying within the heap of landscapes and negatives. Its bottom flap was sealed with a star sticker—unopened. *How did I miss this?*

Intrigued, I made my way over, studying the lone small envelope. Turning it over to its front, I found no postage stamp or return address. Just my name—Natalie—handwritten across its face.

Without hesitation, I slid my finger underneath the flap and opened it, unfolding the small piece of lined paper sealed inside. A letter—addressed to me:

Natalie,

Congratulations on your completion of the eighth grade! I am very proud of you! While I acknowledge that I have not always been available, I want you to know I will always support your dreams. As you continue your high school studies, I know you will figure out your calling along the way. The process is not always easy, but if you stay true to your faith and never compromise your personal values and convictions, you will find a path, even in the darkest days. Do not ever doubt yourself; you are much stronger than you realize! I look forward to watching you grow into an amazing young woman!

"Shoot for the moon. Even if you miss, you will land among the stars."

Love,

Dad

P.S. Justin is a really good guy. He's a safe place for you. I hope you hold onto his friendship.

At a loss for words, I felt my chest grow heavy, overwhelmed by my current circumstances—my mom's confession, my argument with Justin, and now, a long-lost letter from my dad. It was as if a cinder block were placed on top of me, making it hard to breathe.

I watched as a lone water droplet splashed onto my jeans. It took me a moment to realize that the droplet belonged to me. A tear. I brought a hand to my face and felt wetness across my cheek.

I was crying. My emotional reserves had run empty. As I leaned against the closet door, I brought my legs to my chest, resting my forehead on my knees—releasing the floodgates, once and for all.

After a few minutes, I heard a soft knock on the door.

"You ok in there?"

It was Justin. Apparently, my sobbing was loud enough for him to hear.

"Can I come in?" he asked me after a moment of silence.

"Yes," I replied hoarsely.

Justin proceeded to open the door, observing me and my hot mess. Embarrassed, I tilted my head down toward the floor.

"Natalie, I am so sorry for losing my temper," he apologized, sitting beside me. "I was in shock—from everything you told me. It was like my whole life, as I knew it, was turned on its side. I still can't make sense of things. My dad—your mom. I mean, what the hell am I supposed to do with that? I'm already estranged from my family as it is. And now, add an affair to the mix? Shit."

He took a deep breath. "But, I know I shouldn't have overreacted like that, getting upset with you. I know you were only trying to help."

I nodded. "I'm sorry, too. I never meant to overstep any boundaries. This whole mess with our families has been driving me insane. I'm barely holding myself together, weighed down by the gravity of it all. I never meant any harm to you."

My vision suddenly blurred with tears. "I'm fine dealing with my own stuff, moving forward. It'll be easier that way for both of us."

Through my kaleidoscopic vision, I saw Justin reaching out and pulling me in for a hug. "No, you're fine, Nat. Really."

I felt the vibrations of his calm, soothing voice. "You're more than fine," he said reassuringly. "You're wonderful, sweet, caring. And I'm so thankful you're back in my life."

As we pulled apart, I gazed at him, noticing my vision had cleared.

Justin extended a hand toward my face, gently wiping a tear from my cheek. "I love you."

I felt the knot in my throat unravel. I leaned my forehead against his, feeling the warmth of his skin. "I love you too."

He smiled at me as he reached for the lined paper between us. "What's this?"

"A letter from my dad."

"May I?"

I nodded.

Justin smoothed out the letter as I watched his eyes scroll down the page. He let out a small chuckle as he reached the last line—about him. My dad never beat around the bush; that was for sure.

"Very cool. Where did you find this?" he wondered, handing me the letter.

I gestured toward the pile of photos and negatives. "It was hidden behind the negatives, I think."

Justin nodded. "Did you know about that before—what he wrote about your calling?"

I shook my head. I honestly didn't know what I'd believed. I'd always assumed that my dad would encourage me to continue on his medical legacy, but I never really gave it much thought beyond that.

At that moment, things were finally making sense: my dad had always wanted me to be my own person with my own aspirations. He believed in me even when I didn't. If he were still alive today, I knew he'd be proud of me, regardless of whether or not I had a graduate degree. Once again, I felt tears beginning to well up.

"What's wrong?" Justin whispered.

"I miss him," I replied, wiping away the tears. "Terribly. I-I never let myself think about it. I always feel like I have to keep moving on, you know—like I've got my act together. It puts everyone else at ease, thinking I'm ok ... even when I'm not. For so long, I've put on this act. I've perfected it."

I sniffed. "After the funeral, the people I trusted most—my friends and family—weren't there at the time when I needed them the most. Like my mom—I couldn't even talk with her. She refused to acknowledge anything was wrong. No one did. She resumed her daily activities as normal, barely mentioning my dad in conversation, and only gave a passing glance at the photos of him on our wall. I now know why she did what she did, but it still stings, you know? This isolation. Picking up the pieces on my own, trying to figure out what the next chapter of my life is supposed to look like."

I let out a huge sigh. "I never had a chance to properly say goodbye, either."

Justin stroked the top of my hand with his thumb. "I'm so sorry, Nat—for everything you've had to go through. You never should've had to do it alone. I wish I could've been there to support you. Any way I could help, I'd do it."

I gave him a small smile. "I appreciate it, Justin. Can you do me a favor?"

"Absolutely. What do you need?"

"Can you stay with me? I don't wanna deal with this sadness alone." My voice abruptly broke off.

"Of course." Justin wrapped his arm around me. "Come here."

I leaned into his embrace, resting my head on his shoulder, his arm snugly holding me close—as I truly grieved for the first time in my life.

Chapter Twenty-Five

"Don't you wish your life had a soundtrack?" Olivia asked as we came to the entrance of the beach.

I propped my foot on the sidewalk, adjusting the straps of my sandals. "You mean, like the songs on your playlist? Wouldn't the lyrics distract you?"

"I'm not talking pop music so much—though I wouldn't mind hearing 'Happy' when I'm happy!" Olivia tossed her hair over her shoulder. "I'm talking about instrumental music—you know, like a musical score. It's just so epic! You feel like you're on an adventure, even doing something mundane, like going to the mailbox. No wonder you actors get so caught up in your work!"

Olivia turned to face Justin. He adjusted his baseball cap as he watched a distant boat float along the horizon.

"You know, the score is added in post-production, right?" Justin pointed out with a smirk.

"Yeah, duh. I just think it'd make life more exciting if we had a soundtrack to accompany it!"

"But what if you suddenly hear ominous music in the background?" I wondered. "Does that mean you should start running for your life? Personally, I think I'll pass on the suspense!"

"In that case, I'd prepare myself for the unexpected—you know, like a huge tidal wave." Olivia gestured toward the tranquil lake.

"Oh, you mean a huge tidal wave forming from a lake?" Justin remarked with a laugh. "Yeah, I'd like to see that one play out!"

She shrugged. "I don't see why not. I mean, if sharks can spawn from tornadoes, then anything's possible! Cinematically, of course."

"Speaking of which, how's everything going with your new role?" I asked Justin as we edged closer to the rocky shoreline. "You've seemed to be on more calls lately since returning from Montana last week."

"Going all right," Justin answered. "Just some minor location changes, that's about it. The casting hasn't changed if that's what you're getting at."

I shook my head. "No. Just curious, that's all."

"Wait—does that mean you're no longer going to New Zealand?" Olivia wondered.

"No. Still filming in New Zealand," Justin clarified, "but now, also shooting a few scenes in Iceland."

Her eyes widened with excitement. "Iceland?! With the glaciers and hot springs? How cool! Isn't that like, on the other side of the world from New Zealand?"

"Yes." He looked down at his sneakers, biting his lip nervously.

"Not a fan of the travel involved?" I asked him.

"Not really." Justin took a deep breath. "I have a fear of flying."

Dang. I wasn't expecting that.

"Really? But you travel all the time," Olivia said.

"Yep, I've gotten very good at distracting myself: listening to music, watching movies, popping in a sleeping pill, if all else fails. The lack of control bothers me, as I'm not the one flying the plane. So, the more distractions, the better."

"Ah. That's why you were adamant about driving to Ville du Lac," I realized, raising a finger at my sudden discovery.

Justin nodded.

"Yeah, I always wondered why we didn't simply take a private jet over here," Olivia commented. "Celebrities do that all the time, right? Especially whenever they wanna avoid LA traffic?"

"Olivia. 'Simply' and 'private jet' do not belong in the same sentence," I explained to her.

"They do if you're famous or won the lottery—which reminds me..." She faced me with a focused expression. "What do you wanna do for your birthday tomorrow?"

Oh, yeah. My birthday. I'd almost forgotten, as that summer had left me in a bit of a brain fog—for good reason. After our argument, Justin and I agreed to move forward from the chaos of our families' past—it wasn't worth the added strain in our relationship. Subsequently, my mind was now allowed to explore other, more optimistic avenues of thought.

"That's right. Your birthday's in the summer," Justin remembered. "What are you thinking?"

I paused briefly. "Well, it'd be nice to go out to eat someplace and explore downtown a bit more—including Mudgy Hill. How about this: What if I got lunch with Olivia first and then walked with you around downtown afterward?"

"Yeah! Sounds awesome!" Olivia agreed.

Justin sighed. "What if you and I did our own thing, like going out on my boat again? And maybe you and Olivia go to the city together?"

"But you haven't been there yet." I studied his apprehension. "Are you worried about being spotted?"

"Yeah." He removed his aviator sunglasses, inspecting the lenses as he fidgeted with the hinges. "The press—they're everywhere. And right now, it's tourist season. If there's people, then there's press."

"Well. Your disguise has been working pretty well so far. We could stay outside—so you'll never have a reason to remove your hat and sunglasses. We'll choose more secluded paths and stay clear of any crowds. Would that work?"

"Still not sure about that. It takes just one person to figure it out. After that, the rest is history."

Olivia massaged her temple with her index finger. She was definitely up to something. "So, Natalie wants you to join her, but you still have some reservations about going out in public, is that right?"

"Yep," Justin replied, still fiddling with his sunglasses.

"Uh-huh," she said, in a pensive tone, as if she were trying to diagnose a medical condition. "So, what if we left it up to fate? Whether to visit the city."

Justin and I stared at Olivia blankly.

"You wanted a rematch, didn't you?" Olivia grabbed two flat stones by the shoreline and handed one to Justin and me. "So now's the perfect opportunity: you two go to the city if Natalie wins. If Justin wins, you go boating instead. How about that?"

I traced the stone with my thumb. "Yes, but no two out of three like last time—just a one-and-done."

Justin pushed his sunglasses over the bridge of his nose. "That's fair."

"Great!" Olivia exclaimed. "So, Natalie, your birthday: do you wanna go first or last?"

"Last," I answered promptly.

After all, studying my competition beforehand was in my best interest. That could only prove to be advantageous.

Justin focused on the lake as he lifted his arm in anticipation. Swiftly, he swung his arm—his stone skipping steadily across the surface.

"Now, you can say you've skipped five times," I pointed out, as a reference to our last competition.

He nodded. "Yes. But can you ... live up to your name?"

I smirked at him. "We'll see about that!"

I bent my arm, bringing my hand and stone close to my face as if I were preparing to bowl a set of pins. I then released my arm to my side, quickly snapping my wrist as I curved my arm, letting go of the stone. I watched as it bounced off the lake's surface and continued to bounce for a total of eight times before it sank below the surface.

Mesmerized and confounded simultaneously, I looked back at Justin. His focus remained on the lake as he gaped, astounded.

"Well. You better start fine-tuning your disguise, Justin Daniel!" I playfully pushed down on the visor of his baseball cap. "You're gonna need it!"

Chapter Twenty-Six

"Mudgy Hill. Good to be back," Justin stated as we stopped at a lookout point.

He wrapped his arm around my shoulders as I wrapped mine around his—the two of us admiring the massive lake and its glistening waters.

"So, how are you enjoying your birthday?" he asked.

Surprisingly, everything had been running according to plan: I had lunch with Olivia first, and then I met Justin for a walk around the downtown district. We kept our distance from others, who responded to us like they would to anyone else—with a quick glance or occasional greeting. So far, no one appeared to suspect anything out of the ordinary.

"My best one yet!" I replied. "How's it for you? Feeling normal for once?"

Justin chuckled. "I guess you could say that. Close to it, at least."

He let out an elongated sigh. "Damn! I realize I didn't get you anything for your birthday."

"Don't worry about it," I said. "You took care of my debt. That's more than I could ever ask for in a lifetime!"

He shook his head. "That's not the same as a gift. That's just a financial transaction."

"A pretty big financial transaction!"

"Regardless, I wanna buy you something else."

Justin looked out at the horizon, seemingly deep in thought. A light breeze swept a lock of his hair to the side, framing the top of his cheekbone—one of his many stunning features. I couldn't help but smile.

"Well, while you think of a gift idea, could you do something for me right now?" I asked earnestly.

He nodded. "Sure, Nat! What is it?"

I took a quick glance around us, confirming we were alone. "Kiss me."

With a relaxed smile, Justin took off his sunglasses with one hand and stroked my cheek with the other. He gently held the side of my face as I closed my eyes. Pushing off his baseball cap, I leaned in closer until I felt his warm lips touching mine. I ran a hand through his hair as I breathed deeply, my lips melting into his.

After a long, satisfying moment, we pulled apart. I opened my eyes, gazing into Justin's briefly. I looked beyond his shoulder, to my side, and behind me as he slipped his sunglasses back on. We were alone, just as before.

"So, I have to ask. Have you been able to remain anonymous in a highly public place before, like in a store?" I wondered.

"Sometimes," Justin answered, bending down to retrieve his hat. "Really depends on a couple different factors; who I pass by, how many distractions there are, the time of day. Pretty much, you don't wanna draw attention to yourself. You act normal; people think you're normal. Try not to give them a chance to watch you, so movement is key—which reminds me..."

He gestured toward the trail ahead of us.

"Oh, right." I side-stepped onto the path as we continued our hike.

"Also, the store itself would have a play in that," Justin said. "I mean, that's why I haven't been back to Costco. I was ambushed in the dairy section and trapped there for a while—the free sample lines converging into a photo line—I was freezing out of my mind and couldn't wait to get the hell out of there!"

He laughed. "Yep, I didn't make the same mistake twice!"

"I guess the moral of the story is...free samples equal free publicity!" I giggled.

"You got that right."

After a few minutes of walking, we turned a corner away from the lake. We headed into the wooded portion of the hike—the dirt pathway surrounded by lofty evergreens. We then came to a wooden suspension bridge. Across the way, I noticed a small bench where a very pregnant woman with dark-brown hair sat. As Justin and I crossed the bridge, I studied her for a moment.

She appeared to be late in her third trimester, close to term—somewhere in the 35-week range. She was carrying lower, which meant her baby had probably dropped—labor was not too far behind. She massaged her lower back with a hand, seemingly in discomfort. In response, I began to fiddle with the ends of my hair.

"What's wrong?" Justin asked.

"That lady, over there," I said quietly, "I think she's in labor."

He watched her for a moment, his eyebrows scrunching together in puzzlement. "What? Really? How can you tell?"

"A few things. I'm not completely sure, however. I just ... have a gut feeling."

"So, what do we do?"

I took a deep breath. "I can talk to her—to make sure. I'll come back over here once I'm done."

"Ok. Sounds good."

Justin backtracked to the front of the bridge as I progressed toward the expecting lady. *You can do this.* I took a few more deep breaths for good measure. Questioning soon-to-be mothers was something I'd grown accustomed to during my hours of clinicals. Probing a random pregnant woman on a hike, however, was a different matter entirely.

"Hi!" I greeted her. "Are you feeling ok?"

The woman nodded. "Mostly. Just some back pain. I was told to exercise more, but now I regret it!"

"If you don't mind me asking, how far along are you?"

"36 weeks and counting."

I clasped my palms together, bracing myself for the awkward conversation about to take place. "Kind of a random request, but would you mind if I asked you some more questions? I'm a resident OB, so any real-world experience I can get would be helpful for my practice." Half-true, but still. How else was I supposed to word this request without it coming across as interrogation?

She straightened up. "Oh, of course! The more help, the better! First-time mother here."

"Well, first of all, congratulations! I know it's not always easy, but you're doing great! Hang in there a bit longer. Do you happen to remember when your last appointment was?"

"Yes, I believe it was last Thursday."

"Cool. Did you have a cervical dilation exam?"

"Yes."

As I advanced with my line of questioning, I tried to refrain from cringing at myself. *This was much harder than any of my clinical rotations!*

"Ok. Last question: can you describe your back pain a bit more? Like, is it a sharp pain or more of a dull pain?"

"A dull pain, mostly centered around my lower back." She pointed to the corresponding region of her body.

"After sitting down, did you notice any improvement at all?"

She shook her head. "Not really."

A jolt of energy suddenly pushed through my veins. "I appreciate your participation. I don't quite know how to put this, but I believe you're experiencing signs of early labor. Preterm labor, more specifically, since you're at 36 weeks."

She stared at me, perplexed. "That can't be right. My contractions haven't started yet. Plus, isn't my water supposed to break before I go into labor?"

"Contractions aren't always the first signs of labor—they can come later in the early labor stage. As for your water breaking, that's typically one of the final signs of labor. It doesn't happen naturally for most women, but if it does, it'll be more of a trickle than a big gush—unlike what you see in the movies."

I snuck a peek at Justin, who was off to the side of the trail, his gaze focused down at his phone. Just a regular guy on a hike ... he was playing the part well.

"Got it! Is that your boyfriend over there?" the woman asked, observing Justin.

"Yes. I'm Natalie, by the way." I reached out my hand, quickly changing the subject.

"Kim," she responded, shaking my hand.

"Do you have a car nearby?"

Kim shook her head. "Not right now. My husband is driving it as we speak. I think he's getting the oil changed. He should be back in about an hour."

"Oh, ok. For preterm labor, your doctor will want to see you, but waiting for your husband should be fine. Would you like us to wait with you in the meantime?"

"Are you ok with that? Because I'm feeling all right, other than my back."

"Yeah, that's not a problem. I'll be right back."

I crossed the bridge back to Justin.

"Well?" he wondered, slipping his phone back into the pocket of his shorts.

"She's definitely in early labor. I told her we'd keep her company until her husband returned. I'd hate for her labor to progress with no one around."

Justin nodded. "Makes sense."

We walked over to Kim. With a look of gratitude, she stood up from her seat.

"Thank you so much for all your help!" Kim turned to Justin with an extended hand. "What's your name?"

"Justin," he responded quickly, shaking her hand.

"Nice to meet you!"

Just as Kim was about to sit down, she sprung up again—awestruck. *Uh oh! I know where this is going...*

"Wait—you can't be! Are you—the actor, Justin Anderson?" Kim stammered.

"Yes," Justin replied.

"For real? You've returned—to Ville du Lac? I-I can't believe it! I never thought I'd live the day when I'd meet you!"

Suddenly, as if it were on cue, I observed the darkening of the bottom of her dress as a stream of liquid flowed to the ground. *Well, isn't that ironic?*

"Shit! That's not good." Kim stared down at her wet dress in shock.

I placed a hand on her shoulder. "Everything's going to be ok. You can relax. We're here to help. First thing: can you call your doctor? Let them know your water has broken, and we're on our way to the hospital."

"We are?"

"Yes, since you're preterm, you'll need to get help straight away. We can drive you there; you'll want to tell your husband to meet us at the hospital."

"Really? Justin Anderson is driving me to the hospital ... what a story!"

I directed my attention toward Justin. "Can you please call Olivia and tell her to meet us at our rendezvous point ASAP—in the library parking lot, next to the moose statue? And ask her to bring some towels. At least two, but preferably more."

He sighed, seemingly nervous about the implication behind the towels. "Sure."

As the two of them initiated their corresponding phone calls, I unzipped my backpack in case I had something useful for the scenario at hand. I fought back a tear as my fingers brushed against my dad's landscapes.

My dad would've been a pro in this situation, I realized. On the other hand, I was fumbling around, not quite knowing what I was doing or saying. It's a relief that I quit the medical profession when I did—before I could embarrass myself further.

At that moment, I remembered the letter from my dad—more specifically, when he wrote *'you are much stronger than you realize'*. He wasn't only referring to my vocational path but also to all my life circumstances in general. I only saw a fraction of my capabilities. Now, it was time to broaden my view—as with my view of Lake Awl on that one particular hike with Justin a month ago.

"Ah!" Kim sounded, clutching her stomach with a hand.

And so it begins. "Hold my hand. Take slow, deep breaths. You'll be ok," I reassured her.

She grabbed my hand firmly as she closed her eyes, inhaling slowly.

I glanced at Justin, who had just ended his call with Olivia.

He rushed over to us, returning his phone to his pocket. "Everything ok?"

"Yes. Kim is having contractions," I whispered as she continued to hold onto my hand.

After about a minute, Kim released my hand, sighing with relief. "Oh! Thank God that's over!"

"How's your back pain level—on a scale of one to ten?" I questioned her.

"Two, maybe three?" she guessed.

We could work with that. "Ok. We're gonna help you down the hill. We're close to the bottom, but feel free to stop and take as many breaks as needed. Does that sound good to you?"

"Yeah."

Without hesitation, I reached my arm around Kim's left shoulder, and as I motioned for Justin to do the same, he immediately slung his arm around her right shoulder.

The three of us began our careful trek down Mudgy Hill. I meticulously watched ahead of us, verifying that Kim's path was clear of any obstacles—or any potential fans, to a lesser extent.

Much to my surprise, we arrived at the base of the hill in no time—less than ten minutes, according to Justin's phone. Even more surprising, we were spared from additional contractions or people during that time. That's convenient ... almost too convenient.

"Natalie! Over here!" Olivia called out, rolling down the window of Justin's Audi.

I took a quick glimpse around us. We were standing in the middle of a parking lot adjacent to a large, two-story library building. I peeked my head over my left shoulder. There's the moose statue.

"Thanks!" I said as Olivia handed me some beach towels.

I quickly laid them across the backseat. Hopefully, that should eliminate any damage to the interior. Justin was very protective of his car. On our drive up to Ville du Lac, he asked us to lay plastic bags over our laps whenever we ate in his car. Plastic bags! That's pure dedication right there!

I slid to one side of the backseat as Justin helped Kim sit beside me.

From the driver's seat, Olivia turned around to face Kim. "Hi there! I'm Olivia!"

"Kim," she responded.

"Congrats on the new baby! Is it a boy or girl?"

Justin cleared his throat, signaling to Olivia to switch places with him.

"Oh, yeah! Your car," Olivia remembered, unfastening her seat belt.

As Justin climbed into the driver's seat, with Olivia riding shotgun, he pulled his car into reverse, then drove onward—to the hospital.

About a minute later, Kim brought a hand to her torso, clenching her eyes tightly. "Ow! They're back."

I firmly held onto her other hand. "Feel free to squeeze my hand. Deep breaths. Breathe in, then out. In, then out. We've got you."

"Man, this reminds me so much of that one scene from 'What Happens After the World Ends'!" Olivia chuckled, turning to Justin. "You know, when your character Brayden's girlfriend gives birth in the back of the pickup truck, as the zombies chase you down. Oh my God, what a classic—I'm telling you! We should watch it again!"

Justin half-smiled in response, his eyes remaining focused on the road.

I rolled my eyes. "Olivia, not helping."

"Sorry!" she apologized.

Out of curiosity, I looked out the back window. While we weren't in the middle of a zombie apocalypse, we did have to concern ourselves with the possibility of being followed by a crazed fan or paparazzi. Thankfully, neither seemed to be near us.

Kim abruptly let go of my hand. "Ah! That's better. Thanks, Natalie!"

"No problem!" I replied. "I believe we're close now."

"Yep, only a block away," Justin confirmed.

Once we pulled into the hospital parking lot, he left the engine idling as Olivia stepped out of the passenger seat, guiding Kim out of the backseat.

"Congrats again!" Olivia said. "Ooh, so exciting! I can't wait to hear all about your new baby! Well, Natalie can forward you my number. You're going with her, right?"

I followed Kim out of the car. "Yes, until her husband arrives."

"Call us when you're done," Justin told me. "We'll be driving around a bit. Less noticeable, that way."

"Will do," I said as Kim and I made our way over to the Labor and Delivery double doors.

As it turned out, Kim's husband was not too far behind, arriving ten minutes later. By that time, Kim had progressed into the active labor stage—yet still no baby. That was a relief.

At the end of it all, upon returning to Justin's car, sliding into his passenger seat, I let out one audible exhale. That was one heck of a birthday! Hopefully, we didn't draw any unwanted attention in the process, I thought. All we could do was wait and see.

I looked over my shoulder at Olivia in the backseat. A grin swept across her face. "Now, who's ready for some dessert?!"

Chapter Twenty-Seven

I opened my eyes, stretching out my arms in anticipation of the new day. Except that it wasn't a new day. Judging by the way the light illuminated across the bedroom, it appeared to be late-morning by that point. I yawned as I thought back to the middle of the night when I'd awoken from a fairly disturbing dream...

I was standing alone in an abandoned warehouse. The walls were dilapidated, and the windows were aloof—high above me, touching the ceiling, the only source of light in the entire room. Suddenly, I felt the ground tremble below me as I heard the most deafening thunderclap rip apart the sky. I looked up to see the surrounding walls crumbling around me as if they were made of Styrofoam—until the building collapsed altogether, extinguishing my vision and breath.

Everything faded to black as I found myself lying awake in the darkened guest bedroom—my body paralyzed from the residual effects of dreaming. Even with my almost immediate regained mobility, the panic of my impending death was enough to keep me wide awake for the majority of the night.

While I was fully cognizant of the obvious—it was only a succession of images and cognitions that my mind self-generated—the dream felt much more real than that. Almost as if 'The Dalí Effect' bore some truth to it, after all—as if there were a thin line separating dreams from reality.

I sighed, rolling over to my side, staring at the nightstand. *I'll likely forget about this dream within the next few hours.* I might as well get a start on my day in the meantime.

I reached for my phone, unplugging it from the charging cable, as I read the status bar at the top. Thirty-eight missed calls and fifty-five unread text messages. I froze. *What's going on here?* Even on my birthday two days ago, I received a fraction of the messages. I doubted I even had that many people stored in my Contacts list.

At that moment, a new text message from a number I didn't recognize entered my inbox. Intrigued, I clicked on the contents of the message:

Hi, Natalie! It's Brian Roberts from our Intro to Guitar class at UCSD. I hope all is well. I was wondering if you'd be able to help. I'm trying to get my name out there in commercials, guest spots, whatever I can find. Could you ask Justin to put in a good word for me with his agent? Since you're his girlfriend, I figured you'd be the right one to ask...

I dropped my phone onto the floor out of sheer astonishment. *Girlfriend? How did my old undergrad classmate know that?* Then, it dawned on me. He wasn't the only one who knew.

Anxiously retrieving my phone, I selected the internet app, scrolling down to the Entertainment News headlines. While I was half-expecting to find a headline about our Labor and Delivery adventure, what I came across was much, much worse: Justin and me at the Mudgy Hill lookout, his hand caressing my cheek, mine buried deep within his hair, our lips locking—for the whole world to see.

The. Whole. Damn. World.

I hesitated as my index finger hovered above the headline 'Justin Anderson Caught Kissing Mystery Girlfriend in Idaho Lake Town.' *Do I really want to read this?* I took a deep breath, pressing my finger onto the phone's screen—bringing me to the main article:

'Move over, Erica! It looks like there's a new flame in the sky! On Wednesday, July 22, Hollywood golden boy and 'Midnight Club' alum Justin Anderson was seen passionately kissing his new girlfriend in Ville du Lac, Idaho. The pair was spotted together at one of the area's most iconic—and romantic—tourist destinations: Mudgy Hill. The 'Double Blind' star arrived in town about a month prior for an undisclosed family matter—immediately following the release of his latest flick, 'The Dalí Effect'. Previously, the 27-year-old's whereabouts had been unknown, even to his closest sources. Since the couple was photographed together on Wednesday, Anderson's mystery girlfriend has now been identified as 27-year-old Natalie Baker, a UCSD School of Medicine graduate. After an eight-year run with his previous flame, Erica Rhode, it appears Anderson is ready for a new sizzling summer romance. From the looks of it, the pair isn't ready to slow down. Hot, hot, HOT!'

Oh boy! I thought, returning my phone to the nightstand. How could I be so naive, so stupid? I knew Justin was a megastar. Why couldn't I have taken better precautions? Instead, I did quite the opposite—indulging in my desires to the point of endangering our safety. Oh, why did I ask him to kiss me? I should've just asked him for some flowers, a birthday cake, even an Amazon gift card—anything that would've allowed me to remain anonymous. No wonder Justin was so concerned with keeping a low profile!

After I slipped on some clothes—resisting the urge to roll back into bed—I sauntered into the dining room, hoping to see Justin there. Instead, I was met with the most peculiar sight: four grown men in business attire, seated around the table, partaking in a game of dominoes with Olivia sitting at the head, tallying up their scores with a pen and paper. My grandma's dominoes.

How did they get a hold of her dominoes? And who the hell are these men?

"What are you doing?" I asked Olivia. "And who are you guys?"

"These are Justin's bodyguards," she responded casually, gesturing to the table of men. "Say hello to Ryan, Kenny, Alex, and Nick."

The four men nodded in unison.

"Where's Justin?" I wondered.

Olivia kicked out an empty chair with her foot. "Come join us for a few rounds! With zero points, you'll be in the lead—bumping Nick down to second place. Of course, I'm in dead last again, but not for long!"

I groaned. "No, seriously. Where is Justin? I need to talk to him."

"He's on a call with his publicist," one of the bodyguards answered. "I wouldn't bother him—it's a confidential matter."

"All the more time for some dominoes!" Olivia enthused. "You can go first!"

I shook my head. "I need a drink."

She giggled. "But it's only 10:30! A little early for a drink, even for me."

"No. I mean water."

I trudged over to the kitchen sink, grabbing a glass from the cabinet. *Nothing makes sense right now. If only this day would end already!*

I heard the opening of the main bedroom door as I finished gulping down my second glass of water.

"Nat! How's it going?" Justin greeted me, extending his arm for a side hug.

I leaned into him and remained silent, staring out the kitchen window. Even coffee wouldn't be able to shake me out of my daze.

"I assume you're already aware of the situation?" he asked, reading my emotionless expression. "It happens. Nothing to worry about. PR's got it covered."

He motioned toward his bodyguards, who were intently focused on the path of dominoes on the table. "You've met my security team?"

I nodded.

"They're one of the best. We're pretty safe here," Justin reassured. "The press doesn't know we're here, at this house."

I nodded once again. I was at a loss for words this morning. "I just have to know. How? How were we discovered? I mean, I didn't see anyone at Mudgy Hill."

He shrugged nonchalantly. "They're clever. Very clever—especially with the advent of drones."

I sighed. That would certainly complicate matters.

"Yes, we're continuing to assess the situation," one of the bodyguards explained. "The current threat level is low. More surveillance cameras have been installed, so we'll continue to check them for unusual activity."

"So, then, are we all good?" I pointed to the front door. "If I wanted to go outside, for instance?"

"Around the property, yes," the same bodyguard responded. "Off the premises is a different matter. It'd depend on the risk level associated with that location. Of course, you'll be accompanied by one of us—a secondary agent for backup if Justin is with you. Highly trafficked locations are not advisable at this time."

"So then, I'm assuming downtown—like the shops or floating boardwalk—is off-limits?"

"Correct."

Well, there goes my vacation!

"It's just for a little while, Nat, just until the novelty of our relationship wears off." Justin rested his arm around my shoulders. "By next week, things should be less crazy."

I shook my head. "Next week?! That's too late! You're leaving then."

"Don't worry about me. I'm used to it. Doesn't matter where I am—Idaho, California, or New Zealand. Limited freedom is part of the package, I guess."

"But guess what? There's good news!" Olivia announced, excitedly displaying her phone screen of a newborn swaddled in blankets like a burrito. "Natalie, meet baby Natalie!"

Chapter Twenty-Eight

As the windshield wipers rhythmically swept across the Audi's dashboard, I studied the road before me, looking past the torrential downpour. Only Olivia knew I was on my way to my new coffee shop.

Four days after my relationship with Justin had gone public, my patience had reached a new low—even lower than my last few months of medical school. His security team was on full watch. If I took a stroll through the park, for instance, a bodyguard was required to escort me. No exceptions. Of course, Justin was unfazed by the lack of privacy. To him, it was just another day at the office. As for Olivia, she was allowed the freedom I craved—after all, she wasn't the one who made out with a Hollywood heartthrob at a majestic lookout. She was like everyone else who'd hiked Mudgy Hill: ordinary people, tourists, new Idaho residents hailing from California.

As I drove down the slick street, I observed an older brick building at the corner, with the faint lettering of "Ville du Lac Bank" still etched in its front—my new shop. I pulled alongside the curb across the street. As I stepped outside, locking the car door, I sighed.

I didn't like lying to Justin—or anyone, for that matter. It was the only way to guarantee an outing to the downtown district. Upon receiving a voicemail from one of my landscaping contacts, I knew a last-minute opening for a consultation was an opportunity I couldn't refuse—especially given my strong urge to reside anywhere other than at Justin's house. I desperately needed to refurbish my new shop, starting with removing those precarious trees out in front. I was previously unable to set up a consultation before September, but an unexpected cancellation was just what I needed. As Justin was preoccupied with a conference call, the timing appeared perfect.

As I crossed the street, I slipped off the hood of my jacket—turning my gaze to the gray sky. The rainfall was beginning to subside. A high wind advisory was forecast for that afternoon, but it appeared the storm was on its way out. At least something was going my way, I noted as I opened the door to my shop.

Stepping inside the empty former bank, I inspected the roof for a moment. Much to my dismay, the old, rickety roof hadn't been replaced. The contractor hadn't contacted their respective subs like they'd promised. The interior paint job was also incorrect—the off-white color I requested was as white as snow. I'd have to call the contractor in the morning to address these oversights. Otherwise, what's the point of a contractor?

"Good to see you again, Natalie."

Who's there?! I froze—my heart racing, slowly turning my head toward the source.

There, in the open doorway of the shop, stood a rugged middle-aged man. He had gray-brown hair that was mostly uncombed. His face was unshaven, with a short beard of the same gray-brown shade. He was wearing an oversized T-shirt and relaxed-fit jeans, a lit cigarette in one hand, his other hand resting in his jean pocket. The grip of a black handgun was emerging from his other pocket, partially concealed by his T-shirt.

I gasped in terror as I felt a shot of adrenaline jolt through my body.

"Oh, you don't remember me, do ya?" the man remarked, closing the door behind him and taking a few steps closer to me.

Instinctively, I stepped backward.

"I'm surprised. I mean, look at who you're getting hot and heavy with!" He gave me a wide, oddly familiar smile—an uncanny version of his son's.

"Rob," I realized.

"At your service." Rob made a bowing motion with his free arm. "What'd ya think the 'R' in 'RS Landscaping' stood for?"

I'd been duped! I'd thought I'd been in contact with a reputable landscaping business the whole time. Well, Rob's company was legitimate, but he was not in the process of setting up estimates for tree removals. *Why couldn't I have just told Justin of my whereabouts? Why did I have to be so stubborn? Who knows if I'll ever have the chance to see him again!*

"Long time," Rob said, taking a drag from his cigarette. "Funny. You look just like your mother."

"I-I'm sorry. F-for the complications between you and my mom. Really, I am," I stammered, trying to gain control of my voice.

"Oh! And you even sound like her, too—with the fake tone and meaningless words. You know, she was always great at that—at pretending to give a shit. She had it down to an art! How she could be fucking me one moment and cutting me out of her life the next. Really drives the point home, doesn't it? I give her my world, and she doesn't appreciate any of it—the affair she initiated!"

As he stepped forward closer to me, Rob threw down the cigarette, extinguishing it with the sole of his boot. I moved backward in response, my back bumping against the wall.

"And what does she do instead?" he continued. "She goes crawling back to her weak, pathetic husband who doesn't have the balls of a real man. No! John never gave her the time of day—not like I did! Oh, but everybody loved John. He could do no wrong—delivering half the babies in Ville du Lac, always the center of attention. Such a touching life, I must say! Until it wasn't."

Suddenly, I heard a thunderclap in the distance as the wind began to howl vigorously against the shop window panes. The storm had returned.

Rob lightly tapped the grip of his handgun as I swallowed back a lump of fear. "Yes, I was there when it happened—when John took his final breath. It was ironic, you see. For someone so loved that he was so alone at the end—abandoned, washed up along the riverbank. Like a dying fish...gasping his last."

My stomach lurched—a sudden wave of nausea overtaking me. I held onto the wall with a hand as my knees buckled under the weight of his proclamation. In response, I tried to muster up something, but my throat was dry. Even as I'd suspected Rob was responsible for my dad's death, hearing him confirm it aloud did not alleviate my stupor.

"Y-you don't have to do this," I finally managed to say.

"Do what? Hah! You think I wanna kill you? Your mother was a whore, but that's not enough to justify ending her daughter's life over. No, I need you. You're my collateral, my bait. You see, Natalie, I'm setting my hook on a bigger fish in this pond—one that makes the big bucks."

Rob grinned from ear to ear. "Millions of them!"

Justin.

"Your son won't fall for this!" I retorted.

"Oh, I believe he already has!" Rob stated as I heard the faint beep-beep of a car.

I peered over my shoulder through the adjacent window. A black SUV had parked behind the Audi across the street.

In an instant, Rob seized my arm, pulling me closer to his hunched body. My heart stopped, as I felt the sensation of cold, hard metal meeting the skin of my temple—the barrel of his gun.

Chapter Twenty-Nine

- -

At that moment, the door to the shop swung wide open, as two of Justin's bodyguards stepped through the doorway—armed.

"Drop your weapon!" one of them yelled, as the two men aimed their handguns at Rob.

Justin followed behind them, his eyes widening, lips parted in shock. "Dad?!"

"Hello, son!" Rob greeted him, amused. "Not the family reunion I had in mind, but it'll have to do. You've changed your number, so how else was I supposed to reach you?"

He cackled. "Thankfully, Natalie here was kind enough to invite me to her new coffee shop! Let me guess—a nice little gift for your sweetheart? You hotshot superstars never need to worry about the bottom line, do ya? The dough just keeps on piling high for you! That's a nice problem to have … which reminds me. I need you to do me a favor. Well, favor may not be the right word. Your lovely girlfriend here would agree with that, wouldn't ya?"

Rob squeezed my arm, motioning with the gun barrel pressed against my head.

"Leave her alone!" Justin exclaimed, holding out his hand. "I'll give you whatever you want—money, cars, private jets, you name it. Just please, please let Natalie go!"

"Ah, now you seem to care! Now I know where your priorities lie! Well, son, let me ask you this: do you know what it's like to lose someone who means the world to you?"

Justin focused his eyes on his father, as his body began to tremble. A flash of lightning suddenly appeared outside the window, immediately followed by a deafening boom.

Rob shook his head. "Tsk, tsk. Didn't think so. Happened to me a few times, in case you're wondering—first Donna, then your mother, then you. Well, it's about damn time you learn the meaning of sympathy!"

"Please, don't hurt her! Please, I'm begging you!" Justin knelt on the ground, hand over his mouth, tears rolling down his cheeks. "I'm so sorry I never reached out. I-I was wrong. I'm a mess—a fucking mess! I do care about you. Swear to God, I do! I promise I'll keep in contact. I will. Every day, if you want. Please forgive me! Please release Natalie! She has nothing to do with it. I'm the one at fault, not her!"

Ashamed, he turned his head down, as he continued to weep.

Rob scoffed. "You never cared about me! All you care about is getting drunk at your Hollywood parties and sleeping around with your co-stars."

Gun still pressed against my temple, he turned to face me, reading my muddled expression. "Oh, you didn't know? That my son's quite the ladies' man? That he meanders from one woman to the next—depending on the movie he's filming? Well, you can read all about it in the news, like the rest of the goddamn world!"

I met Justin's gaze. "Is that true?"

He nodded, eyes reddened with tears. "A few times, Erica and I mutually agreed to see other people, when one of us was on location for an extended period."

In anguish, I turned away from him, as the walls seemed to cave in around me. I thought back to my prior conversation with my mom. Was she right all along? Was Justin, like other famous men, not interested in settling down? Was I holding onto a false hope that Justin cared about me as much as I cared for him? In that moment, I felt empty, barren—alone, down to my very core.

"So, is that the kind of relationship you want? An open relationship?" Rob pressed further. "Where he can simply dump you once he's gotten his fix—like your fucking mother!"

"I'd never do that to her!!" Justin stated, his voice breaking. "I love you, Natalie! You know me. I'd never hurt you. I was in a very different place back then, when all I'd ever known was isolation. I had no close ties with anyone—the entertainment world is a lonely place. I'd given up on finding any sense of community. But then you came back into my life. You've connected with me on a level I never thought possible. You've given me a reason to believe, Nat, and I'm a changed man because of you."

He smiled at me as he wiped a tear from his cheek. "And Dad, I do want to restore our relationship—with Mom, too. I was angry. You and Mom weren't available when I was a kid. I was alone most of the time. You were so caught up in your jobs that you never seemed to care about me or Kyle. So, when I got older, I figured it was easier to keep you out of my life—since I was so used to that already. I didn't want to face rejection again. But it was wrong of me. And I'm sorry."

For a long moment, Rob looked at his son, his face softening. Finally, Rob spoke. "I can't be close with anyone. Don't you understand? That's the great cosmic joke—relationships are just a way for the universe to give me the finger. Your mother, you see—her sole purpose was her career—going through the ranks, landing promotions. She was obsessed, to an unhealthy degree. I was supportive at first, giving her the time she needed for her work. But as time went on, that was all she cared about. Not me, or you, or your brother. We didn't talk. We had no sex life. So what was I supposed to do? Divorce her, while we still had two boys under our roof?

"No, I found love through Donna. Unlike Jen, she needed me. John was never around, so it made sense. It was consensual. Donna never once expressed any concerns about us. So, you can imagine my frustration when she decided to call it quits out of the blue—all because she wanted to work it out with John. She never gave a shit that I was battling with depression, and I was on the verge of losing. She was the only piece holding me together.

"The day I chose to end my life, I thought I was alone. From Bayview, I drove well past the street lamps. By the river, it was just me and my Glock—until John showed up. He asked me to lower my gun so that we could talk about it—like he was some fucking therapist. It was too late for that. I still don't know how he did it—all of a sudden, he knocked the gun out of my grasp into the water. Without thinking, desperate for a release from my wretched life, I found the nearest large stone and struck him—harder than I intended.

"When I retrieved my Glock, that was when I saw the blood. I tried to resuscitate John, hoping to stop the bleeding somehow—but when his breathing stopped, I knew he was gone. At that moment, I knew I couldn't pull the trigger. I'd already left one child fatherless—I couldn't do the same to my own two boys. In a panic, I tried to think of where to dispose of John's body. If I left him there, foul play would be suspected. Rapids were what I needed—for his death to be deemed an accident. After transporting the body to the other bank and removing all traces of evidence along the way, I thought I'd be freed from the guilt of manslaughter.

"Turns out I was wrong. I allowed my guilt to fester, driving me mad over time. I chose to take out my anger on Jen—real estate was her only passion, so my reactions felt warranted. After our divorce was finalized, that was the last I saw of any family. I was only left with my maddening thoughts for company."

Rob let out an elongated sigh, as he let go of my arm, removing the gun from my head—tossing it onto the floor.

In response, Justin waved a hand, indicating to his bodyguards to remain as they were—standing by his side, in the shop doorway, guns aimed at Rob. He was still processing his father's statements.

Silently, I pondered to myself, as I heard the wind howling loudly outside.

There was only one thing left to say. "Rob, I forgive you."

Rob turned to face me, dumbfounded. "What?"

"For the death of my father. He would've forgiven you, as well."

He stared at me, mouth open in bewilderment. "That's ridiculous. Why would you say that?"

"Because it's true," I continued. "You don't have to allow guilt to run your life anymore. You can forgive yourself and move on from your past, no matter what you've done. We're flawed and imperfect, but that doesn't mean we're expected to live in defeat for the rest of our days. There's more to life than that. I may have not lived in defeat, but I have lived in retreat."

I reached out a hand, touching the wall behind me. "I used to hide behind walls I fabricated where no one could reach me. I thought I could protect myself, that way. But I was only hurting myself—by preventing myself from becoming hurt, and, at the same time, loved. The truth is, we'll all face suffering, in some shape or form. It's inevitable. But if we're willing to grow from our hardship, allowing it to transform us, we'll find that our lives can be utilized for a greater purpose—a purpose beyond our wildest dreams."

I let go of the wall and looked at Justin by the doorway. "Justin and I finding each other, after all those years, is far beyond any dream I've ever had. More like a miracle. A miracle we wouldn't have witnessed if we hadn't gone through those hard times. A miracle I wouldn't change for the world."

I held onto Justin's gaze for a moment before returning my attention to Rob. "There's always hope to be found. We have to be willing to roll up our sleeves and look for it. Our lives may be broken, but that doesn't mean we're a lost cause. We're works-in-progress until our last breath, so each day is a new beginning—a chance to start anew."

Rob remained silent, seemingly deep in thought. His focus was past me, at the blustery weather outside. "That's all I've ever wanted...a chance to start over. A chance to find hope again."

Suddenly, I heard a sharp, loud crack from outside. Before I had a chance to react, Rob shoved me with tremendous force—sending my body flying toward the doorway, knocking into Justin and his bodyguards, like a row of dominoes. Instantly, without warning, down the roof and sidewall went—collapsing onto itself, windowpanes shattering, as I briefly glimpsed the trunk of a tree protruding from the caving rooftop.

In a split second, it was all over: half of my new shop had crumbled to the ground in shambles—a large tree lying across the empty wasteland, Rob's body crushed underneath the fallen debris.

Chapter Thirty

Sighing, I looked out the window of the private jet, staring at the clouds. Despite his fear of flying, I wasn't surprised Justin had agreed to Olivia's suggestion of a private flight home. After the recent turn of events, we were all incredibly exhausted. Once boarded, Justin reclined his seat, propped a pillow underneath his head, and closed his eyes. He was out—no sleeping pill necessary.

Our last week in Ville du Lac—the week following our confrontation with Rob, was a mess—almost reminiscent of the days after my dad's death. As expected, with the collapse of the building, Rob did not survive the impact. His death was recorded as an accident, and no further details were released to the public. Aside from the police, only Justin, his security team, and I knew what happened between us and Rob. His last wish was for a clean slate, so we'd figured Rob should be remembered as a father—not a hostage-taker.

During the process of settling Rob's affairs, Justin called his mom, not only to inform her about her ex-husband's death but also to engage in a deeper conversation about his upbringing—keeping his vow to his father and himself. I never once inquired about the outcome of their talk, but

Justin appeared to be wiping a tear from his eye shortly after their phone call. Additionally, he mentioned they'd scheduled another call for the following week. A breakthrough was certainly made between them.

During the same week, I also reached out to my mom. She seemed much calmer than when we'd last spoken during my visit to Montana. After telling her about Rob, I suggested that she confide in Jen about her affair. Jen was writing a book about personal growth and healing—therefore, she'd likely be more receptive to the whole situation than in years past. In typical Mom fashion, she responded that she'd consider it.

Eventually, the press lost interest in my relationship with Justin—a few days later, in fact. Rob's passing and the sudden breakup of another high-profile couple were valid enough reasons for the public to redirect their focus elsewhere—allowing Justin and me to return to a relative sense of normalcy. The normalcy lasted less than a week until our departure for California.

As I replayed the past week's events, I found that my mind was still not at ease. The absurd phenomena of the thunderstorm and the destruction of my shop were unfathomable. Even more so, the situation with Rob. He'd sacrificed his life for me. In his final moments, he'd chosen to forgive himself—the only reason why I was still breathing today. I had no idea what to think of it all. I was downright speechless.

Watching through the plane window as we approached the deep canyon terrain of San Diego, I felt my heart grow heavy. Our last week together was a solemn one, but I was happy to be there for Justin during his time of grieving. From personal experience, I knew he needed me. The revelation of Rob's corrupt past and their strained relationship made it very difficult for Justin to process the death of his father. He sought answers to his most probing questions about life, death, and the hereafter. I shared with

Justin the insights I'd discovered from my faith journey, hoping they'd help strengthen his. They did. For that, I was eternally grateful.

A time of loss is always a challenge, but it can draw us closer to the ones we love, who support us as we navigate a new normal. Justin and I had never felt any closer than during that week—making it harder for me to process that we'd be apart for quite a while. Even though his current estimate was about three months, I knew the filming timeline was not set in stone. And after what I'd learned at the shop, I wondered if our relationship bore the same truth. Justin had a history. A history I wasn't aware of until that point. Though I believed every word he said about himself and his changed outlook on relationships, my doubts were still there—the only safety net between me and irrevocable heartbreak.

***

Peering through the car window, I recognized the narrow palm tree and square lawn to the side of my aunt and uncle's house, illuminated by the golden light.

I took a deep breath as Justin's bodyguard pulled the sleek black Range Rover into the driveway. Stepping out of the car, suitcase in hand, I took a moment to observe my relatives' residence. It felt like it'd been forever since I'd last seen their two-story suburban home, with the Spanish-style roof and the door off to the side—their three-car garage taking up most of the front, like every other house on the block.

Though their house was unchanged, I realized how much I'd changed since last standing in their driveway. Who was I since last standing here, in this exact spot—anxiously waiting for Justin to pick me up in his sports car while simultaneously dismissing the butterflies in my stomach? A girl whose entire life was built upon the medical profession she'd secretly dreaded? A girl with no social or dating life that Olivia didn't drag her into? Ultimately, I didn't regret my decision—moving to the other side of the country to begin a new job, residence, relationship ... a new life. I just hadn't realized it'd be so bittersweet.

Plodding up the front steps, holding Justin's hand, I rang the doorbell. Aunt Liz promptly opened the door.

"Natalie! You're back!" she greeted me, beaming at the two of us. "And I see you've brought company. Welcome!"

"Well, Justin's only dropping me off. He still needs to drive back to LA," I explained. "And sorry for the delay. We had to drop off Olivia in La Jolla along the way."

"Oh, not a problem! Come in, come in!"

Aunt Liz opened the door wider, letting us through. "Chris, guess who's here?!"

As I entered their house, I saw my uncle in the kitchen, attempting to open a bottle of wine. When he noticed Justin and me, he lost his concentration—the cork of his bottle projecting across the room, ricocheting off the wall.

"Well, that's a sight I didn't expect to see!" Uncle Chris quipped. "Justin Anderson in my house. Wow! Good to meet you! I hope my niece didn't give you too much trouble. I'm kidding, of course!"

He met us by the front entryway, extending his hand.

"No, not at all," Justin replied, shaking my uncle's hand. "She's great!"

"Yes, she is!" Aunt Liz affirmed. "Though, I was surprised to learn you weren't visiting your mom's side, like you told us. But I get it!"

She winked at me. "Your mom called me about a week ago. She told me you two were neighbors. That's so sweet!"

"Now that you mention it, I recall John saying something about the two of you once," Uncle Chris remembered, retrieving the fallen wine cork. "He told me he hoped his daughter would end up with the boy next door or something similar. It's funny that it's you, Justin Anderson, who he was talking about. Small world!"

Placing the cork on the countertop, he returned to us. "Nice picture, by the way! I wanted to make it my desktop background, but your aunt wouldn't let me. Would've been a nice backdrop for my home office—kissing on the top of a scenic cliff like that!"

Aunt Liz playfully elbowed him as Justin turned his gaze toward the floor, blushing.

"Why don't we give them some time to give their goodbyes?" she suggested, changing the subject. "We should clean up the gym a bit more. That elliptical is too far pressed against the sidewall."

I gave my aunt a puzzled look. "Gym?"

"Yeah, while you were gone, we converted part of the garage into a gym," she explained, "but your uncle here decided to assemble the elliptical before there was any room for it."

"There's room in there!" Uncle Chris pointed out. "We just need to park one of our cars in the driveway."

Aunt Liz sighed. "And that's how this whole mess of a project began. Well, we'll be in the garage if you need us. It was very nice meeting you, Justin! I wish you well in your future film endeavors!"

"You as well. Thank you," Justin responded with a nod.

"Take care!" Uncle Chris said as he and my aunt headed into the garage.

Justin and I stood silent momentarily as I felt a sudden rush of nerves through my arms and legs.

I breathed deeply. "Well, I guess that's the end of our trip."

Justin turned to face me, taking hold of my hands. "Yep. I'm not ready to leave. Wish I had more time with you."

I paused briefly, unsure how to form coherent sentences from my incessant train of thought.

"Thank you, Justin—for pursuing me after all that time," I finally said. "These past few months have been the craziest, most amazing months of my life. One moment, we're riding across the lake, leaving our cares in the breeze. The next, I'm being held hostage in the midst of a freak windstorm. I don't know what to say—except I'm glad you were with me throughout it all."

"Likewise. It was a lot...of everything." An air of seriousness swept across his face. "You know, that was the scariest moment of my life, back at the shop—not knowing if I'd lose you at any point. It's unthinkable, even now. I couldn't live with myself if that ever happened."

"That's not your fault. If it's anyone's fault, it's mine for not informing you or your security team. I was reckless and impatient, all because I got a little stir-crazy. I'm sorry."

Justin nodded. "Just—don't do anything like that again in the future, promise?"

"I promise."

I was instantly reminded of a similar vow—a vow between a father and daughter thirteen years earlier. All because a girl loved her father and couldn't bear the thought of losing him.

"So, onto New Zealand, then," I said, weaving my fingers between Justin's.

"Yup," he replied.

I swallowed the lump in my throat, looking into my best friend's eyes—those vibrant blue eyes. A trickle of moisture suddenly rolled down my cheek. Despite my greatest efforts, the rest of my tears followed in line, streaming down my face.

"It'll be ok, Nat," Justin reassured. "I'll make sure we have regular time to talk. I promise—even if it's in the middle of the night for me."

I shook my head as I continued to cry.

He searched my eyes. "What is it?"

"You'll be gone for three months. A long time," I began, trying to regain my composure. "I can't begin to imagine how I'd feel if you decided to see other women in the meantime, like you did with Erica. I–I don't think I could handle it. I–"

My voice abruptly broke as I choked on my tears, my head hanging low.

Justin touched my shoulder, the other gently guiding my chin as my teary eyes met his gaze. "I'd never do anything like that, Nat. I will never hurt you."

He sighed heavily. "In those last years, Erica and I were pretty detached. I was withdrawn, and so was she. We stayed together mostly for the press, which was positive PR for us both. So, we left the option open—to see other people whenever one of us was away, mutually agreeing to it beforehand. I know it still wasn't right. Even in the beginning, when we started dating, I never really loved her—just the idea of it. The idea I developed when I developed feelings for you—when you lived on my street. I've never loved anyone as much as you. I don't know how I'll make it through till November. I'll miss you too much."

My eyes locked on his; I reached a hand to his face, stroking his wavy hair. "I'll miss you, too."

Justin caressed my cheek softly as I leaned into his touch, eyes fluttering closed. As he pressed his lips onto mine, I rested my arms around his neck, moving in close. I kissed him long and slow, basking in those final tender moments with him—the boy who'd stolen my heart.

Chapter Thirty-One

"I still can't believe you and Grandma are here in Ville du Lac. On such short notice, too," I said to my mom as the three of us and Olivia walked along the floating boardwalk together.

"Well, a little bird told me you needed a bit of cheering up," Mom replied, "so here we are!"

I turned my focus to Olivia, who was snapping some photos of the lake. "Thank you, Olivia. Really, thank you. I needed this. I know I haven't been in the best mood lately since moving in. I'm sorry."

"Ah, no worries!" she replied. "I'm enjoying the adventure. I never knew Idaho could be so beautiful!"

"It is!" Grandma smiled, taking in the scenery. "Say, do you ever see any wildlife around here?"

"Deer, sometimes," I told her. "I've seen them hang out on the lawn by the library—near the other end of the boardwalk."

"You know, I haven't taken any selfies with the wildlife yet," Olivia remarked, studying her smartphone. "Can you believe it?"

I chuckled. "That's probably for the better!"

"I mean, I'll keep my distance, for safety's sake. Why don't we check out that lawn? Maybe the deer are hiding over there—like the bunnies in Montana!" She grinned at my grandmother.

"Aww, yes! I never grow tired of seeing those bunnies," Grandma agreed. "Selfies are not my forte, but I'd love to walk with you."

"Awesome! I'll show you how it's done!"

"I'll join you in a few minutes. Are you ok with that?" I asked them.

"Of course! You both come when you're ready. You'll probably catch up to us." Grandma laughed. "My pace is not what it once was!"

As Olivia and Grandma continued their stroll, Mom and I stopped to observe the sunlit view of Mudgy Hill—beyond the boardwalk, across the lake.

"How's your new coffee shop going, by the way?" Mom wondered.

"Not the greatest," I admitted. "We decided to demolish the remainder of our shop—most of it was destroyed by the storm, anyway. We'll sell the plot of land and look for a new property—hopefully soon."

"Do you have one in mind?"

I shook my head. "I wish."

"Well, I wouldn't worry too much about that. I believe you'll find the right place, all in due time. Just requires some patience—like all things in life."

I adjusted the hair tie of my ponytail, sliding Justin's baseball cap back into place on the top of my head—a souvenir of our summer in Ville du Lac together.

Mom took out her sunglasses from her purse. "So, how did Uncle Chris and Aunt Liz enjoy their visit? They stayed for a week, correct?"

"Yeah, they left last Saturday. They liked it here," I answered. "Uncle Chris went paddleboarding on the lake, which he prefers over the bay in San Diego, surprisingly. That was very nice of them—driving halfway across the country to help Olivia and me settle in."

"Well, that's what family's for." Mom took a deep breath. "Though, I haven't been treating you like family lately. Honey, I have to apologize for how I acted during your visit. Truth be told, I refused to forgive myself as a reminder of the horrific life choices I made. I never allowed myself any grace—like a self-inflicted punishment. Lately, I've been meeting with a therapist so I can finally move on with my life. She's been a tremendous help. I also talked with Jen and told her everything—affair included. She took the news better than I thought. Sweet lady. I can see where her son gets it from."

I nodded. "That's great! I'm proud of you, Mom."

"I was wrong about Justin. I got the chance to talk with him. He had nothing but kind words to say about you. Very grounded, even for someone as famous as him. I was impressed."

I sighed, trying to ignore the knot in the pit of my stomach.

Mom lowered her sunglasses. "What's wrong, Honey?"

"Well, honestly, I've been struggling since Justin left for New Zealand. At first, it was fine, you know—chatting with him every day or every other day. But lately, it's been less. This week, I haven't heard from him at all. The last time we talked, he said he was very busy on set trying to figure out some things with work but otherwise doing okay. I just don't know if I can handle it—a long-distance relationship. It's only been a few weeks, and I'm already missing him like crazy."

I massaged the side of my face with a hand. "Is this how it's gonna be every time he travels for a film shoot or a press tour? I'm starting to doubt we'll be able to make it work."

"Of course you will! I believe in the two of you. So does Jen. Your relationship has already stood the test of time—thirteen years. So what's another few months?" Mom wrapped her arm around me for a side hug.

I leaned into her embrace, looking out at the clear blue lake. "Thanks, Mom! I really appreciate it."

"Don't mention it! You're my daughter, after all, and I'm proud of you and all you've accomplished. I love you, Honey!"

Turning my head to look at my mother, I felt the knot in my stomach dissipate. "I love you too!"

***

Upon parking my Volvo underneath a canopy of trees, I paused for a moment, observing my old stomping grounds. Since my move, I hadn't thought of stopping by my old neighborhood for a walk. It never even crossed my mind. I guess that just proved how much I'd been keeping my nose to the grindstone lately, with kick-starting my new business and all, I acknowledged.

As I locked my car door, I reached into my backpack for my phone, double-checking the address my mom had texted me earlier. She and my grandma were already in the area, per her message—after they'd spent the morning exploring the downtown district with me.

It honestly took me by surprise that my mom wanted to take a stroll by our old house. For so long, she adamantly refused to go anywhere with sentimental value—places that reminded her of my dad. The current date was August 29th, the day before the anniversary of his death. It made sense that Mom was willing to pay her respects by revisiting the one place Dad had cherished the most—our home.

Walking down the familiar tree-lined streets, I breathed in the warm, late-afternoon air. I tilted the visor of Justin's baseball cap upward as I studied the various house numbers along the way. None of them matched the address in my mom's text, our meeting point. *Was that a typo? Maybe I should give her a call, just in case.*

Just as I was about to select the "Call" icon on my phone screen, I noticed a small handwritten sign staked in the grass, off to the side. It read my name—Natalie—with an arrow pointing toward the adjacent street. The street across from the lake. *Huh.*

Intrigued more than ever, I followed the arrow down the lakefront street. I thought back to my nostalgic walk with Justin and Olivia—one of my many favorite memories of our trip. It was a beautiful day then. Almost perfect. If only our treehouse were still standing rather than being converted into a housing development ... then I'd consider the day perfect.

Coincidentally, as I turned my head, I was met with the site where the old treehouse had been. Except it wasn't a vacant lot anymore, as it was two months prior. It was instead converted into another sable treehouse—a larger, grander version of its predecessor. The most amazing treehouse I'd ever seen.

In awe, I circled the site, observing each of its features. At the base, I passed by four cushioned lawn chairs surrounding a rustic fire pit. To the right, I saw a lit staircase spiraling around the sturdy trunk of a tree. Catching a glimpse through the open window, the interior of the second floor appeared to be a kitchen of some sort with a stovetop and microwave. The same staircase also led to the third floor—the top floor. I wasn't able to peer inside as its shades were drawn. The bedroom, I presumed. Above the rooftop, I noticed a series of lights lined in a circular pattern, like a constellation of stars—the way *I'd* design it.

Suddenly, I realized: *I knew this treehouse!* It was a manifestation of my ideas from our walk all those weeks ago. *Its architect must not be too far away.*

Turning my gaze to the top floor, there was Justin, sitting on the ledge, his legs dangling over the side—reminiscent of our last time at a treehouse together.

Shocked and ecstatic, I gave him an amused smile. "Justin Daniel—I figured this contraption was your creation!"

"Too much?" Justin asked with a chuckle. "I can totally change it. I was just trying to remember all the details you said before."

I shook my head. "It's perfect!"

He smiled widely at me. "Glad to hear!"

"I believe this belongs to you." Slipping off his hat, I attempted to fling it up to him like a Frisbee, but it plummeted onto one of the lawn chairs by the fire pit.

Justin began cracking up. "I've really gotta take you disc golfing one of these days!"

"Well, this is why we can't have nice things!" I joked.

"Oh, God! You still *remember* that?" He continued to laugh. "That is one of the worst one-liners known to man! Please don't ever say that again."

"Oh, really? Not even to my grandma? It'd be a great addition to her joke collection. She could tell *two* jokes with cheesy one-liners!"

Justin smirked at me. "Yeah, no. That's not happening."

"Don't worry. Your cheesy one-liner's safe with me!" I took a moment to calm my giggles. "You know, you're pretty far away from New Zealand."

"I know that." He looked unfazed.

"Is everything ok with your new film?"

"I've turned down the role."

Justin's statement piqued my curiosity. "How come?"

"My heart's not in the role." He sighed, tracing the sides of the ledge. "In fact, my heart's not in my work at all. I'm sorry for not communicating much with you lately. It's been a process—selling the house and retiring at the end of the year. I should've been better at keeping you in the loop."

Even more surprised now, I fixed my gaze on Justin. "I understand. That sounds hectic, for sure! But I have to ask. If you're retiring from acting, what are you gonna do with your life instead?"

He climbed down from the top floor, joining me by the fire pit. I realized his answer must require some additional context.

"It's been one hell of a summer, hasn't it?" Justin remarked, brushing a few strands of hair aside. "Still don't know what to think of it all. I've been told everything happens for a reason, and I believe these few months were no different. I found you again – well, *you* found *me*, actually. Thank you for that, by the way."

He smiled sheepishly at me.

"I was lost in a world that wasn't a home," Justin continued. "Far from it. I was sidetracked, distracted by the limelight. Not sure what kind of off-road detour I've been traveling. But I can finally say I'm home again—the home I remember, with you."

I found myself beaming at his statement.

"You asked me what I wanna do with my life? Well, I'm not sure yet." He shrugged nonchalantly. "No idea. The only thing I'm sure about is who I wanna spend the rest of my life with."

Justin slipped a hand into the pocket of his jeans. Instantly, my heart began to pick up speed.

"Nat, I'm sorry I never bought you a birthday gift. Never been the best at buying gifts, to be honest," he admitted. "I know it's a bit late, but I hope this'll make up for it."

I gasped in wonder as he pulled out a small box—*a jewelry box*—from his pocket. He opened the box, revealing a ring. A dazzling diamond ring—clearer than the waves of the lake, with a sparkle only matched by the stars themselves.

My eyes widened in astonishment. *I can't believe this is happening!*

Without hesitation, Justin knelt on the ground on one knee, his blue eyes intently focused on me. "Natalie Kathleen Baker, will you marry me?"

Overwhelmed with exhilaration and amazement, I brought my hands to my face, my vision blurring with tears of joy. I felt my heart bound out of my chest as I proceeded to nod—the most definitive I'd been about anything in my life. "Yes!! A thousand times, yes!!"

In response, Justin stood up from his spot and scooped me into his arms. My feet hovered above the ground as he gently lifted me up, spinning me around—me reveling in the beauty of it all.

As my feet touched the ground, my head dizzy and breathless, I rested my hands upon his chiseled face, admiring my best friend for a moment. He smiled at me—stroking my cheek, forehead, and hair—as I closed my eyes, absorbing his tender touch. I felt him softly tug on the tie of my ponytail, releasing my brown hair to my shoulders. I then did what came naturally: sliding a hand through his hair, guiding him closer to me, as I sunk my lips deep into his. Justin returned the favor, pressing his mouth onto mine, holding me close to his chest, our breaths matching in time—our lives finally in unison.

We were home.

Epilogue

“**I**’m so, so happy for you both! Childhood friends first, now spouses!" Olivia moved the microphone from her lips—the twinkle lights of the reception hall reflecting in the Maid-of-Honor's champagne glass. "To Natalie and Justin!”

Olivia lifted her glass and drank from it as the rest of the guests followed in line—Justin and me included, our arms linked together—notwithstanding the accidental elbow bump.

“Shoot! I’m sorry, Nat!” Justin apologized as he quickly grabbed a cloth napkin, dabbing the spilled cider on the heart-shaped neckline of my dress. “Never done that before.”

“Really? Not even in one of your previous roles?” I asked.

“Nope. I did, however, have the honor of colliding into a wedding cake.”

I gave him an intrigued look. “Scripted or unscripted?”

“It was later written into the script.”

I giggled. “Well, then, let’s keep you far away from our cake—until cutting time!”

Justin nodded. “That’s fair.”

I glanced over at the circular table where my relatives were seated. "I should probably say hello to my family."

"Sure, I'll go with you."

Justin and I made our way over to my family's table.

"Well, if it isn't America's Sweethearts!" Uncle Chris joked.

Aunt Liz nudged him with her elbow. "Congrats, you two!"

"You look so beautiful, Natalie! Absolutely stunning!" Grandma enthused. "That dress almost reminds me of your mother's wedding day."

Mom rolled her eyes. "Not even close, Mom! I wore shoulder pads. It was the '80s, remember?"

"That is one style I'm glad went by the wayside!" Uncle Chris quipped, taking a swig from his glass. "Loved the taco bar, by the way! Interesting idea. Not too shabby for a dry wedding, I must say. Though, a glass or two of some hard cider wouldn't hurt!"

Aunt Liz gave him a warning stare as she looked back at Justin and me apologetically. "So, where are you two headed for your honeymoon?"

"New Zealand," I replied.

"Why New Zealand?" my cousin Brad inquired.

"I was working there for a bit last year, but I never really got a chance to explore the country," Justin responded. "They've got some legit landscapes. We're planning to visit the sites of 'The Lord of the Rings' films—hoping to make the journey from the Shire to Mordor, like in the trilogy."

"You better not ask for a speeding ticket this time!" I teased him with a smirk. "We have normal-people jobs now. No more money growing on trees."

"Where do you work now?" my cousin Rosie asked him.

"I'm helping Natalie with her new shop—Lakeside Rendezvous," Justin replied, "managing the financial side of things, along with the music venue bookings."

"It's a coffee shop with a shared music venue," I added. "Bands are able to perform small concerts in the space next to the bakery. Olivia also helps us with the marketing and social media."

"Weren't you planning to open a self-employed workspace or something like that?" Rosie questioned me, baffled.

"Yeah, Justin convinced me to go down this route instead," I explained. "It's still the same concept—a place for professionals to come together. Except in this case, the professionals are musicians. We wanted to give local artists a chance to get their name out there while providing free concerts for the community."

"Cool!" Brad remarked.

"Will you ever perform there, at your shop?" Grandma wondered. "You both play the guitar now, right? You could perform a duet together."

Justin shrugged, smiling slyly. "We'll see about that!"

"Our music tastes are quite different," I said. "You listen primarily to hard rock, but I prefer indie or soft rock more. But at least you're not into metal, like your brother. I can't handle all that screaming!"

"Harsh vocals is the technical term," he corrected me.

"Regardless, just whatever you do, please don't invite any metal bands into our shop. I'm not looking to scare away our customers!"

Justin let out a small chuckle. "Will do!"

At that moment, Jen approached our table.

"Ah! There you are!" she said, directing her attention toward her son. "Remember Cheryl—my old coworker?"

"You've had many coworkers," Justin pointed out to her.

"Yes, but you'd remember her. They used to host those 4th of July block parties on their cul-de-sac every year when we lived in Ville du Lac."

He shook his head. "Still don't remember."

"Well, anyway, she brought her teen daughters; they're dying to meet you. They're sitting over there." Jen gestured toward the other end of the reception hall. "I told them you'd be more than happy to take a photo with them."

Justin sighed.

"Well, we should let you go!" Aunt Liz said. "Wouldn't want to keep the fangirls waiting!"

"Of course not! Congratulations again to you both!" Grandma said.

"Thank you!" I replied.

As Justin and I left my family's table, hand-in-hand, I looked over at the dance floor. The local band we'd hired was still setting up on stage. In the meantime, a DJ was currently playing "Never Gonna Give You Up." Some guests had already begun dancing—Olivia and our friend Becky included. Kyle and one of Justin's groomsmen, his friend Blake, stood off to the side.

Olivia waved us over. "Come over here! Can't get these guys to dance—can you believe it? Maybe if you start, they'll join in!"

Justin pointed to the nonexistent watch on his wrist. "Can't. We've got someplace to be."

We continued past the dance floor, Justin guiding us toward the edge of the reception hall—outside.

"Wait—aren't we supposed to meet Cheryl's daughters?" I asked.

"Not immediately," he replied. "They can wait."

Walking onward, we reached the white picket fence bordering the lake—the twilight-blue sky stretching across the horizon.

"You weren't wrong. We *did* have someplace to be!" I commented.

Justin nodded, wrapping his arm around my waist snugly as the two of us stared out at the vast lake—the glowing moon and stars reflecting in its serene waters.

"You know, this reminds me of that one night a year ago on the back patio," I remembered.

"Ah, yes. The back patio. How could I forget?" Justin said. "I was a nervous wreck back then. Everything that came out of my mouth was either awkward or dumb. I was constantly afraid of pushing you away, thereby ruining my one shot with you."

"You never pushed me away. Actually, I find your quirks to be some of your most endearing qualities."

"They're not, trust me." He kept his gaze on the moonlit horizon.

"I'd say so. Like your story about watching the sunrise over the Pacific and falling asleep reading in the grass. Makes you more genuine, spontaneous. And those are certainly positive qualities!"

Justin lifted a finger in recollection. "Hey, wait a minute—we did both of those this summer, didn't we? Watching the sunrise *and* camping in our backyard."

"So we did."

"Crazy, huh?"

"Well, I'd say you've redeemed yourself, Justin Daniel. You weren't facing in the wrong direction of the sun this time!" I brought a hand to my mouth, giggling.

He turned to smirk at me. "Thanks, Nat."

"But, in all seriousness, you've come a long way."

"So have you."

"Yeah, it's hard to tell when I'm looking at myself day-to-day. But I guess that's the purpose of memories—to remind us how far we've come."

I sighed as I felt my throat tighten. "I wonder what my dad would've said if he had been standing here with us. I wish he could've been here, celebrating with us today."

Justin lightly squeezed me. "I'm sorry. I know he would've been proud of you. From what I've gathered, it sounded like he always was."

"And your dad—I know he always loved you, too."

We both nodded in mutual understanding as we continued to admire the view.

"Shall we head back inside?" I asked after a moment of silence.

"Not yet. Just one last thing."

I turned to face him in curiosity. "What is it?"

Without warning, Justin wrapped one arm around my shoulders—keeping the other around my waist—as he slowly bent me backward, leaning in to kiss me. After a second to respond, I relaxed my lips into his as I reached my arms around him—allowing them to rest around his tux. Gently, he guided me back up to standing, his hands moving to cup my face, our lips still touching.

Eventually, we pulled apart—me taking a moment to catch my breath and adjust the neckline of my dress.

"*That*," Justin responded assuredly.

I shook my head in amazement. "*Wow!* What was that—a scene from a movie of yours?"

"No. It'd have to be raining in that event."

I swung my head back in laughter. "Well, then, let's get inside before it *does* rain on us!"

"Sure thing!"

With one final glimpse of the view beyond the lake, we returned to the reception hall amid the loud music and commotion—a sharp contrast to the evening twilight ambiance of the lake, mountains, and starlit sky.

Justin's and my journey in finding one another is all part of a greater plan, the bigger picture—one we can never truly understand. And that's ok—to be clueless about all the twists and turns along the way. Because, at the end of it all, we can always look up at the stars to find our way back home. The same stars that gleamed their glorious light when I took my first breath and will continue to dazzle the night sky even after my last. The sort of light that never really fades away, radiating through the darkness. Always present, never ceasing, shining brightly, above it all.

About the author

Denise had always dreamed of writing her book. As a child, she loved to write stories with memorable characters and positive themes. She carried this passion for writing into her adolescence and early adulthood, hoping to publish one of her stories someday. However, as with any story plot, there were obstacles to reaching this goal. At Pepperdine University, she began to study accounting, a degree that required intense concentration and countless hours of studying and memorization. In addition, it was around that time when her older brother's chronic medical condition took a turn for the worse – leaving him in almost constant pain and removing his ability to hear, speak, and see well. His parents transitioned into full-time caregivers who sacrificed their time and energy so that their son could live another day.

For Denise, this devastating life change meant taking a step back from her hobbies, instead focusing on her family and establishing herself in her career. Sadly, her brother succumbed to the complications of his condition five years after her college graduation. She appreciated the precious time she had with him and the positive impact he left behind. Although she continued her accounting profession after his passing, she knew the corporate world wasn't where she wanted to remain.

A few years later, Denise and her husband moved from sunny San Diego to the forested terrain of Post Falls, Idaho, to plant their roots—buying their first home and expanding their family. That was when she finally found the inspiration to pen her first book, "Among the Stars"—originally an idea she wrote for her creative writing class in college. From there, she continued to push forward despite a decade-long writing hiatus and several bouts of writer's block. She is thankful that God has provided her with the words to share with others through her book, touching on the themes of forgiveness, redemption, and hope while also paying homage to the notable people in her life, including those who have passed. She hopes this tale of first love, friendship, and family connection will bring joy and encouragement to those who need it.